Why did she have
vulnerable—and

Like a man in a trance, K[...]
her good-night on the ch[...]
the last time, when she'd turned her head and her lips
had brushed against his.

Kirk stepped back, releasing her as if she were
suddenly too hot to hold. And maybe she was. If he
continued holding her any longer, he knew that he
would kiss her, not as a friend, but as something a
great deal more. And that would lead to other things.

Rachel touched his cheek. "Don't be afraid of me,
Kirk."

He'd been referred to as fearless by some, as well as
reckless. Her warning now sounded almost amusing.
He shook his head slowly, his eyes remaining on hers.
"It's not you I'm afraid of. It's me."

Dear Reader:

We at Silhouette® are very excited to bring you this reading **Sensation**™. *Look out for the four books which appear in our Silhouette* **Sensation** *series every month. These stories will have the high quality you have come to expect from Silhouette, and their varied and provocative plots will encourage you to explore the wonder of falling in love— again and again!*

Emotions run high in these drama-filled novels. Greater sensual detail and an extra edge of realism intensify the hero and heroine's relationship so that you cannot help but be caught up in their every change of mood.

We hope you enjoy this **Sensation**—*and will go on to enjoy many more.*

We would love to hear your comments and encourage you to write to us:

Jane Nicholls
Silhouette Books
PO Box 236
Thornton Road
Croydon
Surrey
CR9 3RU

Callaghan's Way

MARIE FERRARELLA

*Silhouette, Silhouette Sensation and Colophon are
registered trademarks of Harlequin Books S.A., used under licence.*

*First published in Great Britain 1996
Silhouette Books, Eton House, 18-24 Paradise Road,
Richmond, Surrey TW9 1SR*

© Marie Rydzynski-Ferrarella 1994

ISBN 0 373 07601 0

18-9612

*Printed and bound in Great Britain
by Mackays of Chatham PLC, Chatham*

Other novels by Marie Ferrarella

Silhouette Sensation®

*Holding Out for a Hero
*Heroes Great and Small
*Christmas Every Day
 Caitlin's Guardian Angel

Those Sinclairs!

Silhouette Special Edition®

It Happened One Night
A Girl's Best Friend
Blessing in Disguise
Someone To Talk To
World's Greatest Dad
Family Matters
She Got Her Man
Baby in the Middle
Brooding Angel
Husband: Some Assembly Required

Books by Marie Ferrarella writing as Marie Nicole

Silhouette Desire®

Tried and True
Buyer Beware
Through Laughter and Tears
Grand Theft: Heart
A Woman of Integrity
Country Blue
Last Year's Hunk
Foxy Lady
Chocolate Dreams
No Laughing Matter

To Leslie Wainger.
The best is yet to be.
Trust me.

Chapter 1

He watched her for a moment. Watched her as he attempted to cut a silhouette from the past and attach it to the woman he saw in the corridor now.

He failed, yet he knew it was her. Knew by the turn of her head, by the set of her shoulders, by the very way she moved.

It was her.

Rachel Reed had just locked the classroom door behind her and was attempting to juggle her attaché case, a stack of term paper booklets, her purse, and several oversize textbooks. Visions of the unruly spring breeze dispensing blue term paper booklets throughout the campus once she went outside convinced her that some reorganization was going to be necessary here.

It was only ten in the morning, and already she felt overwhelmed.

"Funny Face?"

Rachel had her back to the foot traffic in the corridor, and didn't see the man who had spoken.

She didn't have to.

She knew who it was, knew even though she hadn't seen him in over nine years. No one else called her that. Ever.

The slightly harried expression on Rachel's face melted away as if it had never existed. Her eyes opened wide, a combination of surprise, anticipation and disbelief mingling in them. She began to turn around just as her textbooks and attaché case slipped from her hands to the floor. A blue blizzard of term papers descended on top of the scattered heap. She hardly noticed.

Kirk Callaghan.

Here?

Everything else—the students, the lights, Bedford University itself—momentarily faded into oblivion as she watched Kirk approach her, moving like a hunter returning home from the hill. The last she had heard, Kirk was halfway around the world, in Asia somewhere. What was he doing here?

"Funny Face, is that really you?"

For a moment, she forgot, and wondered why he was looking at her so oddly. And then it came back to her. Dummy, she chastised herself. The last time they were on the same continent together, she had been eighteen and still all bones and angles topped off with an oddly round face. She had been what her mother had always promised her she would be—a late bloomer. The past nine years, and particularly the past two, had seen Rachel blossom and emerge into a lovely woman, even by her own self-deprecating standards.

Temporarily forgotten papers and books surrounded her like a haphazard pyre as Rachel held out her arms to the man who had been her brother's best friend and her own surrogate other big brother.

She laughed. "Why don't you give me a hug, stranger, and find out?"

The slightly uncertain look vanished from Kirk's face. With a small laugh that was equal parts amazement and amusement, Kirk pulled her into his arms and gave her a rough equivalent of a bear hug. She leaned into him awkwardly, the fallen books and papers a barrier between them.

"Yup," he pronounced, his voice deep and husky. "You still feel the same, Funny Face. Like a soft boy."

A soft boy. It was an old joke between them, rooted in the days when she had wanted nothing more than to be like Cameron and Kirk—a boy. If there was an unusual trace of awkwardness in his voice, as well, Rachel attributed it to his amazement. By definition, Kirk had never been awkward. He had always been so confident, so self-assured. The dark, brooding prince every high school girl had secretly sighed over.

Aware of the students staring at them as they passed by, Kirk and Rachel drew apart at the same moment. Each studied the other.

Rachel had forgotten just how much she had missed seeing him, talking to him. Friends—especially close friends—were people you took for granted, she thought, until they were gone.

Lord, he looked magnificent. She noted the way some of the female students were eyeing him. If the words *tall, dark and handsome* had ever had a poster model, Kirk Callaghan was it. Wearing chinos and a light blue shirt carelessly rolled up on his forearms, he looked better than anything that had ever stepped out of *Gentleman's Quarterly*. Except, perhaps, that he looked just a little worn around the edges. There was a gauntness to his face that she didn't recall.

He looked, she thought, like a wounded warrior. A tall, noble wounded warrior, determined to remain strong despite his wounds.

She wondered what was going through his head right now. He was staring again, his sky-blue eyes sliding slowly along the contours of her face. She saw a distant, appreciative light there. It pleased her more than she would have thought.

There had been a time, she remembered, when she would have given anything to have him look at her like that. She'd been sixteen, and hopelessly, silently, in love with him. It had been just a teenage crush, and she had gotten over it. But even now it was gratifying to see the look of admiration in his eyes. *Didn't think I had it in me, did you?*

Tucking a stray lock behind her ear, she grinned. "Careful, Kirk, your eyes are going to pop out of your head."

He realized he was staring. He hadn't meant to. It was just that she had caught him by surprise. But then, it had been a long time since he had seen her. A very long time. It was a fact of life that people changed, that they matured. But somehow he had thought, perhaps even hoped, that she would remain the same. He had come home searching for sameness. Searching for the past, because the present had become too hard to endure.

Forcing his attention to the paraphernalia on the floor, he stooped down to pick it up. "I think the proper expression is *Wow*."

"If it isn't, I'll accept it anyway." Humor shone in her eyes.

Yes, he remembered those expressive indigo-colored eyes. Kirk had never met anyone who could say so much with just a glance.

Rachel joined him on the floor, her short pleated skirt floating down like a dark green puddle around her long legs. Quickly she gathered the blue booklets together, then deposited them into her cavernous purse.

"Still clumsy after all these years," Rachel murmured with a laugh as she stood up.

"Nice to know that some things don't change," Kirk countered.

She could have sworn that he sounded wistful, even sad. But that was silly. Why would he be sad? He had it all. Just as he had said he would.

It was uncanny, Kirk thought as he rose to his feet. The Rachel Reed he had known for most of his life had been somewhat on the plain side. The Rachel who stood before him now was light-years away from that girl. The difference he saw was the difference between a moth and a butterfly.

It made him almost uncomfortable. He wanted the moth back.

Her features appeared regal, almost elegant, now. Though she still wore that bouncy ponytail she had always favored, she was different. It wasn't even the make-up she wore, or the smart clothing. There was something he couldn't quite define.

Somehow he had never really thought about her growing up and changing. He'd expected her to look just the way she had when he left town. To look like the freeze-frame photograph he carried in his mind.

Kirk knew he must seem like an idiot, but he couldn't help staring.

"Funny Face—" he handed her back her books "—you've become downright alluring."

She hugged the books against her chest and laughed, a little self-consciously. "Just clean living, I guess. It's bound to pay off sometime."

"If it paid off like that, everybody'd be pounding on the monastery doors, clamoring to get in."

Kirk placed his hands on her shoulders. Where had this woman come from? he wondered. Had she been there all along, and he hadn't noticed? The almond-shaped eyes were the same, and the way she held her mouth—a little defensively, despite its softness—was the same, but the rest had changed markedly.

Her face, now devoid of the slight layer of stubborn baby fat, was oval and just this side of thin. Her prominent cheekbones gave her a wild, sensual look he was totally unprepared for. It caught him by surprise, as did the quick sexual pull he felt and immediately blocked, annoyed and confused by its intrusion. He wasn't here for that. He was here to heal. If not here, then nowhere. Returning to Bedford was his last chance. Bedford was where it had all begun.

Kirk was studying her as if he were attempting to absorb her into his system. "Wanna see my teeth?" She bared them, her eyes laughing at him.

Two students looked at her oddly as they walked by, then fell into whispers.

"Terrific," she muttered to Kirk, looking at the students. "Now they'll think the new criminology instructor is ditzy."

Kirk dropped his hands from her shoulders. "I'm sorry. It's my fault. It's just that I can't get over you."

She waved away his words. "Don't apologize. I'm eating this up."

He looked at her, the affection he always felt for her rising up, spinning a hole through the depths of his despair. He forced a smile to his lips again.

"So, do you have to beat them all off with a stick these days?"

She shook her head. "Not even with a toothpick." She had taken her turn at love, and the dream had become a nightmare for her—and for Ethan. But that was all behind her now. She had no time for that kind of relationship. The stakes were too high. "Nobody's breaking down my door."

"You're probably just not giving them a chance," he guessed.

"Maybe." She shrugged vaguely. The divorce, and what had come before, had left too much of a bad taste in her mouth for her to be comfortable with the idea of attempting another relationship. "I'm too busy for that right now, anyway."

"You always were a dedicated whirlwind." The words were almost teasing. He'd forgotten he had that in him. It felt good.

She didn't want to talk about her, she wanted to talk about him. Kirk had lived life on the edge ever since he left Bedford. A highly respected photojournalist, he'd always gone to the world's trouble spots. He'd led a life of excitement and daring, while she had gone about the business of mundane living.

"How did you know where to find me?" She fumbled a little with her purse, tucking away her keys. She hoped she'd be able to find them when the time came.

"I stopped in to see Cameron right after I arrived back in Bedford late yesterday." Cameron had offered to put him up for the night. Kirk had agreed, not wanting to walk into his old house. He wasn't quite ready for that yet.

She looked up, surprised, when he mentioned her brother. "Cameron?"

Kirk nodded. "He told me where you were."

She drew her brows together. "Did he know you were coming back?"

The touch of feistiness in her voice had a familiar ring. He gathered it to him the way a poor man would a crust of bread. "Yes, I wrote and told him."

"You *wrote?* You wrote to my brother? And he didn't tell me?" *I'll get you for this, Cameron,* she promised the absent man silently.

Kirk reached for the comfortable ground he and Rachel had always shared. Somehow, even though more than nine years had gone by since they had really talked, he had just assumed nothing would have changed between them. They had grown from children to young adults together, and nothing had changed during that time. He didn't want things to change now. He *needed* them to be the same.

"Probably just slipped his mind. You know how Cameron is." Kirk looked around as students passed them in the hall, moving a little more urgently than a moment earlier. "Listen, am I keeping you from something?"

Rachel twisted her wrist to glance at her watch. "Oh, God, yes. I've got another criminology class to teach in ten minutes."

"Criminology," he repeated.

He couldn't quite see her teaching a course like that.

She detected the surprise in his tone. "And why not, I'd like to know?" She stood straight and arched her shoulders in a defensive movement. It was an old habit, one she did for his benefit.

Kirk held up his hands in mock surrender. "No reason that I'm willing to mention and run the risk of being pummeled to the ground." The smile she had always loved tugged at his lips.

"That's better. C'mon, walk me to my next class." Moving briskly, she led the way down the long corridor.

Kirk lengthened his stride to catch up to her. "Walk or run?"

"Exercise is good for you, Callaghan. Besides, the next class is in another building. If I don't move fast, they're bound to start without me." She shifted her books slightly to keep them from falling. "I've got a classful of eager beavers."

Out of the corner of his eye, he saw her struggle. He took the textbooks from her. "Here, give me those. I might as well carry your books, too."

"You never did before," she reminded him, although she gratefully surrendered the research books.

"It's the new me."

"There was nothing wrong with the old you." She noticed that he didn't respond. Something *was* wrong.

Kirk held the swinging door open for her, and they stepped outside.

The campus, a relatively small one, was respectably old and ivy-covered. It gave off an aura of stability, like an ancient Southern grande dame who had gracefully aged in the role of a matriarch. He hadn't attended college here, had been eager to get away. But Rachel had gone here, as had Cameron. For the first time, as he looked around, Kirk wondered what he had missed.

Rachel stopped on the bottom step and turned to look up at Kirk, a question preying on her mind. "Tell me more about this correspondence you and Cameron shared, O so-called friend. You two wrote regularly?"

Kirk shrugged. "If you could call once or twice a year regular."

Rachel resumed walking. All around them, new shoots of grass were pushing their way out to form a green carpet on well-tended lawns. Here and there, black birds hopped about, searching for worms.

It was spring, the time of birth and new promise. But for the moment, Rachel's mind was in the past. "I would have called it regular, if the letter had come to me. Why didn't you answer any of my letters?" She'd written to him on occasion, but he'd never responded. She'd assumed the letters had never reached him, and after a while she'd stopped writing.

She was looking straight ahead, and he couldn't tell if she was baiting him, or if she was annoyed. If she was, he couldn't really blame her.

"I know, and I wrote back."

Then he had gotten them? It wasn't like Kirk to lie. Rachel looked at him dubiously. "I never received any letters."

He gave a small, self-deprecating laugh. The few notes he had addressed to Rachel had all wound up as crumpled pieces of paper in the trash.

"That's because I threw them all out."

They passed an ancient willow, its long, wispy green fingers strumming idly along the tops of the blades of grass like an indolent guitar player strumming his instrument.

"That makes it hard for the mailmen to find them and do their job. They're supposed to buck rain, sleet and gloom of night, not search for letters hidden in wastepaper baskets."

"Some of the places I've been," Kirk told her quietly as he remembered, "didn't even *have* wastepaper baskets. Besides," he added ruefully, "I was never very good at putting things down on paper."

"I would have taken inkblots, you idiot, as long as you had sent them." She had missed being in touch with him all this time. "You wrote to my brother."

He shrugged evasively. "That's different."

"Yes," she agreed dryly. "*Those* letters you put stamps on."

Kirk stopped just before they came to the entrance of the building. He peered at her face, looking for signs he could recognize, signs he associated with the Rachel he had known, the one who, along with Cameron, he had returned to see. "Are you angry with me?"

"Yes," she answered honestly, although a smile was fighting hard to surface. She could never be angry with Kirk, at least not for long. "We were supposed to be friends."

"I'd like to think we still are," he said quietly.

She let the smile capture her lips, silently wondering why he sounded so serious. Didn't he know that they were friends for life, whether or not he remembered to drop her a line? Of course he did. He was probably just suffering from jet lag, or something equally transient.

But there was something in his eyes that bothered her, a look she didn't recognize. A look that had nothing to do with the Kirk she knew.

"I guess I should take pity on you. You're probably down to your last friend."

Kirk opened the door of the building and held it wide as she stepped through. "Something like that." Two more students ducked inside before he released the door.

Rachel waited for him to join her, then continued walking. She struggled to sound breezy as a legion of questions suddenly crowded her mind, all of them centering on Kirk. "So, how many people did the fine young photojournalist alienate in his world travels?"

"Whole countries," he answered, without a smile. *And myself.*

The corners of her eyes crinkled as she smiled. "You haven't changed, then."

"That's just it." The words were low, quiet, as if he were speaking to himself, rather than to her. "I have." *And I've lost sight of who and what I am, or what I'm supposed to be.*

When he didn't elaborate, she stopped to look at him as carefully as he had looked at her. Something instinctive told her to tread lightly.

"Well, you don't look that different than when you left. Oh, there's a line or two around your mouth that I don't recall." Her fingers feathered lightly along his face. She saw a line tighten in his jaw, and pretended not to, though its emergence bothered her. "Undoubtedly those are laugh lines," she said teasingly. "And you look a little more gaunt than you did when you finally galloped off to thumb your nose at the immediate world, but on the whole, I have to say that you look pretty much the same."

She resumed walking and led the way up a flight of stairs. Her heels clicked on the metal steps. "You're as good-looking as ever, and you know it." She tossed the words over her shoulder flippantly.

She turned and pushed the exit door that opened on to the second floor.

"That's what I came back to hear." Kirk laid his arm across her shoulders as they walked down the hall. "Flattery."

"I would have been a lot more flattering if you had written."

He had the good grace to wince. "I'll make it up to you," he promised.

Rachel looked up at Kirk. A full five inches separated them. "You'll write me a long letter from your next port of call?"

"No."

"A short note?"

He shook his head.

She pretended to sigh. Kirk would always be Kirk. "Hard to teach an old dog new tricks."

"No, the old dog isn't going to any more ports of call, at least not for now." He smiled, but she noted that his eyes didn't join in. "I'm staying put for a while."

"Oh?" His statement would have pleased her a great deal more if he had looked happier about it. "Then how do you propose to make it up to me?"

The sound of her voice, of her banter, warmed him. It always had. A bud of hope began to evolve, pushing its way up, just like the shoots on the lawn. Maybe returning home had been the right thing after all.

"By taking you out to dinner."

"Dinner?" She lifted a brow, then tapped him on the chest to emphasize her words. "I don't get bought off that easily, Callaghan."

I've missed you, Funny Face. "C'mon, have dinner with me tonight. It'll be a start," Kirk urged.

She paused, pretending to think it over. In reality, there wasn't anything she'd like better. "Okay," she agreed. "Scanlon's."

The name brought memories ricocheting through his mind, like pinballs bouncing from buffer to buffer. He'd gotten her a fake ID to get in one night, and then sat back and vicariously enjoyed her enthusiasm for the place.

"Is it still here?"

"Sure. Hardly anything in Bedford goes away—except for you." The troubled look in his eyes worried her. "Your sudden appearance out of nowhere caught me off guard. I didn't get a chance to ask you—what are you doing back in Bedford, anyway?"

Kirk lifted a broad shoulder and let it drop carelessly. He avoided her eyes when he answered. "Nothing much. Just looking up old friends."

He wasn't telling her the truth. She could sense it. She stifled the urge to prod him. He'd tell her the real reason he had returned when he was ready. He had always been honest with her before. It was what she had treasured about their relationship, what she had missed when Kirk was gone.

"Smile when you say 'old,' partner."

He looked back at her, still trying to reconcile the changes he saw with the image of Rachel that existed in his mind. "At twenty-seven, I wouldn't exactly say you're over the hill."

"Ah—" she held up a finger "—you remembered my age." Her eyes narrowed. "So how come you couldn't remember my address?"

He laughed, relieved at the switch in subject. "You're going to make me pay for not writing, aren't you?"

She cocked her head, a smile playing on her lips. "What do you think?"

"I think that I'm going to have dinner with a lovely woman."

"Flattery is not going to get you out of it this time, Callaghan." She glanced down at her watch. "I've really got to get in there and set things up. Give me my books, quick." He piled them into her open arms. She spun on her heel. "Talk to you about dinner later. See you."

She slipped into the classroom and closed the door behind her. Kirk stared through the thick glass window in the door and watched Rachel put her things down on the front desk. Hurriedly she began writing notes on the long green chalkboard.

He let out a heavy sigh and leaned his shoulder against the wall.

All right, he was back. But was it too late?

Chapter 2

The sound of the door opening startled her. A piece of chalk broke against the board and went flying over her right shoulder. When she turned to look, Kirk was slipping into the classroom like a truant student. He gave her a quick smile tinged with that old spark of mystery she remembered so well.

She might have known he wouldn't stay out.

It took her a moment to regroup and put some distance between herself and the girl she had once been. As Kirk slipped into the first available seat in the back row, Rachel willed her palms dry.

This was silly. He wasn't observing, he was just killing time. And she was a good teacher. No reason to feel nervous. No reason to want his approval the way she once had.

Her students were looking at her expectantly. Rachel squared her shoulders. With the toe of her shoe, she nudged the chalk that had fallen on the floor. It rolled under her desk. "It seems that we're being observed, class. Let's be worth observing."

"You already are," a masculine voice murmured from the back of the room.

Kirk was mildly surprised to see that the comment had generated a flash of annoyance. It momentarily creased her brow before fading away again.

Rachel zeroed in on the budding Romeo. Because she looked no older than some of the students, she knew there were a few who thought that they could get away by being charming, and trade compliments for grades. They had a surprise coming their way.

"Appearances, Mr. Hughes, are deceiving. I thought we had already covered that lesson. What you see isn't always what's there." She noted an ironic smile lifting the corners of Kirk's mouth, and wondered if something she'd said struck him as funny. "A good criminologist learns to look beneath the surface, beneath the trappings." The words rang with a little more passion than she had intended as she scanned the classroom. Maybe she was coming on a little too strong.

Rachel took a slight cleansing breath, then smiled. "All right, so much for review. Let's get on with today's lesson."

Two dozen pairs of feet had shuffled over the threshold before Kirk rose. Rachel laid aside her notes and waited for him to reach her desk, slightly nervous in spite of herself. Kirk's opinion had always mattered. It seemed that some things didn't change with time.

"So, what's the verdict?" Her voice echoed in the empty room.

"I'm impressed." One look in his eyes told her that he was being honest. Kirk folded his arms across his chest. "You're a hell of a teacher."

She placed her notes in her open attaché case, then looked up. Pride, as well as pleasure, shone in her eyes. "You bet I am."

He rested his hip against the corner of her desk. "Well, that hasn't changed any."

She stopped piling books in the attaché case and stared at him, confused. "What hasn't changed any?"

"Your cocky attitude."

She raised her chin, reminding him of the pugnacious little girl who had always tagged along behind him and Cameron when they were children. The faithful shadow who lingered in the corners of his mind. "That's not cocky, Callaghan, that's positive. It's a tough world these days, and a girl's gotta survive."

There had been a time when she didn't think she would. But she managed. She had had to. Because of Ethan. Ethan was what had grounded her until she got her bearings. Ethan, who was now slipping away from her.

His eyes washed over her again, slowly. It was still somewhat of a shock to see her like this. "You're not a girl, Funny Face." His smile grew serious. "From where I sit, you're all woman."

Unsettlingly so. He didn't like the fact that it disturbed him—not emotionally, but as a man. On a very basic level. A level he wasn't equipped to cope with now. Not when it came to Rachel.

She laughed lightly, though she wondered at the sadness that embroidered his words. "And don't you forget it."

He was at loose ends, and they felt as if they were close to unraveling. He didn't want to be alone just yet. That was what had prompted him to enter her classroom, rather than simply leave.

"Look, dinner tonight seems so far away, and I've got nothing pressing at the moment. Why don't we have lunch together, as well?" Her desk was cleared of extraneous matter. Kirk casually pushed down the lid on the attaché case.

There was a note in his voice that she couldn't quite place. Desperation? Despair? It didn't seem possible, not in Kirk. "Now?"

He shrugged, a little too carelessly. "Why not?"

She shook her head. "I'd love to, Kirk, really, but I'm afraid I can't right now. I've got another class to teach in an hour, and—"

"Got a cafeteria around here?" He snapped one lock closed.

Rachel laughed. "We're not exactly backward, Kirk, no matter what you might think. We've done a lot of growing since you left. It's not that small a town anymore." She saw him eyeing her, waiting. "Yes, we have a cafeteria around here."

He snapped the other lock shut. "Food any good?"

"No one's died recently."

"Good enough for me." He picked up her attaché case. With his other hand, he hooked his arm through hers, striking a carefree pose, though he didn't feel that way. "You talked me into it, Funny Face."

As if anyone could ever talk him into anything, she mused as she led the way out the door.

"Kirk, I'm a teacher here," she reminded him. "I don't really think you should keep calling me 'Funny Face' where someone could hear you."

"Okay." He shrugged casually. They made their way down the corridor and to the front exit. "Professor Funny Face, then."

Rachel laughed. She remembered the first time he had called her that. She had been six years old, a couple of years younger than Ethan was now, and given to holding her breath whenever Kirk and Cameron conspired to leave her behind. Kirk had christened her Funny Face, and it had stuck. Rachel didn't mind him calling her that, though she had pretended to when they were younger. It was a nickname only he used, a symbol of their special friendship. She thought of it with affection.

"All right, to you I'm Professor Funny Face."

He stopped walking as they were crossing the campus lawn. Disregarding the people around them, he touched her face in an oddly tender gesture that completely mystified her.

"Yes, you are."

There it was again, she thought. That flash of pain in his eyes. What was it that was bothering him? She struggled to keep a tight rein on her impatience. Why couldn't he just come out and tell her what was wrong?

Because he was Kirk, and he didn't do things like that easily, she reminded herself.

"C'mon, all this talking is making me hungry." She pulled him toward the school cafeteria.

Humanity and its accompanying din engulfed them as soon as Kirk and Rachel stepped inside the cafeteria. It was almost as if they had hit a physical wall of noise and shuffling bodies. Kirk found it oppressively overwhelming. A flash of a scene snared him. For a moment, he was back in Bosnia, lost in the shuffle of fleeing bodies as they ran toward the Red Cross food distribution trucks. He shuddered and blinked twice, erasing the image from his mind. But not from his soul.

He caught hold of Rachel's hand to prevent being separated from her. Kirk raised his voice. "Is it always this bad?"

"Always." She felt the pressure of his fingers, hard, clutching, on hers. Something telegraphed itself to her, stirring her concern further. But when she looked at him, his face was a blank mask. She was letting her imagination run away with her, she thought, upbraiding herself. It came from years of romanticizing Kirk and his life. "But then, I've only seen it at lunchtime."

Kirk shook his head. "And to think I came here to get away from it all."

There was an odd note in his voice that she couldn't quite fathom. Rachel glanced over her shoulder to see whether or not he was kidding. It had never been easy reading between the lines with Kirk.

The cafeteria was divided in two, meeting at the rest room and pay phone area. A good many of the students were congregating there, waiting for their next class.

"This way." Rachel motioned Kirk toward the larger of the two dining areas. "We'll probably be able to find a couple of seats here, once we get lunch. This place is like a large parking lot. The farther away you get from the hub of activity, the greater the probability of finding some empty spaces."

Kirk looked doubtful. "It *all* looks like the hub of activity." He gestured to her to move forward. "Okay, lead the way." As she did, Kirk tightened his hold on her hand and raised his voice again. "Not too fast. I don't want to be sucked up by the crowd."

She shouldered her way into the dining room on the right. "Don't worry, they're a harmless lot, for the most part."

"They look more like a mob to me," he quipped as he followed her to the self-service area.

Rachel got in line behind a student with sun-whitened hair and tattered jeans. "That's just because they're hungry. That's when the beast tends to come out. I get pretty grouchy myself on an empty stomach."

She smiled to herself as she thought of the enthusiasm of some of her students. She had been that way herself not all that long ago, before Don had tried to rob her of that zest for life.

Rachel inclined her head toward Kirk so that he could hear. "They're so full of their own missions in life. They plan to set the world straight, to undo all the mistakes of the last generation." It was a hopeless, eternal dream that kept being rediscovered by each graduating class. And redefined by every middle-aged adult. "They're going to do all those wonderful altruistic things that filled our hearts and minds, oh, about nine or ten years ago."

Rachel handed Kirk a dingy gray tray still damp from its spin through the dishwasher and then took one herself. She rested hers on top of her attaché case, which was perched unevenly on the iron railing that ran the length of the steam table.

"I remember."

Or did he? Kirk wondered. He searched, trying to recall what it was like to hope, to dream. Nothing materialized. It was as if he were looking at the pages of someone else's past. There was no recognition whatsoever on his part. It felt as if he hadn't even existed.

And if he had, it was too long ago for him to clearly remember.

It wasn't her imagination, Rachel thought, his voice did sound wistful. There was almost an ache in it. But what did he have to be wistful about? she wondered. She had kept track of his career. Kirk had done everything he had set out to do. He had seen the world and made a name for himself. All the things he had talked to her and Cameron about during those long, lazy summer evenings when they lived next door to one another—he had accomplished them.

Had the dream somehow gone sour for him?

The girl in front of Rachel was taking an inordinate amount of time trying to decide between the different salads perched drunkenly on a bed of melting ice. If she was going to get something to eat and get back to class in time, Rachel thought, she was going to have to hurry this process along.

Rachel reached around the girl to pick up a puny offering of chef's salad, and placed it on her slightly warped tray. The dish immediately slid to the edge. Shreds of lettuce rained down around the perimeter of the plate. With a sigh, Rachel took her tray off her attaché case. Holding it in one hand, she picked up the case with the other.

Kirk looked down skeptically at the half-filled dish. "That's lunch?"

"That's lunch."

He eyed the serving and shook his head. "I guess it doesn't take much strength to teach criminology."

She laughed. "You'd be surprised."

Rachel thought of the student who had been in her tiny cubbyhole of an office yesterday afternoon, asking her question after endless question. There had been a point when she despaired of the session ever being over, but finally, the student had left, albeit reluctantly. Rachel had had the distinct feeling that the student was more interested in her than in the actual lesson. It all came with the territory, she supposed.

Rachel picked up a large paper cup and pressed the soda machine spigot. Clear liquid gurgled as it spurted out. "I need all the strength I can get. They all think of themselves as budding Sherlock Holmeses—or, more modernly, budding Columbos."

Kirk's tray remained empty except for a straw. He took a worn stoneware cup and filled it with coffee. He hoped the coffee was better than the rest of the offerings here. "And Columbettes?"

Rachel smiled, amused. "That's a sexist remark, you know. There's not supposed to be a difference in gender anymore, or hadn't that information reached you where you were?"

Kirk wasn't hungry, but for form's sake he knew he should go through the motions of getting something to eat. He indicated to the bored-looking student behind the steam table that he wanted the ham steak. With slow, halfhearted movements, the tall, gangly youth shoveled the serving onto a hot plate and listlessly dropped it on the glass counter between them.

"Oh, I've heard, all right." Kirk gingerly picked up the hot plate. The kid had to have asbestos fingers, he thought, feeling his own sting. "But I've always liked the fact that there's a difference in genders myself."

"Chauvinist." Rachel grinned and glanced around. "That kind of talk might get you lynched in a place of higher learning." She motioned toward the shortest checkout line.

Kirk watched a vacant looking girl in tricolored hair drift by. They were children, he thought, just children. He felt decades older than the age on his driver's license. "I find it rather difficult to associate the term 'higher learning' with people who wear lime-green hair. No, let me get it." He pulled out his wallet just as the amiable older woman behind the register rung up Rachel's tab.

"Thanks." Rachel stood aside as she waited for Kirk to pay. "Every generation has its own thing. The sixties had flower children, gurus, love beads and long hair," she reminded him. She looked at some of the more outlandish outfits in the area. "Maybe it's making a semicomeback."

Lifting his tray again, Kirk fell into place beside her. "Maybe, but the only rainbow colors that they sported were on their jeans or shirts, not on their hair."

Rachel located two empty places side by side near the rear exit. She nodded toward them for Kirk's benefit as she began to move in that direction. Her chef's salad slid from one side to the other, courtesy of the glob of ice that still clung to the bottom of the plate. "Like the man said, the times they are a-changing."

And Kirk had changed, she thought. Changed a great deal. She'd felt it almost from the moment she looked into his eyes. He looked like a shell-shocked soldier coming home and not quite knowing where it was that he had arrived.

"How about you?" Kirk held his tray close to himself to avoid collisions as he followed behind her. "Have you changed?" He tried not to make the question sound as important as it was to him.

She didn't answer until she reached the table and put her tray down. "No, I don't think so. Not really. Just learned to be a little more skillful with makeup and gained a pound or two in the right places, but on the whole, I'm exactly who I was nine years ago."

It wasn't true. She'd lived an entire lifetime in the past nine years. But it was easier saying what she had than going into explanations, even with Kirk—at least for now.

Kirk set down his tray. Cameron had written to him about her marriage to Don Mitchell and her divorce. There were huge gaps he hadn't filled in, Kirk realized as he looked into her eyes. He wasn't the only one who had been wounded, he thought suddenly.

For both their sakes he attempted to keep his voice upbeat. "Nice to see that that ex-jock of yours didn't turn your mind to mush." He saw something flicker in her eyes as he casually referred to her ex-husband. It was raw, he thought, though she hid the wound well. Protective instincts surfaced. He'd always felt that way about Rachel. Kirk bit back an urge to hit something, preferably her ex-husband, for whatever it was he had done to generate that look. "It would have been a great loss for me. I always liked listening to your opinions."

Rachel ignored her salad. She rested her head on her upturned hand and looked at Kirk thoughtfully as she slowly stirred the melting ice in her diet drink with a plastic straw. "Did you?"

"You know I did."

Yes, she did. She'd just wanted to hear him say it. It was comforting, somehow. As she thought back to those years they had shared, a bittersweet fondness flooded through her. Things had been so much less complicated then.

"Yes, I suppose you might have, at that. At least once in a while," she told him teasingly. She turned her attention to the salad and tried to regain her appetite. It was a lost cause. "It would help if they used fresh ingredients," she muttered, poking at the dried bits of cheese.

He looked about, trying to get comfortable, searching for a niche that continued to elude him. He folded his hands before him as he turned toward Rachel. She was studying him quietly. Any second now, she was going to ask questions, questions he couldn't answer. Questions that had no answers. Not yet.

"So tell me, Professor Funny Face," he said, a little too quickly, "why'd you become a teacher? I can remember when making a speech in class made you sick to your stomach."

He was trying too hard, she thought. *What's wrong, Kirk? You can tell me.*

She lifted a shoulder, then let it drop. "I thought I had something to say, something to give. I realized that I was just as good as everyone else—less than some, more than others. You did that for me." She smiled into his eyes, remembering. He had been the source of her courage. And other things. "You made me feel important. When I talked, you listened. That meant a lot to me." She let out a breath self-consciously.

She didn't want to talk about herself. What she wanted to do was to get some answers about him. And find out the reason for that flat, distant look in his eyes, for the pain that crept into his voice at unguarded moments.

"So," Rachel began casually as she shifted ever so slightly in her chair, "what have you been doing with yourself for the past nine years, other than winning Pulitzers, dodging bullets and scowling?"

He retired his knife and fork. He wasn't quite ready to discuss himself or his life just yet. It wasn't that easy. As much as he wanted to, as much as he thought he should, it wasn't that easy. He should have realized that it wouldn't be.

"That sums it up neatly."

She sensed his withdrawal and felt frustrated. Kirk had never been one to be summed up neatly. She didn't like him shutting her out. It wasn't something she would have expected from him.

"Kind of terse for nine years, isn't it?"

"Terse and empty," he said, more to himself than to her.

Rachel laid a hand over his, her fingers soft, coaxing, as if attempting to draw words out of him. "Why did you come back, Kirk?"

"I already told you why."

This time, she wouldn't let it go. "You gave me a reason that would have fit nicely into a sit-com. Tell me the real reason."

She saw through him, Kirk thought ruefully. She always had. At times it had irritated him, but it always kept him straight with his own emotions, had always helped him keep his own feet on the ground. But now it didn't seem to be enough. He still couldn't manage to open up. Not yet. Opening up was painful. It was like ripping tape off a gaping wound that hadn't healed.

The smile that touched his lips was cynical. It was a smile he had acquired since the last time she had seen him, she thought. Rachel couldn't help wondering about the things he had seen and done that had created it.

Flippancy came easily. It was a cloak he used to cover the uglier things in his life. "Is that a polite way of saying get lost?"

Rachel shook her head. When had she ever said those words to him? Why would he anticipate that she'd say them now? "No, that's a nosy way of trying to find out what you're doing here after all this time."

He wanted to tell her.

He couldn't. What could he say? "I'm looking for answers"? That sounded too vague, even though it was the truth.

It had been so long since he had put his feelings into words that he wasn't altogether sure that he was able to anymore. Nor that he was even able to feel. For the time being, just listening to her was enough for him. It was all he could manage.

Kirk looked away. "I thought it was time to see if I should sell the house or not."

The house. His parents' house. They had been dead for over three years, having died within six months of each other. He hadn't returned for either of the funerals. It didn't make sense. Why now, suddenly? There had to be more to it. Why was he being so evasive with her? Had the past nine years done something horrible to him?

She couldn't get herself to believe that. Not about Kirk. Kirk was a crusader, a crusader with a charmed life. An untouchable. Lancelot had magic in his veins. No wounds were fatal to him. No wounds ever penetrated.

Kirk had been her Lancelot.

But wounds had obviously penetrated. Something, or someone, had hurt him badly. Rachel took a deep breath. For now, she would let him play this game. "I see. So, how long are you staying?"

He knew by her tone that she wasn't buying it. Kirk was grateful that she wasn't pushing. "Until I make up my mind what to do."

That much was true, he thought. But it wasn't the house that he had to make up his mind about. It was his life. There wasn't any meaning to it anymore. The things he had seen had stripped him of the carefully swaddled idealism he had managed to preserve, even after the childhood he'd had. He was tired of strife, tired of the cheapness of lives traded and lost. Tired of bored, beautiful women who didn't matter. And the solutions he had found at the bottom of a bottle had shaken him so badly that he had taken flight and wound up here.

He'd fled when he saw his father at the bottom of that bottle. Fled because he feared he was turning into the thing he loathed most. His father.

Kirk realized that Rachel had grown quiet and was looking down at his left hand. He looked down himself and saw nothing that could have garnered her attention. "What's the matter?"

She looked up at Kirk. "I was just looking for a wedding ring."

A wedding ring. He laughed cynically, thinking that at least he hadn't dragged anyone else down with him. "I'm not married."

Part of her was glad, though she couldn't begin to understand why he wasn't. Although it would have hurt her to find out that he had gotten married without at least dropping her a line to tell her, she had fully expected him to be. He had always been the kind of dark, brooding hero women fantasized about. She certainly had.

"Never?"

He shook his head and smiled. "Never."

"Why?"

He shrugged carelessly. There had been a sea of women between then and now, and not a drop of feeling amid all of them. It had been just a way of making it through the night. He hadn't wanted it any other way. If any of them had, he hadn't been made aware of it.

"I never met the right person." It was a nice, safe, pat answer.

Rachel nodded, accepting that for now, as well. They needed to talk, in depth, but the cafeteria wasn't the place for it. She rose, taking her tray with her. He followed mechanically. Stopping at the conveyor belt, she angled her tray onto it as the damp, dark rubber snaked its way slowly into the kitchen.

He hardly glanced at the belt as he placed his tray on top of hers.

"I've got to be getting back," she told him.

She walked rapidly out of the cafeteria. Kirk had to move rather quickly to keep up. He wasn't more than five inches taller than she was, and he had maybe a couple of inches on her leg-wise.

"Now you answer a question for me," he said. She glanced at him, waiting. "Why did you become a criminology teacher? You never talked about being interested in criminology when we were younger."

"No," she agreed, "but I always loved mysteries."

"Yes, you did at that." Kirk remembered her obsession. She'd *always* been reading some mystery or other. It had been around then that he became aware of just how sharp her mind really was. "You were the only one I ever knew who could solve an Agatha Christie mystery. Still have the novels?"

He had given her a leather-bound set of the mystery writer's novels as a parting gift when he went off to make his mark on the world. It had been a costly gift he could ill afford. The gift had been that much more precious to her because of that.

"Every last one."

He followed her up a short stairway to another level of the university. A domed building rose into view, like the sun lighting the horizon at dawn. "I thought you'd have tried your hand at writing them, not living them."

She shook her head. "Writing's too hard. Trying to solve them is more gratifying."

As they hurried to her next class, Kirk took in the campus's peaceful setting. The scenery appeared almost idyllic. It was a sharp contrast to the desolation he felt festering inside of him.

There were only a few people in the hall when Rachel finally stopped in front of a classroom. "Well, this is where my next class is."

A bell rang, and people poured out of classrooms along the corridor. He knew she had to go. "Scanlon's tonight?"

"You're on." Maybe he'd talk to her then. "Pick me up at eight."

He suddenly realized that he didn't know where she lived. He still thought of her as living in that small blue-and-white house on Maple. The house that had seemed to radiate warmth and love. "Where do you live now?"

"Right next door to you." He looked at her with such a surprised expression that she laughed. "I moved back after the divorce. Mom and Dad live in Arizona now, so I bought the house from them. It seemed a shame to let the house stand empty. Like your house."

His house. A chill came over Kirk, the way it always did when he thought of the house where he had lived as a child.

Rachel saw the slight shift in his expression, the tiny hardening of his jaw. Speculations multiplied like aphids in the spring, yielding nothing tangible. She felt compelled to shift the mood. "Bring your credit card. I feel a huge hunger coming on."

He noticed several of her students giving him the once-over as they filed into the classroom. "I'm in between jobs."

"I have no mercy." She winked. "See you later."

"Right." Kirk shoved his hands in his pockets.

On impulse, she brushed her lips lightly along his cheek. "Stay out of trouble, Callaghan."

Warmth flooded him at the barest touch of her lips along his skin. "You take all the fun out of everything, Funny Face." He slid his fingertip down her nose, as if that reinforced their relationship, freezing it in the position it had been in nine years ago.

Kirk turned and walked away.

Rachel watched the set of his shoulders as he disappeared down the hallway. They were almost rigid, as if he were bracing himself for something. As if he had been bracing himself for something all along.

"I'm going to find out what's wrong, Kirk," she whispered softly under her breath as the last bell rang. "Even if you don't want to tell me."

Chapter 3

At first glance, there was nothing to set the house apart from any of the other homes on Maple Apple Way. It looked as lived-in, as settled, as the rest. It was the way he felt about it that made it different.

Kirk brought the battered minivan to a stop in the driveway. Cutting off the engine, he remained seated where he was, staring at the house. Waiting for the courage to get out of the vehicle and walk up the front steps.

It hadn't changed in nine years, even though the voices that had once rung out here had been stilled. The outside still looked the same, except that there were daisies growing in the front yard now. There had never been any flowers before.

Until recently, the house where Kirk had grown up had been rented out to a family of five, the Fosters. They had relocated when Mr. Foster had gotten a better job offer in northern California. The real estate agency Kirk had left in charge of the house after his parents' death had contacted him through his publisher. They'd asked if he wanted to have the house rented out again.

That had been three weeks ago. At the time, it had seemed to Kirk like a call to come home. He had been burned-out, bone-tired, and utterly weary of the life he was leading. All his reasons for leading it had abruptly vanished. On impulse, Kirk had terminated his contract with the real estate agency and returned.

But when he had arrived in Bedford last night, the impulse had already faded, transforming into foreboding and dread. Instead of coming to the house, Kirk had looked Cameron up. His old friend, delighted to see him, had invited Kirk to stay the night at his apartment, which he had gladly done. There was something almost surreal about returning to the house of his youth at night.

If he had returned last night, he thought with the barest hint of a smile, he would have known that Rachel still lived next door. There was a measure of comfort in that. Maybe that had even given him the strength to come here now, knowing that the best part of his childhood still existed next door.

It was time to face the ghosts. Or at least some of them.

Kirk slid out of the cab of the minivan, his eyes on the house. Like a man about to face down an unpredictable enemy in hostile territory, Kirk approached the weathered two-story house with measured steps.

He heard the insistent cry of a crow flying overhead as he took the key from his shirt pocket. Maybe it was an omen, he mused, slipping the key into the lock. He turned it slowly, then tried the doorknob.

The door opened soundlessly. No telltale creak greeted his ear as if he were opening the door to a crypt. Yet there was no denying that was the way he felt. As if he were stepping out of the light, into a tomb.

The tomb of his childhood.

Kirk squared his shoulders. He hadn't returned to Bedford to embrace these four walls, these memories, he reminded himself. It wasn't in this house that he had found the seeds of his strength, the roots of his identity, though it was what had happened in this house, never a home, that had partially formed him.

And perhaps, in an odd sort of way, some of his strength *had* originated here. Strength to withstand what had gone on behind these walls.

Secrets he had never told anyone.

Certainly not Rachel. Rachel, with her worshipful eyes and her nurturing manner. He'd been too embarrassed, too angry about his life, to tell her.

Not even Cameron, with whom he had shared every other thought.

Fingertips lightly braced against the door, he pushed it open the rest of the way, his movements mimicking those of a gunfighter expecting to be ambushed when he walked into a room.

Sunshine burst into the house over his shoulder, eager to bring life into the living room. There were various pieces of furniture scattered about the room, draped in white sheets like children engaged in a game of impersonating ghosts. He'd called the storage company and had the furniture moved back into the house after the Fosters moved out.

Kirk looked around, then forced himself to step inside. He had no inclination to lift aside a single sheet. It was as if the sheets, left in place, could somehow suppress the secrets, suppress the memories.

Light pushed its way through windows that had only now begun to become dusty. It gave an artificial cheerfulness to the house that he knew wasn't there. At least it hadn't been before.

Perhaps the Fosters had been happy here.

He dragged a hand through his unruly black hair as he looked around. God knew the Callaghans hadn't been, he thought.

As he remembered it, it had been a house of sorrow. A house filled with somber expressions and drunken recriminations.

A house of violence.

A shudder threatened to slide over him. He braced his shoulders, blocking it. Kirk frowned, wondering how wise it actually had been to return here. But to remain away from his past was to remain away from the solution, the key to why he had withdrawn so dramatically. Why everything had fallen apart for him. It was here. He knew it was here.

It had to be.

He needed to find himself, to discover who and what, after all these years, he was.

To rest and regroup.

And to attempt to untangle the skeins of his badly tangled soul by returning to where it had all begun. To the heart of it.

Or, if not the heart—for the heart had been all but beaten out of him here—then the creative force that had spawned him and molded him into the man he'd been destined to become.

Kirk passed the fireplace. His eyes were drawn to the rusting poker that stood off to one side like a discarded sentinel. Obviously the Fosters hadn't been much for fires on cold winter nights, he mused. And they hadn't discovered the extraneous uses of the poker, either, the way his father had.

He closed his eyes and took a deep breath, but he could still almost feel the sting of the iron on his back, on his flesh. All these years later, he could still feel it.

Restlessness pervaded his body, but he forced himself to remain, even though he had somewhere else to go if he chose. Cameron, now a detective with the Bedford Police Department, had given him a spare key to his apartment this morning before he left. The latter had sensed without being told that Kirk might not want to spend the night on his own territory.

They'd always been so tuned in to one another, Kirk thought. He and Cameron. And Rachel.

Tension had his body almost rigid as he roamed about. He shoved his hands into his pockets, and his fingers came into contact with Cameron's key. He curved them around it, debating.

With a sigh, he pulled his hand out and hooked his thumbs on his belt as he continued to wander slowly about the house.

He hadn't returned just to run again. The time for running had passed. He realized now that that was what he'd been doing ever since he left Bedford. Running away.

Echoes of memories whispered softly in the shadows of his mind as he moved silently through the rooms. The day was warm. Kirk felt cold. There had been no laughter here, no pride, no joy. Never once, in all the years that he'd known them, had he ever invited Cameron or Rachel into his house.

He hadn't wanted them tainted.

He hadn't wanted them to know his shame.

Neither of them had ever questioned, ever asked why. They had accepted the situation as a given and moved on with their friendship, treasuring Kirk, not any external trappings associated with him.

There was no air in the house, despite the fact that he had left the door open. He felt as if he were suffocating. Quickly he crossed to the closest window and threw it open to let in some air. He needed the feel of clean air sweeping away the dust, the stale cobwebs that had begun to form.

He wanted it to sweep away the debris of the past.

Looking out, he realized he was facing Rachel's house, across the way. The structure was partially hidden from view by a squadron of towering Italian cypresses.

They had to be well over twenty feet tall by now, he judged. When he was a young boy, Kirk had thought of them as an armed military guard, fashioned in the likeness of the Wicked Witch's guard in *The Wizard of Oz*. And he had believed that they, like those guards, had been posted there by his father to keep out the good. To keep the evil in.

On dark, moonless nights, the trees had appeared particularly oppressive.

Their heads nodding sagely in the light spring breeze, they looked pretty harmless now.

It had all been due to the overactive imagination of an unhappy little boy, Kirk thought detachedly. In a way, it was as if he hadn't been that boy. As if he had never had a childhood at all. And perhaps, in some ways, he hadn't.

In other ways, ways involving Cameron and Rachel, he had, Kirk recalled with a smile as he looked past the trees. He could just about make out the bright blue-and-white stucco house.

It seemed an odd twist of fate that she had chosen to move back into the house just at the time when he had returned to his roots. To either strengthen them or pull them out completely and replant them somewhere else.

Fate, he supposed, was a very strange thing. He only had to review some of the events of his life to be convinced of that.

The sun shone so that it threw his reflection back at him in the window. Kirk looked down at his rumpled work shirt and realized that he was wearing the exact same clothes he'd worn last night, when he had appeared on Cameron's doorstep.

Kirk wrinkled his nose. If he didn't watch it, he was going to become eccentric. Or at least gamy. He needed a shower, he decided, and a change of clothes.

He needed a hell of a lot more than that, but the shower was a start. Things had a way of propelling themselves if you gave them an initial push. He still believed in that. Sort of.

The window remained open as he walked away.

Ethan watched her move about the living room through sullen, dark eyes. Sullen eyes that held so little of the boy she'd adored in them.

As she approached him to straighten up the mess he had left behind while playing with his toys, he raised his chin defiantly.

"You're dressed up."

Did he know how much he sounded like his father? How the cadence in his voice emulated the man he'd hated? Rachel purposely tried to sound cheerful. She didn't want to argue. Not tonight.

"That's because I'm going out."

Ethan dug fisted hands into the sofa as he sat up, his feet planted beneath him as if he were about to spring up at any second.

"On a date?" It wasn't idle curiosity in his voice, but hostility. As if he were daring her to lie to him. As if he were daring her to tell him the truth.

Either way, he wasn't going to be pleased. She knew the signs by now.

Rachel stacked several videotapes on the television set. Tapes she meant to watch but never found the time to view.

"Not really." She was going to remain calm, she swore to herself. Ethan was going to see that he couldn't bait her. They were going to find a way to get along, or she was going to die trying.

Ethan cocked his head to see her face more clearly. "But it's with a guy."

Tension shimmered between her and her son, the way it always seemed to these days, without cause, without provocation. It was there, lying in wait for her, as soon as he opened his eyes in the morning. It was like attempting to cross a mine field. She had no idea how to successfully circumvent it. It was especially frustrating because she and Ethan had once been so close.

Until her divorce.

And the reason that had prompted it.

She smiled slightly as she concentrated on Ethan's words and not the accusation behind them. A guy. Kirk was far from being "a guy" in the way Ethan meant.

"An old friend," she told him.

Rachel brushed one hand against the other. The tape jackets were dusty. Showed how often she got to watch television, she thought. Life was galloping away from her. And taking Ethan with it, she thought with a deep-seated pang.

Ethan rose to his knees as he knelt on the sofa, turning to keep his mother in his range. "Old?" he echoed. "How old?"

Rachel stopped fluttering around and crossed to him. "Older than me."

She ran her hand along Ethan's cheek, then fruitlessly attempted to block the stab of pain when he jerked his head back, his eyes flat. She doggedly maintained her sunny tone of voice.

"He's picking me up here in a few minutes." She watched as Ethan rose from the sofa. He was retreating to his room. In the past six months, he always seemed to be either attacking or retreating. No middle ground.

"I'd like you to meet him," she said softly.

Suspicion creased the smooth brow, mingling with his perpetual scowl.

"Why?"

She let out a breath. Where was the child who had been so happy? Who had enjoyed her company, and life? Don had destroyed that. And somehow, unintentionally, she had helped.

"Because he's someone I grew up with. Your uncle Cameron and I were best friends with Kirk Callaghan for years. He lived in the house next door."

Rachel looked in that direction now, though there were walls in the way that obstructed her view. If she tried, she could almost envision Kirk there now. Having him back, for however long, somehow helped her cope. In an odd way, it negated some of the worst parts of her life. The parts with Don in them.

She placed her hands on her son's slender shoulders and held tight as he tried to shrug her off. He'd never succeed in that, she thought. Never. Tenacity was something she prided herself on.

Her eyes held his. "Ethan, I want to share things with you."

The suspicion deepened its mark. Distrust and wariness were stamped all over his face. "Why?" he repeated, with more feeling.

She wanted to shake him, to shake this cloak of ugliness from him somehow. She restrained her impulse. It wouldn't accomplish anything.

"Because you count. Because you're my son." Rachel stared down into the defiant eyes. Eyes that mirrored Don's so well. "That should be enough reason. I don't need any more reason than that." Her grip tightened slightly, as if that would help him absorb her words. "You shouldn't, either."

This time Ethan succeeded in shrugging her off. "I've got homework to do."

He did, she thought, but he wasn't going to do it. He was just evading her. In the past six months, Ethan's schoolwork had suffered. There had been a bevy of notes from a discontented teacher, littered with words such as *potential* and *waste*. And "failure." And yesterday Ethan had dropped out of his Little League team. He'd turned his back on baseball, a game he adored. She was still trying to get to the bottom of that.

To the bottom of all of it. She had tried talking, pleading. When that had failed, she'd asked Cameron to talk to him. That hadn't helped, either. It seemed inconceivable to Rachel that she was losing touch with her son, the person who mattered most to her in the world. And yet she was.

She had no one to blame but herself.

And she had no one but herself to rely on in order to win him back.

"Your homework can wait." Her words stopped him in his tracks. "I want you here, with me."

A defiant retort formed on his lips just as the doorbell rang.

Startled by the sound, Rachel's eyes darted toward the front door as she sucked in her breath. She knew that Ethan was watching her reaction.

There was a sneer on his lips. "If he's just a friend, how come you're acting as if he's a date?"

The accusation was sharp. And he was partially right. She *was* behaving as if this were something more than an evening with an old friend. But that was because she'd once had a crush on Kirk, because she'd been more than a little in love with him when she was in her teens. In some ways, she supposed, he was still her idea of Prince Charming. A brooding, troubled Prince Charming, but a Prince Charming nonetheless.

"That's just your imagination. I'm excited about seeing him again after all these years, that's all."

Crossing to the door, she threw it open, a greeting hovering on her lips. It dissolved in a sigh as she stepped back to admit her brother.

"Oh, it's you."

Cameron kissed the top of his sister's head as he walked in. "Nice to see you, too." He looked around. Kirk was nowhere in sight. "Weren't you expecting me?" Rachel had asked him to stay with his nephew while she went out with Kirk.

Rachel closed the door behind Cameron, chagrined at her reaction. "Yes, but..."

Cameron looked at her knowingly. "But I'm not Kirk," he completed for her.

Rachel waved her hand, dismissing his comment—and the blatant meaning beneath it. She'd just gone through all that with Ethan. She wasn't about to live through an instant replay. "Sorry. Ethan and I were talking, and I was preoccupied."

Cameron nodded, accepting the excuse. He looked at his nephew. The boy's slender build clearly indicated that he took after his mother, rather than his athletic father. Or him, for that matter, Cameron thought. Only the scowl belonged to Don.

"How's it going, Ethan?"

"Okay, I guess," he mumbled.

"I ran into Pete Kelly." He mentioned the name of Ethan's baseball coach as he made himself comfortable on the sofa. "He tells me that you quit the team."

Ethan studied the worn creases on the toes of his sneakers. "Baseball's for dorks."

Cameron and Rachel exchanged looks. Ethan had lived and breathed baseball for the past three years. It was because of him that Cameron maintained season tickets for the Angels and Dodgers.

"I don't know. Some of those dorks can hit pretty well," Cameron said.

Ethan jammed his hands into his pockets. "I don't like baseball."

"Since when?" Cameron asked, his surprise evident in his voice.

"Since now," Ethan spit out. Before Cameron could say anything further, Ethan looked at his mother accusingly. "What's he doing here, anyway? I'm eight years old. I don't need a baby-sitter."

"No," Rachel countered evenly, "what you need is someone to teach you some manners. But for the time being, your uncle is going to stay here with you while I go out."

Frustration had tears welling up in her eyes, and she turned away, walking toward the dining room.

Torn between attempting to talk to his nephew and coming to his sister's rescue, Cameron seemed to decide that she needed him more. Following her into the other room, he placed his hands on her arms. Rachel was forced to look up at him. Both were aware that Ethan was hovering in the background, looking annoyed with them. And with himself.

Diversion had always been a good tactic to employ in emotionally charged situations. Cameron had learned that on the force. It was no less true in personal matters. "You look awfully good tonight, Rach. Trying to make him see what he missed out on?"

Rachel sniffed once to draw back the tears that threatened to fall, and looked up in surprise at Cameron's obvious attempt at diversion. "I haven't got the faintest idea what you're talking about."

"No?" Humor curved Cameron's generous mouth and moved into his eyes. The young, vulnerable Rachel had been too frail to tease. That was no longer the case. "Then I guess you didn't lead the same life I did."

Rachel's eyes narrowed. She had the uneasy feeling she knew what he was getting at. "Cameron..."

He ignored the warning note. "Seems to me I remember a very starry-eyed younger sister who would have very easily sold her soul if she could have gone out with Kirk Callaghan as something other than just a friend."

So, she hadn't been that successful in hiding her feelings, she thought, her amusement rising. Trust Cameron to make her feel better.

She pretended to sniff at his scenario. "Scanlon's has a dress code. No bag ladies allowed."

Cameron dropped his hands and stepped back to give her a thorough once-over. She was wearing a simple black dress that accented some very unsimple curves.

"You're a hell of a long way off from being a bag lady." He grinned at her, then grew serious. "All kidding aside, you look great, Rach. It's about time you put your life back into gear." He looked toward the living room. Ethan was back on the sofa, flipping channels on the television set. "For both your sakes."

Rachel shrugged, smoothing down a wayward curl. "That's not how Ethan sees it." She glanced over her shoulder at her son. "He thinks of it as a betrayal."

Cameron looked at his godson. He'd witnessed a bright, happy boy descend into his own private hell in the matter of a few baffling months. "Whose? His?"

"Yes." She could only guess at the rest of it. "And perhaps his father's." There wasn't anything else she could think of.

"Don's dead." Cameron set his mouth grimly. "Besides, he wasn't much of a father when he was alive." If the man hadn't died, Cameron was afraid of what he might be driven to do. Every time he thought of Don mistreating Rachel, of what he had put her through, a rage seized Cameron that was in direct contradiction to the affable man he usually appeared to be. "You should have told me sooner about him, you know."

The words were said mildly, as if merely in passing, but Rachel heard the suppressed emotion. She shrugged, helpless either to combat the past or to change it. Helpless to change the effects it had had on her life, and her son's. That was the worst of it. The way it had affected Ethan.

"I thought he'd change." *Hoped.* She raised her eyes to her brother's face. "And maybe I was ashamed to let you know. I honestly believed that I could straighten it all out."

She pressed her lips together, her heart aching as she attempted to push back the memory of those days.

Her voice lowered, choked with emotion. "It wasn't until I saw him raise his hand to Ethan that I knew we had to get out." A sad smile twisted her lips. "Even then, Ethan wanted to stay. Now he acts as if I was the heavy, instead of Don." She sighed. "I don't understand that boy."

Cameron placed his arm around her shoulders in a familiar, comforting gesture. "He doesn't want to be understood. This is what they call the difficult age." He released her and crossed to the living room.

The difficult age. A popular phrase that served as a catchall for any and all problems that couldn't be addressed or solved.

"How long does it last?"

"I don't know." Cameron laughed softly. He saw Ethan raise his head in his direction, his suspicions refreshed. "I'm still in it."

"Great help you are," Rachel muttered, following him into the room.

"I try, Rach, I try." Cameron looked toward the door when he heard the bell. "Poor old Kirk."

Rachel stopped and looked at her brother. "What makes you say that?"

The broad grin threatened to split his face. "He won't know what hit him."

"No, but you will," she countered, one hand on her hip. "And it'll be me, if you don't stop."

Cameron laughed and nodded toward the door, an innocent look in his sea-green eyes. "Want me to get that?"

She could feel Ethan's eyes on her, and she did her best to remain playful. He was going to come around, she swore to herself. Any day now.

"No." When she swung her head, the tips of her light blond hair brushed along her shoulders. "It's my house now," she reminded him. She had bought it from their parents. Somehow, having clear title to it helped center her and place things in perspective. "I can get my own door, thank you." Out of the corner of her eye, she saw Ethan heading for the back bedroom. "You can drag your nephew back out. I want him to meet Kirk."

Taking a deep breath, she crossed to the door and opened it.

This time, Kirk was on her doorstep. Right on time. "You always were punctual."

His eyes washed over her, absorbing her quickly, the way he had trained himself to absorb every fleeting detail in his life. In his line of work, there wasn't always time for second takes or refocusing. Not on the plane he operated on.

"And you were always full of surprises." And never more than now, he thought as the light of appreciation crept into his eyes.

Chapter 4

"Wow."

Kirk remained standing in the doorway as he looked at Rachel slowly, appraising her as a connoisseur would a glass of fine wine. This morning hadn't quite prepared him for the way she appeared tonight. Had she really lived next door to him all those years without giving an adequate hint of what was to be? He found it difficult to believe, and yet here she was, as gorgeous now as she had been plain then.

A smile glimmered at the corners of his mouth, nearly reaching his eyes as they swept up to her face. "Or am I repeating myself?"

"Yes, but twice in one day is fine with me. I certainly don't mind hearing it again." More than that, she could go on hearing it forever, she thought. Rachel grinned as a warm feeling burrowed through her with long, far-reaching fingers.

Because Kirk made no move to come in, she took his hand and ushered him into the house.

Amusement flickered over Cameron's face. "See you still know your way."

Kirk nodded a greeting at Cameron. "Very funny."

There was a tall, thin boy standing next to his friend. Against his will, from the look of the hand Cameron had firmly on his shoulder.

Rachel's son.

Kirk studied the small, defiant face, looking for similarities with his mother. The boy resembled Rachel as she was today. There was very little there to recall the girl she had been. For that matter, the boy hardly looked like Cameron, either. Cameron was large-boned, and Rachel had a slight bone structure, like a porcelain doll. More like his mother, the boy appeared fragile standing next to Cameron. His fine, artistic features could almost have been called pretty.

They probably teased him a lot at school, Kirk guessed.

The scowl on the young boy's face marred the delicate features. No doubt he saw him as a threat, Kirk thought. It seemed rather funny. The only threat he posed these days was to himself.

Cameron cleared his throat as he urged Ethan forward a step. "What time are you planning on getting my sister in?"

Kirk arched a brow, amused by the question, and by the way Rachel's mouth dropped open in stunned surprise. There were some who thought of him as unsavory, as a dangerous renegade who would risk anything for the right photograph, the right story. But he doubted that part of his reputation had ever reached here.

"Playing the role of the worried parent, Cameron?"

"Playing the role of the tired older brother," Cameron told him. "It's been a long day, and I'm not sure I can outlast Ethan here." He nodded at the boy.

There was no corresponding smile on Ethan's face.

A sullen child, Kirk observed, and immediately wondered why. He would have thought that having Rachel for a mother would be the answer to any child's prayer. Kirk had little doubt that Rachel was as warm, as loving and giving, as her own mother had been. Families usually followed certain set patterns.

Which was why he would never have children of his own, he thought. Kindness bred kindness, abuse only abuse. There were things still locked within him that he was afraid to let out into the light of day. Afraid because of what he would find out.

As a child, he'd pretended more than once, as he lay cowering under his blankets, praying for morning to come and his parents' raised voices to cease, that Mrs. Reed was his mother. More than that, when he was still naive enough to wish, he had wanted Mr. Reed to be his father. He would have sold his young immortal soul to belong to their family, to know the unconditional love, the comfort, that Rachel and Cameron knew.

Instead, he had sold his soul for freedom. And lost it in the bargain.

Rachel was embarrassed by Ethan's defiance. Ethan was her pride, her joy, and she didn't want Kirk's first impression of her son to be a negative one.

Forcing a smile to her lips that she hoped would be infectious, she hooked her arm through Kirk's and drew him over toward Ethan.

"Kirk, I'd like you to meet my son."

He'd never been good with children. Even as a child, he'd never been good with them. It always filled Kirk with wonder how a loner like him had attracted the warm friendship of people like Cameron and Rachel.

There was something in the boy's eyes that struck a distant but familiar chord within him.

Kirk put his hand out to Ethan. "Hi, I'm Kirk Callaghan."

Ethan kept his hands at his sides and looked at Kirk's as if it were a strange object being thrust at him. His lips curled in what looked like the beginnings of a sneer.

Humiliation and frustration rose up like a wave in Rachel's throat.

"It's a hand, Ethan," she prompted. "You're supposed to shake it, not examine it."

Ethan's head jerked up in his mother's direction. "I know what it is."

Kirk recognized something vaguely disturbing beneath the angry words. He cut through the rhetoric and took the boy's hand in his, surprising him. Kirk gave it a quick press in greeting before releasing it. Ethan stared at him, his small, light brows drawing together over his perfectly shaped nose in puzzlement.

"Done and over with," Kirk said simply, in reply to the unspoken question. "No big deal, right?"

In response, Ethan shrugged indifferently. It was, Kirk knew, a flippant gesture meant to mask his feelings of awkwardness and inadequacy.

No one recognized the gesture or the significance better than Kirk. He'd been there himself, before Cameron and Rachel had managed to crack his outer shell and befriend him. It had been Kirk against the world then. He saw the same painfully familiar stance assumed by the boy now.

Kirk's eyes shifted from Ethan to Rachel, his brow arched in a silent question.

Rachel merely shook her head slightly. Her apology was in her eyes.

Kirk turned to Cameron, thinking it best to drop the matter.

"In answer to your question," he continued, as if there hadn't been an awkward break. "I should have Rachel back in a couple of hours or so. However long it takes to make amends."

Cameron ran his hand along a cheek that was already beginning to need a shave. "Amends?"

Kirk nodded. He noticed that, although Ethan was attempting to appear disinterested, he was listening. "She found out that I wrote to you."

Cameron was more lost than ever. "And you're apologizing for that?"

"Maybe he should," Rachel cut in, "but he's apologizing for not writing to me, even after I wrote."

The short laugh was knowing and dismissive. "That's because he didn't want to get inundated with ten-page letters." A self-satisfied smile lifted Cameron's mouth as he elaborated for his sister's benefit. "Real men like to be terse, quick. They don't have time for embellishments."

Rachel jabbed an elbow sharply into his ribs, catching him off guard. "And how would *you* know what real men do?"

Cameron nursed his side, shaking his head. "On second thought, keep her out as long as you like." His eyes narrowed to slits as he contemplated the next image before voicing it to Kirk. "Lose her even, maybe."

Kirk laughed, pleasure wrapping itself around him like a warm woolen blanket on a cold January night. The scene before him was reminiscent of so many others that had been played out within these walls.

These walls.

As the laughter slipped away on soft cat's paws, Kirk looked around the house. From what he could see, little had changed here. The feeling of homecoming permeated through him the way it had failed to do when he entered his own house earlier.

No, he amended, it had never been his house. It had always been his parents' house. It had been merely a place where he had eaten and slept. And, at times, wept. Until he was old enough not to care.

Or to believe he didn't.

Kirk saw the expectant look on Rachel's face and knew which side he was going to have to take to find peace this evening.

"I didn't write to her," he explained to Cameron, "because I just couldn't put anything down eloquently enough."

At least it sounded like a good excuse. The real reason was that he had been too busy. And then too tortured by what he had witnessed. Cameron was right about the way men corresponded. A few words were enough. An entire tome wouldn't have begun to adequately cover what he felt. And he hadn't had the time to even attempt it. So he had written nothing.

"I wasn't going to grade them," Rachel protested, then stopped herself. This could go on all night, if she let it. On another occasion, she might have, but tonight she wanted to go out, to get Kirk alone and possibly unravel the mystery that seemed to be cloaking him. "But that's in the past. Now you have to make amends."

She picked up her purse from where she had left it on the table next to the door. Slipping the thin strap onto her shoulder, she turned to the boy who had been watching all this in brooding silence.

Looking at him, Rachel realized that Ethan made her think of a smaller, younger version of Kirk. Withdrawn, unreachable. Kirk masked it better, but there was that same strange, wary, distrustful look in his eyes. It was almost as if there were a link between them.

Thank God for Cameron, she thought, shifting her eyes to her brother.

Cameron saw the flash of gratitude immediately. He smiled reassuringly at his sister. "Make the devil pay, Rach. We're going to be fine, aren't we, Ethan?" He laid his arm around the boy's shoulders.

Ethan flinched before he caught himself and stiffened. Watching, Kirk could feel the movement echoing within him. When he was young, he'd reacted just the same way whenever anyone touched him. Because of what his father had done to him, Kirk had trusted no one. It had taken seeing what life was like in the Reed household for Kirk to realize that ridicule and beatings weren't the norm.

Had the boy been beaten? The question ricocheted violently in his mind.

None of his business, Kirk told himself, shaking off the thought.

Rachel moved toward her son. "Ethan, I want you to behave tonight," she said to him softly. "Please." Her eyes echoed her entreaty.

Ethan looked uncomfortable being talked to this way in front of a stranger. He shrugged indifferently, the weight of his uncle's arm heavy on his shoulders.

"Don't worry, I won't burn down the house or anything."

She cupped his chin in her hand and forced him to look up at her. "That's not what I meant, and you know it." She pressed her lips together, wishing she had a magic wand that would allow her to change her son back to the child he'd been before all this ugly business began. "I know you're a good kid, Ethan," she whispered.

There was more, so much more, but she knew she would only embarrass him if she voiced it now. Embarrass him, and accomplish nothing.

Rachel dropped her hand to her side. Maybe Cameron was right. Maybe this was just a rebellious phase Ethan was going through, and she was making too much of it. Maybe, just this once, if she ignored it, the problem would go away.

But she had ignored a problem once before, and it had just snowballed until it had nearly engulfed her completely. Until Don had nearly destroyed her and Ethan.

Not tonight, she told herself. Tonight was for homecomings and Kirk, not for any troubled memories.

Rachel looked at her brother. "We'll be back after we exceed his credit limit," she promised, forcing a smile to her lips again.

"That shouldn't take long," Cameron commented as he followed them to the door. Ethan had flopped down on the sofa and returned to switching channels. "Have a good time," Cameron instructed. It was hard to tell who the order was aimed at, Kirk or Rachel. "And don't worry." The last comment was obviously directed toward Rachel.

Rachel nodded. "Thanks." She waited until they were both in the car before she said anything to Kirk. "I'm sorry about Ethan."

Kirk kept his eye on the side mirror as he guided the minivan out of the driveway and onto the street. He didn't have to look at Rachel to detect her embarrassment. "Sorry?"

She sighed as she folded her hands in her lap and stared straight ahead. It felt good to get away. Scanlon's was just a nice neighborhood club, yet right now, in her present state of mind, it seemed like an exotic retreat. It had been a long time since she had taken a break from the tension. A long time since she had dared.

"About the way he acted." Rachel glanced at Kirk's profile. "Don't pretend you didn't notice how sullen he was."

For Rachel's sake, Kirk made light of the situation. It probably involved nothing more than a boy testing his limits. There was no point in his reading things into the situation. Ethan wasn't him. "Not everyone comes off like an effervescent champagne bottle."

She saw just the smallest hint of a dimple in his cheek. He was biting back a smile. That alone was hopeful, she thought.

"Is that the way you see me?"

He saw her in terms of rainbows. And himself in terms of dark clouds and thunderstorms. Kirk glanced in her direction as he turned right at the corner. "In comparison to me, yes."

Rachel's laugh was just short of a snort. "In comparison to you, flat soda is effervescent. You were never given to overt displays of excitement." She paused, reflecting. "Now that I think about it, I don't believe I *ever* saw you get excited about anything." It had frustrated her when she was younger and attempted to get Kirk to become enthusiastic about a score of things, all to no avail.

The smile that rose to his lips came of its own accord, and was that much more surprising because it did. "You took care of that department for both of us."

Rachel shook her head. "You make me sound as if I were your familiar."

He had no idea what she was talking about. That, too, had echoes of the past, and was vaguely comforting to him. "My what?"

"Familiar," she repeated. She shifted in her seat so that she faced him. The seat belt dug into her hipbone. "You know, like witches and warlocks were supposed to have." She could see that she wasn't striking a chord. "A pet that carries about the essence of the master within it," she elaborated.

The terrain on either side of the road had changed somewhat, yet he could still find his way around after all this time. Scanlon's was just ahead.

"I never thought of you as my pet." That wasn't entirely true, he remembered with a tinge of fondness.

"No, mascot was more like it." Rachel noted that at least he had the good grace not to contradict her. "You and Cameron both treated me like one."

For a while they *had* thought of her as one, he mused, he and Cameron. She'd dogged their tracks like a faithful, playful puppy. "You were the one who wanted to tag along," Kirk reminded her.

Fiercely, she remembered. She had worshiped her older brother, though in those days she would rather have died than admit it. Some of that worship had been transferred to Kirk when Cameron all but adopted him. "That's because your life seemed to be so much more exciting than mine."

Exciting was the last word he would have used to describe his life back then, he thought. He spared her a glance before taking his foot off the brake. He drove the car through the intersection. "I thought I was as dull as dishwater."

"*You* were, your life wasn't," she pointed out. There was a difference. One that, knowing him, he probably was unaware of, she thought.

Rachel laughed as they drew close to the small strip of restaurants and shops. Scanlon's was located at the very end of the block. "Don't you know that you always had an aura around you?"

"Auras. Familiars," he echoed. "This is all sounding very mystical." Amused skepticism highlighted his angular face.

She wasn't going to be teased out of this. He had to know that he attracted a following. Didn't he? On second thought, Kirk had always been oblivious of the ripples he generated. It wasn't modesty, as much as disinterest, that kept him from knowing, she decided.

"You were brooding and mysterious. I didn't know a single girl in school who wasn't in love with you."

That seemed absolutely ludicrous. He'd hardly dated while in high school, not wanting to become entangled in relationships of any sort beyond the one he treasured with the Reeds. "I don't remember ever tripping over any of them."

That was just typical of him. She shook her head, dismissing his protest. "That's because you never noticed anything as mundane as a worshipful female."

Just before they drove into the parking lot, Kirk gave her an odd look. It made Rachel feel that perhaps he hadn't been as oblivious of the way she felt about him as she had believed.

She felt a blush climbing up her neck, reaching for her cheeks.

Kirk parked close to the restaurant, then pulled up the hand brake and looked at her. He made no effort to suppress the smile on his lips. "Either the heater is suddenly going full blast on your side of the van, or you're turning pink."

She waved a hand at his comment, ready to dismiss it. At the last moment, she thought better of it. "Just a tinge of embarrassment."

"Don't." He said the word so sharply as he got out of the car that Rachel looked at him in surprise. She was still staring at him as she got out herself. "Not around me." Realizing how he must have sounded, Kirk cleared his throat. When he spoke again, his voice was lower, less intense. "Not even if it does look rather appealing."

Rachel rounded the hood to stand beside him, not knowing exactly how to respond to that. Part of her was confused, but another part was reacting to the compliment he'd handed her, however cavalierly. That small kernel of a glow was beginning to grow, like a long-overlooked ember that suddenly found itself near a source of heat once more.

She gestured toward the restaurant. It always looked better at night. In the light of day, all the work that needed to be done was evident. Night hid faults. And secrets.

"Well, here it is." She smiled as she looked at it and remembered the first time he had brought her here. She'd felt so daring, sneaking in on a faked ID. "A little older, a little scragglier than you remember, but still here." On impulse, she took his hand in hers and tugged gently. "C'mon, let's go inside. They're not going to serve us standing out here."

He wasn't given to touching or holding. He wasn't demonstrative at all, so when Rachel took his hand, it sent him back across the years to when she would grab his hand, squealing in excitement as she dragged him off to see something she had done or discovered.

Like an annoying, endearing little sister, Rachel had always sought him out. For his approval, for discussions, and just for the joy of sharing things with him. And he had always gone.

Memories and warm thoughts from the past fought with an entirely different set of parameters generated by the same light touch of her hand. Feelings that had nothing to do with those between brothers and sisters. Or even close friends.

Surprised, annoyed, angry with himself, Kirk drew his hand away.

Rachel turned to look at him, a step away from the front door. He'd pulled his hand away as if he'd been burned by something. It made her wonder again about what was bothering him. Why was he acting so strangely?

He could have sworn there was almost a hurt look in her eyes. "I'm supposed to take your hand," he pointed out quietly.

She was accustomed to taking charge these days. It probably offended some manly bone in his body. But she could live with that.

With a laugh, she held her hand up to him like an offering. "Then do it," she urged.

Kirk wrapped his fingers around hers. The somber look had eased again. "Thanks for not changing too much, Funny Face."

She smiled at the nickname, and at the man who had given it to her. "My pleasure. Now feed me."

Kirk opened the door and waited until Rachel had stepped inside before following.

"Be gentle," he cautioned. When she raised a brow, he tapped the pocket with his wallet in it. "I haven't used my credit card in a long time. I'm not sure it's still in force. Bosnia doesn't have many boutiques."

Rachel stopped at the hostess's desk. She could see a rather minimally clad woman in the distance, coming toward them. Rachel turned toward Kirk. "Was that where you were last?"

He shrugged off her question the way he wished he could shrug off the last few years of his life. "There, among other places." They had different names, but the atrocities, the inhumanities, had all been the same. As had the despair.

Rachel thought of the stories she had read, of the carnage she had watched on the nightly news. There was no way to suppress the shudder that swept over her. She laid a hand on his arm in mute sympathy. The horrors he must have witnessed firsthand. . . .

"God, Kirk, when I think of you being there—"

"Don't." Again the word came a little too quickly, a little too fiercely, propelled by his own denial. "I don't," he said, more easily. He shoved his hands into his pockets. "I think of myself exactly where I am at the moment.'' He purposely looked around, though the darkened atmosphere did not lend itself to close scrutiny. ''In Scanlon's, with an old friend.'' He watched as amusement tugged at her mouth. ''A gorgeous old friend.''

She blew out a breath. She knew a retreat when she heard one, but for now she would let it alone. ''Well, I guess I won't argue with that.''

He laughed softly to himself. ''Probably one of the few subjects you wouldn't argue.''

Toward the end, before he left, they had gotten into some very heavy philosophical debates, the way only adolescents on the verge of adulthood could. ''I've gotten better.''

She had been a rabid optimist, in contrast to his dogged pessimism. He found himself yearning for the innocent past. ''That I'll have to judge for myself.''

You will, she promised him silently. *You will.*

''Well, since you're planning to stick around for a bit, I'm sure you will. By the way, I intend to fill you with a lot of good home-cooked meals during your stay.''

The platinum-haired hostess, in a black spandex skirt that could have doubled as an armband, gave Rachel an amused look as she approached the desk.

Obviously not a domestic, Rachel thought, returning the shallow smile.

''Two,'' Kirk told the woman. The latter gave him a very inviting look before she turned on four-inch heels and led the way to a table.

''An economy of words,'' Rachel murmured as they followed in the hostess's rather provocative wake. Rachel wondered how the woman managed to sit in that skirt. ''Nothing's changed.''

How he wished that were true. How he wished he was still the same man he'd been when he left Bedford. Still able to hope.

Still whole.

Kirk held out the seat for Rachel as the hostess let two menus all but drop from her pencil-thin hand. ''Some things have,'' Kirk told her.

''Yes, you've gotten more manners.'' Rachel folded her hands together before her as Kirk took a seat opposite her at the tiny table. "And become even sexier-looking—and more mysterious."

She said the words like an old friend, telling herself that her pulse hadn't skipped a little when his thigh brushed against her arm as he passed her.

A smile slowly peeled away the layers of somberness around his mouth as he looked at her over a flickering candle that sat in a dim red glass bowl. He reached for a menu.

"You always did have a way of oversimplifying things."

Following suit, Rachel flipped open her own menu. "That's because you were always complicating them. Someone had to cut to the heart of the matter."

Kirk glanced down at either side of the menu and saw nothing. His mind was preoccupied. He wanted to be here with her, yet he couldn't seem to release the restlessness that had a chokehold on him.

He set the menu aside and looked at Rachel. "So, what's your pleasure?"

That was easy. "A glass of wine, a rare steak—" Rachel folded her menu and placed it on top of his "—and a long conversation."

He nodded, looking around for someone to take their order. Someone who looked to be a college freshman was heading their way, an abbreviated apron tied around his waist, a pad and pencil in his hand.

"I'm sure they can accommodate you with two out of three."

Instinct had her laying her hand on top of his, and smiling when she saw something dark in his eyes. "I wasn't thinking of talking to the waiter."

As unobtrusively as possible, he drew his hand away and toyed with his water glass. "You could always talk to anyone," he recalled.

Rachel shook her head. She remembered a different version of her life. "I was painfully shy."

Her protest caused a genuine laugh to rise to his lips. "In a pig's eye."

"I was," Rachel insisted as the waiter arrived at their table. "I just learned to mask it with rhetoric, that's all."

"You did a hell of a job of it, then." She could talk the leaves off the trees if she put her mind to it.

Though the tension was still with him, he made an effort to settle back and enjoy the evening. He was with Rachel, and for now, nothing else was supposed to matter.

Chapter 5

The steak was excellent, the wine fair. It didn't matter. Rachel was far more interested in the man sitting opposite her than in anything on her plate. She retired her knife and fork and thoughtfully sipped her drink while regarding him.

Even in the dim light, with the din emanating from the dance floor and the surrounding area, she could still see that Kirk hadn't shaken off whatever it was that had been bothering him this morning. If anything, it seemed to have become part of the permanent weave of his life.

She had to find a way to unravel it.

The conversation over dinner had been pleasant, but vague and distant, as if they were two strangers feeling one another out, instead of two friends cemented together by experiences, feelings and time. Whenever he spoke, it had been to reminisce, not to go forward.

It was time to get down to it. Because she cared about him, Rachel felt that she had a right to know what was wrong.

She set her glass down and bracketed it with her hands, sliding her thumb slowly along the stem. Attempting to appear nonchalant, she nodded around the large room. "This must all seem rather boring and tame to you, after all the wars and everything else you've experienced."

The barest of smiles curved his mouth. Kirk finished his drink and set it down.

"Oh, I don't know. Tame looks pretty good right now." He leaned back in his chair and watched a couple as they danced in and out of the lights that seemed to spread out over the small wooden dance floor. The figures didn't seem real. "Besides—" he thought of his own personal turmoil "—there are all sorts of wars. They don't necessarily have to be external."

He wasn't looking at her, but she knew he was referring to himself. She also knew that he had never had an easy time of it, but he had never seemed as troubled as he was now.

Rachel leaned forward, raising her voice slightly in order to be heard. "And what sort of internal wars are going on inside of you?"

Kirk looked away from the couple. His eyes held Rachel's. There wasn't a thing she could see in them. She only knew that the enigmatic smile on his lips didn't reach them. "I was speaking figuratively."

She refused to retreat this time. "I was asking directly."

He reached over and slid his hand along her cheek. He thought he saw something flicker in her eyes. In another woman, it might have been desire, but this was Rachel. That wasn't part of the picture. "Funny Face, don't ruin the evening."

It was almost a plea, she thought. Oh, God, she wanted to help him so badly. Why didn't he see that? "I don't want to ruin it, Kirk. I want to get close to you."

A genuine smile bloomed and played on his lips. He pushed back his chair. "The best way to do that is to dance."

"That's not what I meant."

About to rise, Kirk stopped and arched a brow. "Then you don't want to dance?"

Rachel shook her head. He was clearly winning this little battle of wits. She smiled at him. "That's not what I meant, either." She rose to her feet, pushing back her chair. "Yes, I'd love to dance with you."

Not waiting for him to make the first move, Rachel took his hand and led the way to the dance floor, which was already crowded with people.

He lowered his head toward her ear so that she could hear him better. "It's been an eternity, but I still think I remember how it's done. One foot in front of the other, right?"

His breath was fluttering down along her ear and neck. Her stomach churned in response. Rachel congratulated herself on maintaining an unfazed expression as she turned to face him. Inside, there was a miniearthquake going on.

"That's for walking, not dancing." She held her hands up to him. He slipped his arm around her waist, then pressed her hand against his chest, covering it with his own.

They fit together rather well, she thought, a small shiver passing through her. She was the one who had taught him how to dance, all those years ago, insisting that it might come in handy someday. "Don't worry—if you get stuck, I'm good at faking it."

He placed his hand along her spine, lightly pressing her to him as soft, bluesy music enveloped them like a warm fog.

"Are you now?" He glanced down at her. "And what else were you good at faking?"

She had meant it strictly as a quip, but now that he asked, she answered honestly. "Happiness."

The note of sadness in the single word ripped through him. "Yours?"

Rachel nodded. All those years she had spent married to Don had been such a waste. She had gotten nothing good from their marriage, except Ethan. "Yes."

His hand tightened slightly at the small of her back. "Why?"

She had long ago given up seeking that special kind of happiness for herself. She gave him the only answer she could. The only answer that mattered. "For Ethan's benefit."

Kirk thought of the angry, sullen boy he had met in her living room. "Didn't seem to work."

No, not at the end. And not now. But it had for a time. "He wasn't always like that."

She said it so fiercely, Kirk could almost feel her emotion vibrating against his chest. He curved his hand around hers in a mute, awkward gesture of comfort. It was the only kind he could offer. He'd been stripped of everything else. "Oh. How was he?"

She sighed as they moved past another couple. "Happier." She wished Kirk could have seen Ethan then, before the joy had been drained from him.

Without fully acknowledging how it was happening, Kirk felt himself being drawn into her world. "What changed that?"

She lifted a shoulder helplessly. "I don't know." That wasn't entirely true, and Kirk deserved the truth. She had to be honest with him if she wanted him to be honest with her. "No, that's not exactly right. I do know. Partially." She was stumbling over her own tongue and hating her clumsiness. "It had to do with Don and me."

Rachel stopped abruptly. Honest or not, this was painful, and not a subject for a crowded dance floor.

Kirk waited a moment, thinking she was gathering her thoughts together. When she didn't continue, he prodded her. "Go on. I'm listening."

Rachel raised her head and looked up into his eyes. He was, she thought, and he would probably listen to her all night if she wanted him to.

"Yes, but I'm not talking."

Amusement lifted the corners of his mouth as he looked down at her. The tempo of the music picked up, but he ignored it. It seemed too soothing just to sway with her like this.

Soothing and arousing, at the same moment.

Maybe he was going crazy faster than he'd thought.

"Seems to be a lot of that going around tonight." Suddenly aware of the reaction he was having to her warm, supple body, Kirk moved so that they were not quite as close as before. "We each have brittle little secrets we're trying to keep under wraps, I guess."

He made it sound so civilized. So aloof. It brought a chill to her despite the fact that it was warm in the club. "We shouldn't—not from each other."

When she looked up at him like that, she brought the past flooding back to him, the part that he'd enjoyed. The part he'd shared with her and Cameron. "All right," he said, nodding. "You first."

She regarded him skeptically, clearly on to him. "And then you'll follow."

Kirk knew better than to look at her. Instead, he looked over her head as he moved them to another section of the small floor. "Maybe."

Just as she'd thought. Rachel shook her head. "Not good enough."

There was humor grazing her mouth, but her eyes were serious. As serious as his, when he looked into them. "Funny Face, it's the best I can do."

He meant it, she realized, aching for him. For herself. "Maybe you could do better if you called me Rachel, instead of Funny Face."

The request caught him off guard. He had always thought of her with that name. "Does it bother you, my calling you that?"

He almost sounded sad, she thought, although she was probably reading something into it that wasn't there. "No... actually, I kind of like it. But a man can't get serious talking to someone he calls Funny Face."

He looked into her eyes, and for just the faintest glimmer of a moment, he had a feeling that things were going to change for him. How, he wasn't certain, but they would change. And she would be at the core of it.

She already was.

He laughed softly, holding her to him and feeling far from complacent. "You'd be surprised."

Her breath caught in her throat as he drew her closer. She was aware of every part of his body as it touched hers. Rachel could feel herself reacting, not to the friend she cherished, but to the man she had once daydreamed about.

Rachel turned her face away and laid her cheek against his shoulder. For the moment, that was safer.

"Would I?" she whispered. Her question glided along his arm.

Something in his gut tightened like a fist, and Kirk had to concentrate to make it unclench again. Just as he had to concentrate on his words in order not to give her a clue to what he was feeling right now.

Hell, he wasn't sure exactly *what* he was feeling right now.

"Sure. You always did surprise easily." As he spoke, it became easier for him to delve back into the past. Fondness began to spread through him in tandem with his thoughts. "You had just about the happiest hold on life I ever encountered." Kirk tilted her head back so that he could look into her eyes. He saw the marks of sorrow there, and felt angry and cheated at the same time. Angry for her, cheated for himself. "What changed that?"

She shrugged. It was far too complicated to dissect. "It didn't change." She saw the skepticism in his eyes. "Not exactly," she amended. "It just got a little bent out of shape, that's all."

"By Don?" He thought he already had his answer, but he wanted to hear it from her.

There was no use in lying. She wasn't about to protect Don's memory. There was no one to protect it for. Ethan knew what his father had been. Knew more than she wanted him to know. "Yes."

From out of nowhere, Kirk's anger flashed, hot and consuming. "The son of a bitch." There was a silent apology in his eyes, an apology because somehow he had let her down. "I wish I'd been here."

Rachel could only laugh softly. His sentiment echoed hers so closely. "Funny, so did I."

She knew she had surprised him. He pressed her even closer and ran his hand along her back, comforting her, supporting her. Rachel thought how good it was to have him back. How wonderful it was to just talk to him. To have him here like this.

She raised her head to look at him. Something stirred, something different. Electricity sparked through both of them, jolting them to a level of awareness neither was sure how to deal with yet.

"You did?"

She nodded, her mouth as dry as cotton. "Cameron's been wonderful, but before I told him what was going on—" She stopped herself. She was getting ahead of herself. "Before I told him I was getting a divorce," she clarified, when she saw suspicion enter Kirk's eyes, "I secretly wished that you were here." This part was safe to tell him. She didn't want to tell him everything. It hurt too much to admit.

It seemed an odd thing to say, when she'd had her brother here to take her part. Though he teased her, Kirk knew Cameron would do anything for Rachel. They both would. "Why?"

The answer was very simple. "You were my knight in shining armor." She smiled as she remembered the way she'd felt about him, even before she had her crush. Or had that crush been a part of her all the time? Maybe, she mused in retrospect. "I used to think you were invincible."

The silly sentiment almost made him laugh. And yearn a little. That surprised him. He hadn't thought he was capable of yearning anymore.

"I wish you'd been right." If he had been invincible, then perhaps none of the rest of it would ever have affected him. Perhaps he could have witnessed all that misery and not had it leave an indelible mark on him. He had gone to record it, to bear witness to the world's sorrow and to convince himself that he was not alone in his unhappiness. But, by and by, the magnitude of it had managed to overwhelm him. And it had burned him out. Misery didn't love company. It was appalled by it.

"What happened?" She asked the question so softly, he almost didn't hear her at all.

"When?" he countered evasively, knowing he'd said too much, alluded to too much.

She had no idea when this devastation of his soul had begun. She chose the likeliest point. "When you left Bedford."

Shrugging, he avoided her eyes. And attempted to avoid the sensations sweeping insistently through him as he felt every minute part of her body against his, reminding him that he was still a man, with a man's needs, even though he had thought those needs long gone and buried. "I bummed around, freelanced, got a job."

Rachel frowned. He was being deliberately evasive, and it hurt her. "I'm not asking for a chronological development of events, Kirk."

The sharp note in her voice had him looking at her. His own defenses locked into place. "Then what are you asking for?"

She bit back her frustration. This was Kirk, and he needed her, even if he didn't want her butting in. "What happened to your soul, Kirk?"

It was cynicism that curved his mouth this time, not humor. "I pawned it in one of those little out-of-the-way thrift shops along the way, traveling through one ravaged country after another. I don't remember which one, so don't ask."

She wasn't going to allow him to put her off with flippant remarks. "Seriously," she insisted.

The music seemed to fade into the background. He looked into her eyes. "Seriously," he echoed.

He wasn't going to tell her. Rachel let the matter drop. She was afraid she had struck a nerve. Afraid that Kirk had told her more than he wanted to, and more than she could assimilate right now.

She wanted to help, not hinder.

With a surrendering sigh, she rested her cheek against his shoulder again and let the music take her. For a moment, she simply drew comfort from the fact that he was here. Drew comfort from him.

The music pulsed all around them. Kirk wished she didn't smell so good. Like salvation. Like a woman. He'd returned to strike at the heart of his problem, and to take solace as best he could from the friends he'd left behind. Cameron and Rachel. He'd thought of them as a unit. He hadn't wanted to do anything else but be with them, to find a little peace before he completely self-destructed.

Instead, he was having some very definite reactions to the woman he held in his arms. Those reactions had nothing to do with peace, and everything to do with deep, gut-wrenching sexual attraction.

He felt almost disloyal for the stirrings that were curling through him, like a giant coil about to be released.

Rachel silently prayed that the band would go on playing forever. Or at least a while longer. She hadn't felt this good in a long time.

"Hey, honey, how'd you like to wrap yourself around a real man for a change?"

Rachel felt the hand on her arm, cracking the euphoric shell around her. At the same moment that she heard the question, she smelled the pungent cloud of alcohol engulfing her. She raised her head in time to see a dark glint entering Kirk's eyes.

"She's with me." Kirk's voice was low, and all the more dangerous for it, like the warning growl of a cougar.

Rachel turned around to look at the man whose hand was still on her arm. He was heavyset, tall, his eyes squinted into small slits as he attempted to focus them.

"But she can be with me." He exhaled, and Rachel stiffened, bracing herself against the smell. "Why don't we let the little lady make her own choice?"

Beneath her hand, Rachel could feel Kirk's heart pounding, like an old-fashioned engine working up a full head of steam. She knew that at any moment Kirk was going to push her behind him and take the challenge the man presented. There was no doubt in her mind that Kirk had the advantage, even though he was smaller. The man was drunk and out of shape. Rachel had seen Kirk handle himself in a fight just once. She never wanted to see it again.

Instincts had her turning so that she blocked Kirk's reach with her body.

"The 'little lady' *has* chosen," she informed the drunk tersely, hoping that would be the end of it. All around the perimeter she could see that people had stopped dancing to gather around and watch, even though the band continued playing.

But as she turned her back on the man, she felt his hand land roughly on her shoulder. He jerked her around to face him. "Then make it the best two out of three, sweetcakes."

"She said—" Kirk began, attempting to harness the rage he felt.

Too drunk to realize the danger he was in, the man contemptuously planted a hand on Kirk's chest and shoved him back.

"Nobody's talking to you." He turned toward Rachel, ready to claim his prize.

It happened so quickly, Rachel had difficulty absorbing it all. She raised her knee to deliver a strategic blow that would rid her of this nuisance, but she never got the opportunity to follow through. There was no need to. Half a second later, the man was on the floor at her feet, out cold. One punch from Kirk had ended the confrontation quickly.

Scanlon's bouncer came running over to them. The wooden floor vibrated from his hurried approach.

Rachel didn't wait for the man to speak. "He started it." She pointed at the unconscious man, jumping to Kirk's defense.

Concurring murmurs came from the ring of people around them.

The round-faced man grunted as he took an arm and yanked the troublemaker to his feet. "Don't worry, I saw the whole thing," the bouncer assured her.

He slung the unconscious man over his shoulder with no more difficulty than if he were a raincoat. Admiration shone in his small, deep-set eyes as he looked at Kirk. The customer had just made his job easier for him.

"Hey, buddy, you ever want a job here, you come see me." The bouncer turned toward the crowd. "Show's over, folks. Go on having a good time," he urged them patiently. Then he looked over his shoulder at Kirk and Rachel one last time before disposing of his burden outside. "Dinner's on the house."

Rachel let go of the sigh she'd been holding as the bouncer walked away and the crowd began to disperse. She smiled at Kirk, attempting to lighten the tension that had all but sawed through them. "Well, it seems you got out of paying this time."

Taking her arm, Kirk escorted her back to the table. He was accustomed to stalking through life alone, eschewing manners and the finer points of etiquette. Somehow that didn't seem fitting around Rachel. She brought a gentler world into being for him.

He held her chair out and waited until she was seated again. "Does that mean I still owe you a dinner out?"

She raised her eyes to his. "What do you think?"

"I think I can bear it a second time, if need be." Humor faded as he looked at her shoulder. He could make out the faint, smudged imprint of the man's fingers on her collarbone. Kirk sobered immediately. "Did he hurt you?"

That dangerous look was back in his eyes, the one she didn't recognize. She shook her head, quick to reassure him. "How about you?" She glanced at his hand. His knuckles were red. "Your knuckles sting?"

Kirk passed his hand over them reflexively. He'd been so incensed that he hardly felt anything when he made contact, but now his knuckles throbbed. "I've had a lot worse."

She winced. "I'm sure." Perhaps that was the source of his pain, she thought, all those things he had been forced to witness. His beat had been the seamier side of humanity, the side that had fed his basic pessimism until it all but engulfed him. "Will you tell me about it?"

The coaxing note in her voice tempted him to unburden himself. But it wouldn't be fair. He had to do this very carefully, to spare her as much of the horror of it as possible. But he owed her a degree of honesty. He always had.

"Some of it. Eventually." He looked at her. "But not tonight."

She'd known that even before he told her. She'd seen it in his eyes. Rachel sighed. "You know, I used to think you were closemouthed. In comparison, you were positively gregarious then."

He toyed with his glass for a long moment before looking at her. When he did, it all but tore at her heart. "It's going to take me a while, Funny Face."

She studied him. He looked so tortured. "Is that why you came back? To work out the kinks?"

Yes. "No, I came back because I missed your funny little laugh. I even missed Cameron's ugly face."

They weren't even dealing in half-truths yet. But they would get to the truth, she promised herself. They had to.

Rachel reached across the table and placed her hand over his, as if to absorb all the things he couldn't say. "We missed you, too."

The display of emotion made him uncomfortable. He drew away. "You were telling me about your ex-husband before we were interrupted."

Nice try, Kirk. "I was not," she countered with a smug grin. Checkmate.

He leaned back in his chair, determined. "All right, tell me now."

"How come I have to talk and you don't?"

He spread his hands, as if her question had the simplest of explanations. "Because I just rescued you, that's why. You have to grant my request."

Rachel raised her chin defensively. "I could take care of myself."

She probably could at that. Cameron had written that he had taught her some self-defense moves. "Humor my frail ego, okay?"

Because it was Kirk, she relented.

"Okay." She shifted beneath his gaze, uncomfortable with the subject. Uncomfortable with her own failings. She should have bailed out at the first sign, not lingered and hoped.

She took one of the last of the breadsticks and toyed with it, needing to have something to do with her hands. "There's not all that much to tell."

The hell there wasn't. She was afraid of Don. Or had been, at one point. Kirk got down to the crux of it. "Do you think he could give you any trouble?"

Rachel's head jerked up. She looked at him sharply. "You don't know?" She had assumed, that since Cameron and he corresponded, Cameron had told him.

Kirk drew his brow together, confused by the expression on her face. "Know what?"

"Don's dead." Even as she said the words, it still didn't seem true. Don had been such an overwhelming force for her to deal with for so long. "There was a car accident a couple of months after the divorce." She stared at her fingertips. "That's when Ethan really began to change on me." She blew out a huge breath. "I think that he blames me for the accident somehow."

"You had nothing to do with it—unless you tampered with the brakes somehow." Rachel looked at him, surprised at the note of suppressed annoyance she heard in his voice. "And I'm getting the distinct impression that if you did, Don deserved it."

He'd known the triple-letter high school jock fleetingly in school, and hadn't cared for him. He'd been surprised when he learned of Rachel's wedding, three months after the fact.

She shook her head as she placed the broken breadstick on her plate.

"He might have deserved being horsewhipped, or whatever the modern equivalent of that is these days, but no one deserves to be splattered across a highway." She closed her eyes and felt ashamed of the relief she'd experienced because Don couldn't take Ethan away from her anymore. "Especially if he has a son who loves him."

What she was telling him didn't jibe with the vibrations he had picked up at the house from Ethan. "Then they were close?"

She thought of the times when Don had gone out of his way to ignore his son. Of the way Ethan had stood, hanging his head, rejected. He had always returned for more, determined to break through to his father. It had broken her heart. "Not exactly, but Ethan loved him."

Having lived through it himself, Kirk heard what wasn't being said. "And Don? Did he love Ethan?"

She shrugged. "In his own way."

Kirk pressed, determined to get as much of the story from her as possible. "Which was?"

She'd shared all she intended to share for tonight. Kirk had gotten a great deal more from her than she had from him. She had no desire to turn Scanlon's into a confessional.

An enigmatic smile graced her lips. "I think we've exceeded the twenty questions you're allotted in exchange for conquering the hairy beast." She planted her elbows on the table and rested her head in her upturned hands. "I don't answer any more questions until you do."

"Kirk Callaghan, photojournalist," he began reciting. "Social security number—"

She held up her hand, not in surrender, just to stop him for a moment. "This isn't an interrogation."

Kirk grinned at her in reply. "Had all the signs of one."

He said the words lightly, but she read more meaning into them than he had intended. "Have you ever been interrogated?"

"Once," he admitted. "In Iraq. I managed to escape, though, before the situation got out of hand."

His mouth grew grim. His escape had cost another man his life that night, leaving Kirk with a debt he could never hope to repay. He sent money to the man's widow regularly. But he knew money fell painfully short of repaying her for her husband's life.

She saw pain flicker in his eyes. It was still too raw. "Sorry, I don't mean to stir up any bad memories."

Kirk shrugged. "Not your fault. That's all there seem to be right now."

She had seen his work in newspapers, magazines. She couldn't believe that some of the pride she felt about his accomplishments hadn't managed to catch up to him, as well. "They were all bad?"

The conversation was descending to depths where he didn't want it to go. He didn't know how it had managed to get away from him.

"Depends on the point of view." He looked at her empty glass. "Want another drink?"

"No." *I want answers. I want you to really smile again. Most of all, I want to help.*

"Want to go?" he suggested.

She really didn't want the evening to end just yet. But what they had to say to each other couldn't be said with a sax blaring in the background. "Some night air would be nice."

He felt a smile over his lips. She could always draw them out of him. "I think I might be able to scare some up for you."

Kirk took her hand and rose from the table, drawing her up with him. For a moment, an odd feeling sauntered through him. He felt as if he were a man on a date with a woman.

He had given up simple things like that a long time ago. Subconsciously, he'd wanted to be alone, wanted to eschew relationships, because he couldn't open up to anyone. It was all basically simple. If there was no relationship, there was no pain.

Besides, this wasn't a woman he was with, it was Funny Face. Funny Face, who mattered far more to him than any other woman ever could.

"Come on. I think they have a fresh supply just outside the door." Kirk underlined his urgings with a wink just before he led her out.

The minute movement brought a flutter to her stomach. Rachel remembered the effect that wink used to have on her. It was sexiness encapsulated.

She reminded herself that she was light-years away from that young girl with the crush.

"You sure do know how to entertain a woman," Rachel told him with a laugh as they walked outside. "Free dinner, free drinks, free air." She turned to look at him. "Careful, you might turn my head."

"Never happen," he assured her. They stepped aside as a couple, very obviously in love, passed them to enter the club. "You were always the most grounded person I knew."

She let out a sigh and shook her head. "You make me sound boring."

He looked at her for a long moment, and saw her the way she had been. Affection slipped into his voice. "Not boring, Funny Face. Never boring."

He took her hand. And they went for a walk, staring into the darkened windows of the closed stores along the strip and sharing memories.

Chapter 6

The drive home was far too short for her liking. Rachel wanted to stay out longer, to talk more. She had a feeling that, with enough time, things would start to fall into place. And it would take time to peel away the thin, sinewy layers that years and distance had put into place between them.

But for now, she'd made very little headway. It was like shadowboxing with the wind. She knew no more about what had happened in the years between then and now than Kirk wanted her to know.

Frustration was chewing tiny holes in her. The gaps would be filled in only when Kirk was good and ready to fill them in. She knew that. Yet impatience drummed long, pointy fingers on her soul. She hated being kept at a distance like this. Distance had never had a place between them before, and yet here it was, keeping them apart.

When Kirk brought his minivan to a stop in her driveway, Rachel made no move to get out. Instead, she turned toward him. She maintained a purposefully innocent expression, masking her curiosity.

"You know, you never got around to answering my question. What are you planning on doing with yourself while you're here?'' She raised her eyes to his, waiting to see if he would attempt to get out of telling her again.

Kirk ran his hand slowly up and down the steering wheel. For a moment, Rachel had the image of him running his hands along a woman's body—her body. She blinked and blew out a breath.

"To be honest, I hadn't planned that far." It had taken all his concentration just to get here.

"You? Without a plan?"

Rachel grinned as she thought back to those long, hazy nights when he would sit outside, talking about his long-range goals, and the ways he would reach them. He'd had everything so well orchestrated, positive that he could meet all contingencies. He'd been so sure, so adamant. It was hard to believe he'd changed that much.

"Now that's a first. You always had everything so mapped out."

That was because it had been the only thing that kept him going, Kirk thought. Having goals had kept him sane.

He stared straight ahead at her garage door. The paint was beginning to chip in a couple of places, he noted absently. "Maps don't always lead you to where you want to go."

And he'd discovered that his plans hadn't led him to where he wanted to go, Rachel realized. "And where's that, Kirk?" she asked softly. "Where did you find you wanted to go?"

He continued staring, seeing something beyond the wood and stucco. "Never-never land."

The words had just popped out of his mouth without any thought. His answer seemed to surprise Rachel almost as much as it surprised him.

Was he kidding her? Rachel stared at Kirk, attempting to understand. He'd always been such a realist. Had that changed, too? "Like Peter Pan?" she asked.

Kirk laughed disparagingly at his own folly. He shook his head, dismissing what he'd said.

But Rachel was taken with his answer. "You'd have to wear tights, you know." Humor lit her eyes like bright candles as she lowered them for a better survey. "Might be rather interesting at that."

For a moment, because it amused him, because he liked hearing her laugh, he played along. "Everyone knows that Peter Pan was a girl."

"That was Mary Martin. To the audience, Peter Pan represents the eternal boy." She reached out and touched his cheek before she could think better of it. "There was never anything boyish about you, Kirk, even when you were one."

Kirk pressed her hand to his cheek, taking the comfort she so blatantly offered. In that single moment, he allowed his guard to lower just a bit, and a little more of Rachel slipped through.

If it hadn't been for the bucket seats, Kirk would have pulled her into his arms, giving in to the sudden, strong impulse that rumbled through him.

Rachel's heart felt as if it were engaged in a fast and furious game of jump rope. If it beat any harder, she was certain, he would see it. As it was, it took her a moment to remember that breathing was necessary to perpetuate life.

"You were always too much the man," she ended, her voice almost a whisper, her eyes on his face. Oh, God, she thought, she wanted him to kiss her.

Kirk struggled to regain control over his feelings. "You'd better go in."

It was almost an order, but Rachel remained where she was, searching for a reason to linger. If staying here with him just a little longer hadn't felt so important, it would have made her smile. It almost seemed like old times, those long-ago summer nights when she would search madly for excuses to be with Kirk just a few minutes longer, under the guise of friendship.

That same old feeling was beginning to come back to her. In spades.

Oh, no, not again. She was twenty-seven years old, divorced, with a child to raise. She couldn't be falling for him again.

Could she?

Her palms dampened.

No, she couldn't. It was just her reaction to the pleasant memories that they had shared tonight. He just represented a happier period in her life. Nothing more. She certainly wasn't going to delude herself into thinking that she . . .

That she felt something for him. Not in *that* way.

She was too sensible to do something so stupid. Loving Kirk held no future. What she was experiencing was nostalgia.

Nostalgia wrapped heated tentacles around her, making the air within the minivan very, very warm.

"Why don't you come in?" she suggested. "Ethan's probably asleep by now, and I'm sure that Cameron would like to talk to you." Maybe Cameron could draw Kirk out better. Maybe between the two of them . . .

She thought he wanted to avoid her son, Kirk thought. He shook his head slightly.

"Ethan's fine," he assured her. "Cameron, on the other hand, looked as tired as hell three hours ago. I'm sure he just wants to crawl into his own bed." Kirk thought of last night, and a trickle of fondness seeped through. "I kept him up half the night, talking." Kirk saw the skeptical look that entered her eyes. "Actually, he kept me up half the night talking."

Now that was something she could believe. Kirk had never been talkative, even at his best. Cameron was the loquacious one.

"That sounds more like it." She saw Kirk place his hand on the ignition key again. "Walk me to my door?" she urged quickly.

Things were happening inside him that he didn't quite understand. He felt differently about her tonight, and until he managed to get things into perspective, he thought it best just to leave. "I . . ."

She wanted him to walk her to the door. She wanted every moment she could get. Somehow, it seemed important, though she wasn't exactly certain just how. She smiled at him, amusement mingling with a beguiling she wasn't aware that she possessed.

But Kirk was.

"Surely that's not such a difficult request for a slayer of dragons."

The romanticized version was typical of her. "That was a drunk, not a dragon," he pointed out. "And I didn't slay him."

She thought it prudent not to mention the dark look she had seen in his eyes a second before he sent the intruder into slumberland.

"Only because you didn't have a sword in your hand." She was making light of it, and yet some faraway part of her had secretly been thrilled. It was like a childhood fantasy come to life. He'd been her protector, just the way she had once envisioned him. "You should have seen yourself. I'm surprised lightning didn't come from your brow."

He left the key in the ignition and slid his hand to his thigh. "You always did have a penchant for exaggeration."

She didn't quite agree with his assessment, but she was willing to split the difference. "I might embellish a little now and then—"

"Embellish? Is that what it's called now?"

"Just to be more colorful," she continued, as if he hadn't said anything. "Of course, being more colorful than you isn't difficult, since you're usually about as colorful as snow, but my point is that I don't have to embellish this time," she concluded. "An angered Kirk Callaghan is a fearsome sight to behold."

He laughed, just as she'd hoped he would. "All right, I give in. I'll walk you to your door. Otherwise you'll go on talking all night."

"Ah, chivalry is not dead."

Kirk got out and rounded the hood. Rachel remained sitting in the car, waiting. She was obviously expecting the whole nine yards. Since it cost him nothing, he gave it to her, bowing elaborately as he opened the door for her.

"That's more like it," she murmured, stepping out.

When had her legs gotten so long? he wondered as she tugged her skirt back into place. "It must be a whole twelve steps to your door from the driveway," he said as he closed the door behind her.

Not one to waste an opportunity, she hooked her arm through his. "It's not the distance, it's the company." She saw the way his brow creased. "What's wrong?"

She still thought of him as the young man he'd been. She didn't know that he had been completely emptied. She didn't

know that he had photographed anguish for posterity instead
of saving lives, or that a soldier had died right before his camera's eye. "You don't know the first thing about me, Funny
Face."

She wasn't about to let him beat himself up this way, or drive
a wedge between them, no matter how much he might want to.
She swung around, determination in her eyes. Her hand closed
over his in a silent plea.

"I know *everything* about you." She saw the resistance in his
face and refused to let it stop her. "I know you're good and
kind and sensitive." Her mouth curved a little. "Even if your
scowl does freeze people in their tracks."

She didn't understand. How could she, when she didn't
know. "Funny Face—"

She laid a finger on his lips, silencing his protest. She wasn't
going to stand here and allow him to denigrate himself. Whatever he might have done in the years between then and now
didn't change how she felt. It didn't change what she knew he
was, underneath. A decent human being.

"I don't know what's bothering you, Kirk, but I do know
that nothing you can ever tell me, nothing you have ever done,"
she said with feeling, "could make me change my mind about
you."

He combed his fingers through her hair, touched by her sin-
cerity. She was so innocent. So unsullied by the outside world.
"Don't be so sure."

What? What is it? She swallowed the questions, knowing
now that it was too soon for him to tell her. Instead, she said the
only thing she knew to be true. "I'm sure."

Kirk looked into her eyes and saw that she meant it. God,
had there ever been such innocence touching his life? Had he
ever been part of that world?

He glanced in the direction of the house next door. No, he
hadn't, Kirk thought. Not really. Rachel, the way she thought,
the way she was, was something apart from his life. She was his
peek into a world that could have been—but not for him.

Fondness softened his features. "You are one in a million."

So are you. Somehow I've got to make you believe that. "I
always told you that."

"And you were right." Kirk shook his head and smiled. "Good night, Funny Face. Thanks for tonight." Moved by impulse, Kirk leaned over and kissed her cheek.

She had no idea what made her do it. At the very last moment, she turned her head so that her lips brushed ever so lightly across his.

The jolt, she thought—when she *could* think again—could probably be felt for miles. There was absolutely no doubt in her mind that a power surge had rippled out through southern California, its epicenter right here on her doorstep.

She curled her fingers into her palms to keep from encircling his neck with them. That would only scare him away.

Instant hunger filled his being, and it took everything Kirk had not to pull her into his arms and kiss her the way he wanted to. The way, he realized, he had wanted to all night.

What had come over him? This was Funny Face, for crying out loud, not some woman he had met in one of the countless bars he'd passed through.

Startled, Kirk backed away, the way a man did when he realized that he had almost stepped on a live wire that was dangling before him on the ground.

"Good night," Rachel murmured.

Kirk inclined his head slightly, then turned away and quickly walked to his minivan. His lips throbbed as if they'd gotten burned.

Rachel continued to stand on her porch even after Kirk had pulled away. She wrapped her arms around herself, hugging the shivery sensation to her like an unexpected treasure.

Wow, she thought. Oh, wow...

With an effort, she turned away and let herself into her house. The sound of a television set in the background reached out to penetrate the haze around her.

Cameron was alone. He was sitting on the sofa, his dark blue eyes glazed over as he watched the final minutes of a cop show that relied heavily on car chases and improbable situations to reel in its audience. When he was more rested, Cameron enjoyed pointing out the flaws in shows like that.

He blinked and came to life as Rachel eased the door closed behind her. "What happened to Kirk?" he asked, looking around.

At her brother's question, a little of the euphoric bubble dissolved. "He went home." She dropped her purse on the table.

The look on her brother's face was a mixture of surprise and disappointment. "I think I've been snubbed."

Rachel knew Cameron had a whole host of friends, but Kirk had always been special to him. Perhaps because their differences complemented one another so well. "He wanted to let you get your rest."

He snorted as he retrieved a television guide from the floor and tossed it back onto the coffee table. "He makes me sound like an old man. I'm only two months older than he is."

"Three," she corrected, dropping down next to her brother on the sofa. She tucked one leg under her as she made herself comfortable. "He said you stayed up all last night talking."

"Only half the night," Cameron replied. He shifted and let out a slight groan. "You need a new sofa. This one's not made for comfort."

"It's not made for sleeping, either," she said affectionately, pointing to the cushion next to her, where a faint impression revealed that Cameron hadn't spent the entire evening in an upright position. She blew out a breath, then looked toward the stairs. "So, how did it go with the black prince tonight?"

Cameron laughed. He'd bestowed that name on Ethan the day he was born. The first time he'd seen his nephew, the infant had been scowling. The nickname, Rachel decided, could just as easily be applied to Kirk.

"Ethan settled in after a bit. We watched some television. He played video games on that damned handheld thing of his. He even did some homework, although under protest."

Ethan still had his good moments. She clung to that. "Is there any other way?"

"Probably not," Cameron replied, linking his hands behind his head and studying her face. She looked flushed. As if she were running. Or as if something had made her breathless.

"How about you? How was your evening with Kirk?" he casually asked.

"Interesting," she said evasively. She wasn't quite ready to share the fact that she had kissed him. Not by any stretch of her imagination could she turn it around to say that Kirk had kissed her.

"Interesting?" Cameron prodded. "As in how?"

"As in he punched a guy out." She slanted a look to see how Cameron reacted to that.

"I'm assuming there was a reason for that."

"The man was trying to cut in . . ." she began.

"I'm surprised the guy's alive, then," he deadpanned.

Rachel shook her head. "Let me finish. The man was drunk, and he tried to pull me away."

"Like I said, I'm surprised the guy's still alive." Cameron sat up. "He is alive, isn't he?"

"Last I saw, the bouncer was depositing him outside."

With eyes trained to take in every minute detail, Cameron looked her over. "Are you hurt?"

She smiled. "No. A little thrilled, maybe, or am I not supposed to admit that?"

He laughed at her. "Not to a police detective, unless, of course, he's your brother and used to overlooking a myriad of faults and quirks."

Rachel sat up. "Those are your faults and quirks you're talking about, not mine."

"We'll talk," Cameron promised. He rose and stretched again. "Well, old or not, I'd better be getting home. The captain wants us all in early tomorrow. Something about the mayor holding a meeting to promote a harvest festival." He shook his head at the thought. "Harvest festival," he repeated incredulously. "God, it's only early spring."

Rachel made sympathetic noises. She was only half listening as she followed him to the door. "Cameron, did Kirk seem . . . I don't know—" she hunted for the right word, and fell back on the most common, though it didn't quite describe what she meant "—preoccupied to you?"

Cameron didn't hesitate. "Yes, but then, that's Kirk. You know what he's like. He was never exactly a Fourth of July sparkler." He looked at her fondly. "That was your department."

She ignored the last comment, except to note that in some ways Cameron and Kirk were very alike. Kirk had said almost the same thing to her.

"No, he wasn't overexhilarating. But Kirk was never this sad before, either."

She was really concerned, he thought. Cameron quickly replayed what had been said between them when Kirk had come over last night. He'd been struck by the same feeling as his sister. The lengthy conversation, mostly his, hadn't shed any light on the cause. He'd chalked it up to Kirk being Kirk, only more so. Perhaps it was just a little more difficult for him than for them to pick up a friendship after all these years.

"It *has* been nine years, Rach," Cameron told her. "People change in less time than that. Besides, don't forget, Kirk's line of work didn't exactly take him to the lands of the rich and famous. More like the poor and invisible." He was quoting Kirk directly now. It had been a summation he'd offered Cameron after some prodding. "That sort of thing might tend to get to a man after a while. I've seen a lot of cops drop out of the force for the same reason. They became burned out. Not here, of course. Here we just look for jaywalkers and people easing through stop signs, in between addressing kids in different schools. But when I was in L.A., I saw it all the time. Hell, that's why I put in for duty here when there was an opening, and took a pay cut."

Rachel chewed her lip. It sounded plausible. "Think that's all?"

He wanted to reassure her, but he didn't want to lie in order to do it. "With Kirk, you never know. But if anyone can get it out of him, you can." He skimmed his finger down her nose, the way he used to. "Good night, Rach." He turned away.

"Oh, one more thing..."

Her voice stopped him just as he was going down the last step. Cameron turned and looked up at her. "You sound like Columbo stalking a suspect." He waited patiently. "What?"

She'd meant to ask him this all day, and it had kept slipping her mind. "Why didn't you ever mention that Kirk wrote to you?"

Cameron sighed. "Knew I should have left when I had the chance."

Her eyes narrowed. He'd kept it from her on purpose, she realized. "Don't be evasive with me, Detective Reed. Why didn't you tell me?"

He shrugged carelessly. It was too studied a reaction to fool Rachel and he knew it, but he did it anyway. And crossed his fingers. "It slipped my mind."

She wasn't buying it, any of it. "All these years, all those letters?"

He took the two steps back to her. "Rachel, I'm a police detective. Letters are a low priority on my list, unless they're from a serial killer."

"We've never had any serial killers in Bedford." She stood, hand on hip, waiting.

He shrugged again, this time in surrender. "I knew that he hadn't answered any of your letters, and I didn't want to rub your nose in it."

"How'd you know he hadn't answered? Did he mention it?" Had there been some reason, other than what he said, why he hadn't written?

"No. I knew because you would have told me if he had. You could never keep a secret about anything. Except once."

She knew he was referring to Don's abuse, and thankfully he let it drop as soon as he'd mentioned it.

"Besides, in the beginning, I thought that if I didn't talk about him, it would help you get over that larger-than-life crush you had on Kirk. After a while, it didn't matter. You were married and dealing with your own problems."

Be that as it may, that still didn't get Cameron off the hook. "He was *our* friend, Cameron. You had no right to make that decision for me. Besides, it wasn't a crush."

"So I'm overprotective. So sue me. It's not as if I went into your mailbox and stole your letters from him. In any case, he didn't write all that often. Maybe once or twice a year. Sometimes not even that."

"Okay." Rachel decided she'd kept Cameron twisting in the wind long enough. "But why didn't you at least tell me that he was returning to Bedford?" She would have liked to have that to look forward to, would have liked to be more prepared to see him.

But you didn't prepare for someone like Kirk Callaghan, she reminded herself. You just let him happen.

"Because he'd mentioned it once or twice before and never shown up," he told her, obviously surprised by her adeptness at interrogation. "I really didn't think he was coming this time, until he turned up on my doorstep last night. Kirk didn't even return for either of his parents' funerals," he reminded her.

She hadn't really expected Kirk to. Both funerals had been very sad, lonely ceremonies, attended by her own family out of courtesy. They had gone because they had lived next door to one another for years, not because they had really been that friendly.

She sighed. "Kirk was never close to his parents."

In his own way, Cameron was more of a traditionalist than she was. Certain rules were always followed. "Yeah, but you come for a funeral," Cameron said.

Rachel shook her head. There had been a schism between Kirk and his parents, a wall that had never been breached. He'd never talked about it. It was what he didn't say, rather than what he did, that had told her of its existence. And then there had been that incident she'd witnessed. The one she hadn't mentioned to anyone, not even Cameron. She had a feeling it hadn't been an isolated one.

"Not if you never came while they were alive," she insisted. "What's the point of going to their funeral? Kirk wasn't the type who cared what anyone else said about him. He certainly wouldn't have returned for form's sake."

She stopped and stared across the way. From where she stood, the trees on Kirk's property obscured her view of the house, but she could just make out the tail end of his van in the driveway.

"Why do you think he's back?"

"Maybe he just needed to touch base with someplace familiar, someplace that wasn't ravaged by fighting." Cameron shrugged. "Maybe, like he said, he missed us."

Her eyes turned to his in surprise. "Did he tell you that, too?" She had thought that Kirk was just being flippant.

"Yeah." Affection lighting his eyes, Cameron cupped her face. "Hey, stop worrying about Kirk. He's okay. And you've got enough on your mind as it is." He grinned as he lightly passed his thumb over the crease in her brow, smoothing it. "If you don't watch out, your face'll freeze that way."

She laughed at the old, familiar warning. She hadn't heard it in years. "Great-grandma Reed," she remembered with a surge of pleasure. She had been a tiny gnome of a woman with an old adage for everything. "I wonder if she really believed that."

"Just as much as she believed in tying garlic around your neck to ward off evil spirits—and dates with dirty intentions." Cameron laughed as Rachel shuddered at the thought. "Anyway, I want you to stop worrying about everyone and just think about yourself for a change."

She waved her hand at the suggestion. "Easy for you to say. You're a bachelor. You get to go home, live like a slob and crash wherever you want to. You don't have to worry."

But he did. About her. About his nephew. And his best friend. He just didn't show it.

"Why do you think I stayed a bachelor?" Cameron kissed the top of her head. "See you, Rach." He went down the steps again before he stopped. "Oh, by the way, I thought I'd bring over some videos tomorrow night." She looked at him curiously. "You know, of our high school days. Drum up a few memories, entertain Kirk. Maybe even get Ethan interested."

He was always trying, she thought. "I love you, Cameron."

He spread his hands wide. "What's not to love? I take it the idea meets with your approval."

"Yes." She couldn't have planned a better evening herself. Perhaps, surrounded by old friends and old memories, Kirk would loosen up and relax a little. Maybe, as Cameron said, that was all he needed.

"Great." He fired his parting salvo. "Make lasagna."

Rachel thought of the ingredients and the time involved. Time was always at a premium. She leaned her shoulder against the post and folded her arms in front of her. "That's a tall order."

Cameron gave her an innocent look over his shoulder. "That was always Kirk's favorite meal when Mom used to make it."

She reacted the way they'd both known she would. "I'll see what I can do."

Cameron grinned. "Knew you'd come around."

Chapter 7

There had been no answer at the front door when he knocked. Reverting to old familiar behavior, he'd gone around to the back door and found it unlocked. On impulse, he let himself in quietly. After years of being an unobtrusive extension of his camera, Kirk knew how to move soundlessly.

For a moment, he stood just inside the doorway, savoring the sight he was met with, capturing it in his mind. He wanted to absorb just a bit of the atmosphere before anyone realized he was there.

Rachel was alone in the kitchen, her back to the door. All around her on the counter and the stove were pots and pans and all the preparations needed to make an old-fashioned Italian meal.

She was moving from stove to counter and back again. Every step seemed to be underlined by an aroma that was making his mouth water. It was a pleasant, surprising sensation. He'd long ago stopped eating for the pleasure of it. The consumption of food had become mechanical for him, just a way of taking in fuel to continue going. The scents in the kitchen—the meat frying in the pan, sauce simmering in the pot, bread warming in the oven—all combined to reawaken old memories.

Picture of Domesticity, he thought, framing the shot and labeling it.

Kirk's mouth curved slightly as he thought of Rachel's reaction if he told her the title she'd inspired. Wouldn't the independent, motivated college professor just love to hear that one?

Or perhaps she would, he mused as he watched her reach up to the top shelf for glasses. As she stretched, her breasts moved beguilingly against the taut material of her blouse, causing in him the same warm feelings he'd experienced last night as he held her.

With effort, Kirk shut his feelings away. It took more effort this time than it had last night. Feelings like that about Rachel were totally out of line. He had no business entertaining them. This was a house that had given him his happiest moments, and he wasn't going to mar the evening by allowing his inner turmoil to get the better of him. Rachel deserved him at his best—whatever that was. He sure didn't know these days.

Maybe he never had.

All he knew was that he had always loved being here, where even raised voices were stamped with affection and angry shouts quickly gave way to hugs and embraces of forgiveness.

Remembering, Kirk wrapped his fingers around the bottle of wine he'd thought to bring after Cameron called to extend the invitation earlier today.

She sensed him the moment he approached behind her. She felt his presence above the soft music coming from the radio beside her on the counter, above the echoes of the program on the television set Cameron had on in the other room. Rachel hadn't heard the doorbell ring, but she had sensed Kirk the moment he entered the kitchen, had felt his eyes on her as she worked.

She didn't bother attempting to subdue the pleased smile that rose to her lips.

Rachel debated turning around to greet him, and then decided to stall for a moment longer. She wanted to enjoy the feeling of having him there, of having him watch her. It made her feel . . . pretty. Feminine. It had been a long time since she had felt that way.

Kirk felt a little like a voyeur, intruding. Lately, he'd felt like that a great deal.

Clearing his throat, he tapped her on the shoulder, and was relieved when she didn't jump. "Need help?" he asked as she turned around.

There were three filled pots and one frying pan on the stove, all boiling, frying or simmering. It seemed to Kirk that Rachel was everywhere at once, stirring, tasting, adding. And looking incredibly competent while she was doing it. A hint of admiration filtered into his eyes as he looked at her.

Rachel set the slotted wooden spoon she'd been using on the counter and took the bottle of wine from Kirk. She placed it on the first rack in the refrigerator to chill before dinner.

"Thanks, but I've got everything under control," she assured him cheerfully.

It hadn't been easy, rushing home from the college to pick up Ethan at school and then going to the supermarket to buy all the ingredients. Ethan had balked at being dragged around, but he was too young to leave on his own. Besides, Rachel felt that if she hammered in the point long enough, Ethan would realize that she was going to love him no matter what his mood or behavior, so he might as well settle down.

Kirk nodded at the stove, hooking his thumbs in his pockets. "Certainly looks that way."

He looked as if he felt awkward again, she thought. And it hurt. For her, nine years had all but faded into the background when she saw Kirk. Why couldn't it be that way for him?

A teasing smile lit her face. "Is that why you offered?"

Her smile was infectious. It always had been, he remembered. "No secret that I'm all thumbs—but with good intentions."

She nodded, accepting the excuse. "Park your good intentions on a chair and talk to me." She gestured toward a stool at the other side of the counter. "Cameron's busy communing with the television set, and Ethan's glued to his portable video game. I'd kill for the sound of a human voice that wasn't coming through a transmitter." She said the last sentence wistfully.

"Okay." Kirk slid onto the stool closest to her and folded his hands on the counter as he watched her work. He wasn't accustomed to domesticity. His mother had favored frozen dinners when she remembered to cook at all. If it hadn't been for the Reeds, Kirk wouldn't have known that string beans didn't always come frozen and cut into neat, equally measured pieces.

He watched her as she fished out wide noodles and laid them on a plate to cool off. "Don't I still owe you a dinner?"

Rachel looked up, pleased that he wasn't attempting to wiggle out of it. "You do, and don't let this fool you." She gestured toward the stove. "You're not getting out of taking me out again that easily."

She pushed a wayward strand of hair out of her face with the back of her wrist. It insisted on falling forward into her eyes again. Kirk leaned over and slowly tucked the strand behind her ear. Rachel felt a wave of heat shadowing his fingers as they came in contact with her skin. It took her a moment to force air into her lungs.

"It's just that," she continued after what seemed like an eternity, "as he must have told you, Cameron had other ideas. He thought a dinner at home, the way we used to have, would be a welcome change from what you're accustomed to."

Kirk dropped his hand to his side, his fingers still tingling. "He's right."

"I might also warn you that he's dragged out all the old videos my dad took of the two of you when you played for the Vaqueros."

The Vaqueros had been the name of their high school baseball team. Her father and Cameron had talked Kirk into trying out for the team. To please them, Kirk had gamely tried—and been surprised when he showed an aptitude for the game.

Kirk winced at the thought of viewing the videotapes. "You mean I'm going to top off the meal by watching myself as a scrawny kid in high school?"

She took a moment to sample the sauce and decided that it was ready. "You were never scrawny," she told him. "You were hauntingly gaunt." He'd made more than one girl's heart beat fast. "And very mysterious. The fact that you favored wearing black only added to it."

It had never been his intention to appear mysterious or to create an aura. He had just been very practical. "There was a reason for that."

She rinsed off her spoon and placed it on the rack to dry. "Which was?"

His mouth curved. "Black didn't show the dirt as fast."

Rachel covered her heart and pretended to stagger back a step. "Another myth dies." She dropped her hand, but the amusement remained in her eyes. "Next you'll tell me that there's no Santa Claus."

Kirk laughed, playing along. "Funny Face, there is no Sa—"

Rachel held up the slotted spoon as if it were a sword meant to ward off blows. "That wasn't a challenge, Callaghan. Leave a poor girl some illusions."

His eyes skimmed over her as she began draining the second pot of lasagna noodles. He felt better just being around her.

"Do you still have them?" When she looked at him curiously over her shoulder, he added, "Illusions, I mean."

Her mouth softened. "I don't think of them as illusions. I prefer to think of them as reality."

Knowing what he did of reality, Kirk found that impossible. Illusions had nothing to do with reality. "How?" he asked.

"Because I choose to." It was as simple as that. She had always believed in the basic goodness that lived within each person. Don had shaken that belief, but he hadn't shattered it. "Remember, my glass was always half-full. Yours, you insisted, was always half empty—with a chip in the rim."

That was one way to describe his philosophy of life, he thought. He would have had an even darker view of life, if not for her and Cameron. "I guess I was kind of a somber kid."

Was? She looked at him sharply, the spoon slipping from her hand to the floor. "You've changed?"

He was quick to pick up the spoon and hand it back to her. "No."

Rachel rinsed it off, regarding him thoughtfully. Just by looking at his credits, by looking at the sheer profusion of photographs that bore his name, she would have said that Kirk had accomplished every goal he'd set out to reach. But he certainly didn't look like a man who had reached anything, except perhaps a measure of desperation.

"Wasn't there a pot of gold at the end of that rainbow you chased after?"

His mouth quirked in a disparaging smile. "No, there wasn't even an end of a rainbow. It just sort of vanished when I came close to it." He couldn't quite pinpoint when he had ceased to feel like a witness and begun to feel like a voyeur, recording the world's cankers and sores for all to see.

Rachel moved aside the rectangular pan she'd been alternately layering with cheeses, meat and noodles. This conversation was far more important than any culinary creation she could have come up with. Her eyes held Kirk's in mute sympathy. "Tell me."

He didn't have to be told that she cared, genuinely cared. Kirk knew that. And, while he was grateful, he also knew that this was something that would have to evolve on its own, over time. If it ever did. He wasn't able to talk about anything that was bothering him just yet.

He couldn't. His feelings were like some formless, nebulous thing that refused to be contained, that refused to assume a definite shape. He didn't want to become one of those misanthropic malcontents who dwelled on the downside of life and of themselves.

For the time being, that meant keeping his mouth shut. "Funny Face, I promised myself that I wouldn't get serious tonight."

"Too late." She sighed as she drizzled a handful of mozzarella over a layer of sauce. There was no use pushing it. "Well, I'm here, if you change your mind and want to talk."

It was one of the reasons he'd returned, he thought. Perhaps, subconsciously, the most important reason he'd returned. "I know that."

Abandoning the preparations again, she wiped her hands on her apron. Coming around the counter, she took his hands in hers, enveloping them.

"No, *really* talk," she insisted.

His eyes held hers. As altruistic as she was attempting to be, something definitely felt watery within her when he looked at her that way. She couldn't quite blot out the warm sensations that were trying to break through.

She wasn't reacting strictly as a friend, she chided herself.

It did no good.

"I know," he repeated. But it still didn't make it any easier to talk.

Suddenly self-conscious, feeling as if he could read her thoughts, Rachel dropped her hands to her sides.

"She can't cook if you hold her hands."

They both turned to see Cameron walking into the kitchen. He looked only mildly surprised to see Kirk standing there.

Kirk slid onto the stool again. "If that's the kind of detective you are, I'd say the Bedford police force is in serious trouble. *She* was holding *my* hands," he pointed out. Leaning over, he picked up a strand of shredded mozzarella and sampled it.

Cameron joined in and took a healthy handful. Rachel slapped his hand away. "When did you get here? I didn't hear you come in," he asked his friend.

Kirk nodded in the direction of the living room. "I knocked on the front door, but no one heard me. I thought I should come in before the wine got warm."

Rachel looked pointedly at her brother. "I told you that television set was on too loud."

Cameron leaned toward Kirk, taking the opportunity to pinch a bit of meat from the plate. "She still nags," he confided. Rachel moved the platter of meat to the other side of the counter. Cameron looked at her innocently. "How long until dinner?"

"You keep nibbling," Rachel said pointedly, "and there won't be anything left for dinner." She laid three wide noodles next to each other in the pan. "Not for at least half an hour."

"Great." Cameron motioned Kirk toward the living room. "That gives us time to see a couple of videos."

Kirk looked skeptical about leaving Rachel alone, when she had all this work left. "Maybe Funny Face wants to see them, too."

Ethan had drifted toward the kitchen, following the sound of the voices. "Who's Funny Face?"

He hadn't meant to ask a question, but his curiosity had gotten the better of him. It sounded as if his mother's friend was talking about his mother. But how could he be? His mother didn't have a funny face. She was pretty.

Rachel smiled. Any sort of question meant involvement, and that heartened her tremendously.

"That was my nickname when I was your age," Rachel told Ethan. She looked over her shoulder at Kirk as she took out a fresh container of Parmesan cheese from the pantry. "Kirk insisted on calling me that." Opening the top, she liberally sprinkled the contents over the pan. She glanced at Kirk. "I don't think I've ever heard you call me Rachel."

Now that she mentioned it, he didn't think he had, either. He said it now. "Rachel."

Damn that knot in her stomach, Rachel thought as she felt it tightening, shrinking like leather left out in the sun. Kirk's voice had been low, throaty, and her name—her *name*, for heaven's sake—had seemed to glide along her skin like an invitation to a hot night of passion when he said it.

Maybe it was just the kitchen and the heat, she thought. God knew it was getting to feel hotter to her by the moment.

Her hair was untidily piled high on her head, held in place by hidden pins. It looked as if it would cascade down along her face and throat at any moment. There was a look in her eyes that he recognized as latent desire. Kirk felt an itch taking hold. He wanted to lose his hands in her hair, to bury his face in it and breathe in the fragrance that seemed to cling to it.

He'd been in enough dangerous situations to know when to evacuate. Kirk slid off the stool and crossed to Cameron. "How about being neighborly and offering me a beer? We'll hold off on those videos until later."

Cameron was more than happy to oblige. "My sister's refrigerator is yours." He pulled open the door and moved a few things aside to get to the six-pack Rachel had picked up earlier.

Ethan had turned his attention back to his handheld video game. The musical chimes caught Kirk's attention as Cameron handed him a beer. Kirk popped the top, but didn't drink.

"What *is* that thing?" Kirk motioned toward the game.

Ethan's brow narrowed and puckered over the bridge of his nose. He looked at Kirk as if the latter had just landed on earth in a spaceship labeled Mars or Bust.

He held the game up. "This?" Kirk nodded. "It's a Gameboy." Ethan cocked his head, as if that could help him understand better. "Where've you been?"

"Ethan…" Rachel warned. She flashed an apologetic smile at Kirk.

There was nothing to apologize for. He had been out of touch with things such as games for a long time. The children he had encountered had never had a childhood. Had never had toys.

"Out of the country," Kirk told Ethan.

Interest flickered mildly over the young face. He looked down at the animated game in his palm. "Don't they have this everywhere?"

Kirk shook his head and smiled for the boy's benefit. "Not in the places I've been." He reached for the game, then stopped. "Do you mind?"

Thin shoulders rose and fell in feigned boredom. Ethan surrendered the game. "You can look at it if you want."

He knew what a little attention could do. He'd been hungry for it himself when he was Ethan's age. "How do you play?"

Ethan attempted not to look superior, but failed to carry it off.

"Uh-oh, famous last words," Cameron muttered as he popped the top on his own can of beer. "But, hey, I'm used to sharing you." He winked at Rachel over his shoulder before he followed Kirk and Ethan into the living room.

Rachel returned to placing the final layer on the lasagna. She would have felt infinitely more satisfied about the situation unfolding before her if the nervous feeling in her stomach hadn't been so intense.

Sighing, she splayed a hand over her midsection, as if physically attempting to hold her emotions back. If she wasn't careful, her feelings could get out of hand. And that would ruin everything.

She glanced toward the living room. It looked as if Kirk and Ethan might just begin to draw each other out over something as innocuous as handheld flashing lights and annoying noises.

Whatever worked, she thought, putting the pan into the oven and flipping the dials.

Ethan couldn't pretend that he wasn't listening any longer. Curiosity had egged him on until it all but vibrated within him, like a child waving a hand at a teacher hoping to be called on.

"You were really there when the war broke out?" Ethan blurted out, obviously stunned at the stories Kirk was telling him.

Kirk placed his fork on his empty plate. Three helpings of lasagna was his limit. He wouldn't have eaten that much, except that it had tasted so good. Kirk wasn't certain where or when he had had his last home-cooked meal. Probably in this house, he mused.

"Yes," he answered. It was the first time he had seen interest spark in Ethan's face. "Right from the very beginning."

"I have the news photographs to prove it," Rachel put in to back up Kirk's claim. Lately Ethan had a tendency to doubt everything anyone told him.

Kirk looked at Rachel, mildly surprised.

Cameron obviously saw curiosity etched on his friend's face. "Rachel kept a scrapbook on you."

He clearly caught the warning look that Rachel shot him, but he ignored it. He leaned back in his chair, grinning. "She'd scrutinize every photo in the newspaper, looking for your moniker."

That only made Kirk feel guiltier for not having written. She'd kept far more faithful tabs on him than he had on her.

Rachel shrugged self-consciously, looking for a way to minimize Cameron's words. He made her sound like some kind of lovesick idiot.

"I always liked keeping scrapbooks, remember? You just gave me a reason to." Time to change the subject. She looked around the table. "Dessert, anyone?"

Kirk groaned in spite of himself. Cameron had confided that Rachel had picked up some cannoli. They had sounded a great deal more tempting forty minutes ago. "I don't think I've got any room left."

Cameron raised his brow encouragingly. "I'll take his share."

Kirk looked at his friend. Though large-boned, Cameron had an athletic build that didn't have an ounce of fat on it. He had been eating like a starving man ever since he'd known him.

"Do you still have a tapeworm?" He patted Cameron's stomach and felt his abdominal muscles. They were hard as a rock. "How can you eat like that and not gain an ounce?"

"Luck."

Rachel arranged eight cannoli on a single large platter. Before she was finished, Cameron was helping himself. After a moment's hesitation, Ethan took one, as well.

"Actually," Rachel confided to Kirk, "he's got a portrait in the attic that's been steadily gaining weight for years."

Ethan scowled as he looked from his mother to his uncle. A layer of cream outlined his mouth. "You don't have an attic."

Seeing that Cameron's mouth was full at the moment, Kirk answered for him.

"It's a joke," Kirk told him confidentially, without the hint of a smile on his face. He didn't want to take a chance on making Ethan feel as if the joke were at his expense. "There's a famous story called *The Picture of Dorian Gray.* It's about a man who sold his soul to the devil because he wanted to remain young forever. All the evil things he did became etched into the portrait in his attic, while he remained young-looking."

"Forever?" Ethan asked, plainly fascinated in spite of himself.

Kirk nodded. "Until the end of the story."

"Cool."

It was a delight to see enthusiasm of any sort on Ethan's face, instead of that black look he habitually wore these days. "Don't get any ideas," Rachel warned him affectionately. She leaned over to tousle his hair, only to have him pull back.

One step at a time, she thought, chiding herself for being overly eager.

Kirk felt for both of them. That in itself was a step forward for him, he thought. "It's only a story," he added for Ethan's benefit.

Dark eyes turned on him thoughtfully. Perhaps even a little hopefully. "You have any more stories?"

Cameron exchanged looks with Rachel. This was the most animated and unbelligerent they had seen Ethan in a long while.

"Kirk has lots of stories," Cameron assured him.

"Tell me one," Ethan said challengingly.

Rachel brought over the coffeepot and poured three cups. Her eyes were on Kirk. He looked a little wary, so she gave him an encouraging look.

He folded his hands in front of him. "What kind of story?"

Ethan shrugged. He picked at the pastry on his plate, eating the candied bits first. "I dunno." He raised his eyes to Kirk's. "One of the war ones."

The "war ones," as Ethan called them, were too brutal to tell an eight-year-old boy, Kirk thought. For the most part, they were too brutal for anyone. Pausing, he dug through his memory, attempting to recall something that would not eat away at a man's soul in the wee hours of the morning.

In the end, he settled for one about his escape through enemy lines in the dead of night. He'd been disguised as one of the fleeing refugees, his precious camera equipment wrapped up in rags. His olive complexion and bartered clothing had helped him blend in with a sea of people. Whole cities had found themselves displaced overnight.

He wasn't given to embellishments, but even the facts took time to unfold. By the time he'd finished, Ethan's eyes were huge. His world-weary sneer had vanished, to be replaced by something akin to awe.

"And you really did that? Escaped right under their noses?"

"Yes." It was almost as if he were talking about something that had happened to someone else. The escape *had* been rather miraculous.

Ethan cocked his head again. Kirk recognized it as a movement that echoed Rachel when she'd been the boy's age.

"Weren't you scared?" the boy asked.

Kirk's eyes met Rachel's for a brief moment before he answered. "Yes."

Ethan blew out a breath, disappointed. "I thought you were supposed to be brave."

The story, simple in its narration, had still left her stunned. She hadn't allowed herself to think of the danger he lived with daily. The story forced her to face it. Maybe it was better that he hadn't written. She would have spent a great deal of time worrying about him.

"Brave men are men who are afraid, but still go on and do things anyway," Rachel told her son.

Kirk decided to indulge in a piece of the cannoli. He broke it off from Cameron's plate. Cameron was on his second one. "Still the diplomat."

Rachel shrugged away his comment. "I just see things a little more clearly than you do, sometimes."

Cameron pushed himself back from the table and looked at Kirk. "The videos are waiting."

Rachel wasn't much on cleanup. She nodded toward the dishes. "I could use help stacking the dishes."

"I'll flip you for it," Cameron said to Kirk, digging into his pocket for a coin.

Kirk raised his hand, stopping him. "That's all right, I'll do it. It's probably a two-headed coin, anyway."

"I'm a cop. I have to be honest these days," Cameron said, taking his hand out of his pocket. "But you talked me into it."

Rachel rose. "You two could learn from him," she told them.

"Whatever you say, Rach." Cameron looked at Ethan, who was already crossing the threshold into the living room. "C'mon, Ethan, you can show me how to work the VCR."

Ethan stopped and looked at his uncle suspiciously. "You already know how to work the VCR."

"I'm old, I forget." Cameron began to place his hand on the boy's shoulder, then thought better of it. Ethan didn't need to be crowded, only nudged along.

Rachel turned toward Kirk as the others left the room. "You're the guest for tonight. You don't have to do this." Although she was glad of the company.

He stacked the dessert plates on top of each other. "I don't mind. It's been years since I sat in a kitchen that wasn't surrounded by a tent."

She attempted to think of how that would be, and failed. "Was it really that nomadic?"

Nomadic was far too colorful a term for it. "You have no idea." He laughed.

"No, I don't," she agreed. "But I'll let you fill me in while we load the dishwasher." The more he talked, the more she would know, she thought. And perhaps the more he would heal. She decided that was why he had come home. Not to simply renew old ties, but to heal.

And she meant to help any way she could.

Chapter 8

Funny how he had completely forgotten how much he'd enjoyed playing baseball, Kirk thought as he watched video after video of games that had long since faded into the creases of his mind. Was that really him running the bases? Had he ever looked that young?

Lacing his fingers behind his head, Kirk settled back in the corner of the sofa, studying his image on the television screen. Absorbing the action. As he did, tiny fragments of pride, of the sensation of belonging that he had once experienced, wafted through him. A sensation as elusive as smoke.

As elusive as love. The thought came from nowhere. And faded away to the same place.

"You struck out a lot," Ethan commented to his uncle as a very lanky-looking Cameron was retired by the opposing pitcher.

Cameron laughed. After taking a long pull of his beer, he said, "Yeah, but I had great form."

Cameron's and Rachel's father had been very serious about taking videos. The tape they were watching had all the earmarks of one made by a professional. He'd panned the bench, capturing the expressions of each of the team members. The camera passed smoothly over a tall, restless-looking player.

Don.

Kirk heard the faint, sharp intake of breath, and glanced in Rachel's direction. She had stiffened a little beside him. Not in the eager way a woman might when she saw someone she had once loved, but in the manner of someone unconsciously bracing for a blow.

Ethan was sitting on the floor in front of him. It occurred to Kirk that Ethan might not have seen these videos before. The stunned look on the boy's face bore him out. He turned suddenly and looked up at Kirk. "My dad played with you?"

Kirk barely remembered Don. What he did remember, he didn't care for. He gave no indication of his feelings as he spoke.

"I think he only played a couple of games before he dropped out. Said he didn't like the game." Football had been more to Don's liking. Now that he thought about it, Kirk recalled Cameron saying that Don had planned a career in football.

Cameron cursed himself for not remembering that Don was on this one when he had picked out the videos for tonight. He hadn't wanted to stir up bad memories for Rachel or for Ethan.

"That was only because he was uncoordinated and didn't have the patience or the eye for it," Cameron reminded his friend.

Resentment leaped into Ethan's eyes as he scrambled to his feet. "That's just because he didn't have time for a dumb old game like baseball. Me neither." Like a prizefighter daring an opponent, Ethan stuck his chin out at Cameron.

She'd had enough of deifying a man who hadn't had the time of day for his son. Who hadn't had time for anything except mourning the pieces of a broken dream.

"Ethan, I think you owe your uncle an apology." The look in her eyes was stern.

Ethan turned rebelliously toward his mother. "What for?" He pointed accusingly at Cameron. "He's the one who said bad things about Dad."

He wasn't one to intrude, but this was the closest thing he had ever had to a family. "He wasn't saying anything bad,

Ethan,'' Kirk said quietly. ''He was just making an observation. Your dad was better at football.''

''Yeah.'' Ethan leaped at the way out. ''He would've been
one of the greats, if he hadn't busted up his knee in that last
game.''

He was parroting words about an event he'd heard about
time and again, Rachel knew. An event that had taken place
when he was only a baby.

Ethan looked down at the floor, sighing impatiently. Kirk's
words seemed to have siphoned the air out of his indignation.
''I'm sorry.''

The words weren't entirely sincere, but at least he had said
them, Rachel thought, grateful for any tiny headway that might
have been made. She glanced toward Kirk and offered him her
silent thanks.

''Apology accepted.'' Cameron stopped the videotape, and
a commercial for cat food materialized where the baseball game
had been a moment ago. ''I think it's time that we all called it
a night.''

Rachel nodded. ''I think we've skipped down memory lane
long enough for one night.'' She rose and cleared away the almost empty bowl of popcorn she'd made for the occasion.
Cameron managed to snag one last handful before she set it on
the dining room table.

Kirk stopped to pick up a couple of crumbs from the rug and
deposited them on the coffee table. He dusted off his hands.
''I'd better be going myself. It was a great dinner, Funny Face.
Thank you. Good night, Cameron. Ethan.''

The boy looked surprised to be acknowledged, but he nodded at Kirk awkwardly.

''Get ready for bed, Ethan,'' Rachel urged, though her son
was already out of the room. She hurried after Kirk as he
reached the front door. As she passed, she noted that Cameron seemed inordinately busy gathering his tapes together. He
undoubtedly thought she needed this time with Kirk to make
amends for her son's behavior, and she was grateful to him for
his intuitiveness. Her brother had his moments, she mused.

''I'm sorry,'' Rachel said softly as she walked Kirk outside.
He closed the door behind her and waited. Rachel ran her

hands along her arms restlessly. "The divorce, and then Don's death, seemed to hit Ethan really hard."

He thought of the boy, of the defensiveness in his stance. It was a familiar sign he could relate to so well. "Did Don?"

Rachel looked at him, confused by his question. "Did Don what?"

She looked so vulnerable. He had a sudden urge to enfold her in his arms, and shoved his hands into his pockets instead. But his eyes remained on hers, kind and coaxing. "Hit Ethan really hard."

Rachel's head jerked up as she looked at him sharply. "What makes you ask—?"

He'd struck a nerve, he thought. This wasn't anything that he could just casually go into with her, not from his standpoint. Not yet. "A hunch. Nothing I could really explain to you, just a feeling."

For a moment, reflexes had her wanting to sweep away the question with a denial. But who would she be protecting if she did that? Don? Ethan? The answer, she knew, was neither. Don was dead, and Ethan needed saving. Things like this had to be out in the open, at least as far as the people who cared were concerned.

She took a step farther away from the house, as if distancing herself a little from the subject. She looked out at the inky sky. There were no stars out tonight, she thought. No stars to wish on.

"That's why I left him." She said it so softly, he almost didn't hear her.

The night air was warm, with a hint of a breeze. Her words, and the memories they evoked, made her feel so cold, so abandoned. She looked at Kirk. He was waiting for her to continue. No prodding, no probing. He was just there, waiting. If she said nothing, she knew, he'd accept that. Rachel took a deep breath and made up her mind.

"I could put up with it when it was just me. Looking back, it's a terrible thing to admit, that I was that weak. I made up all sorts of excuses for him. Mostly I kept hoping that he'd change, that maybe he needed to work things through for himself."

Rachel wondered how many of the details he knew from Cameron. She knew she hadn't written to Kirk about it herself. She couldn't.

"That accident with his knee had robbed Don of his identity, of who and what he thought he was, or would be. He couldn't play football anymore, and he'd never wanted to do anything else."

She knew she was making excuses for Don again, but she had felt his pain, his agony, with him. Until it had turned on her.

She bit her lower lip. It was difficult to say the next part without pain, even now. "When he took his frustration out on Ethan—I knew I couldn't afford to wait any longer."

He'd assumed that she was talking about emotional abuse, which was bad enough. But then he realized that she meant something far more horrendous. Something twisted in his gut at the mere thought of it.

Rachel was surprised when Kirk abruptly seized her arms, forcing her to look at him. "He hit you?"

She'd never seen such anger in his eyes. It made her look away, ashamed to be the cause of it.

"A couple of times." Rachel raised her eyes to him, suddenly wanting to make him understand. "It wasn't anything that landed me in the hospital. It wasn't even bad enough for Cameron to see. The few times it happened, they were bruises that I could easily cover up, at least outwardly. And he was always so sorry afterward." She sighed as the emptiness threatened to swallow her up. "But the situation only became worse instead of better." Her mouth grew hard. "And then he hit Ethan."

She could have killed her ex-husband for that, she thought. "I have an awful feeling that Don had done it before, when I wasn't around, but Ethan swore he didn't."

She shrugged, looking off into the darkness. She blamed herself for that, for her son's tolerance of things he shouldn't have mutely tolerated—he'd only had her example to follow.

"Maybe Ethan was like I was, looking for the good, thinking that perhaps in some way he'd done something to deserve a beating."

Kirk swung her around, his eyes fierce. He'd never been anything but gentle with her before, and the sight of his anger overwhelmed her. "No one *deserves* to be battered around, Rachel."

"I know that now." She looked at him in surprise, both at his tone and because he'd used her name. "You called me Rachel."

Very slowly, he released her, cursing his temper. But it wasn't Rachel he was angry with, it was the ghost of her husband. He'd seen so much injustice, so much suffering. Somehow he'd never thought of it as touching those he cared about.

He attempted to smile at her. "'Funny Face' didn't seem to fit this situation."

She nodded. "No, there was nothing funny about it. But it's over." She blew out a long, cleansing breath. "I can move beyond it now." She frowned as she glanced toward the closed door. "If only Ethan hadn't withdrawn the way he has." Rachel felt tears forming, and blinked to force them back. One was too far along and spilled down her cheek. "He won't let me hold him anymore. I just don't know how to reach him."

Moved, Kirk took her into his arms, to offer her what comfort he could. "He'll come around."

She sniffed, feeling like an idiot. "That's what Cameron says." She wiped the tear away with the heel of her hand. "That's what I'm clinging to." A ragged sigh tore loose as she looked up at Kirk. "Sorry he spoiled the evening."

"It wasn't spoiled."

She felt good in his arms, he thought. As if she belonged there. As if he were meant to hold her.

He felt a sexual edginess move to the fore, pushing everything else aside. They'd said good-night to one another a hundred times on this very spot. Why was there tension crackling between them now? Why did she have to look so vulnerable—and so damn attractive?

Like a man in a trance, Kirk inclined his head to kiss her good-night. But then he remembered the last time, when she'd turned her head and her lips had brushed against his. Kirk stepped back, releasing her as if she were suddenly too hot to hold. And maybe she was. If he continued holding her any longer, he knew that he'd kiss her, not as a friend, but as something a great deal more. And that would lead to other things.

The one thing he could count on was her friendship. It was very precious to him. He didn't want it to become tangled up inside something else, something whose parameters he was uncertain of.

He'd been ready to kiss her, she thought, a pang filling her as he drew away. What had changed his mind? What had made him pull away from her?

Rachel touched his cheek. "Don't be afraid of me, Kirk."

He'd been referred to as fearless by some, as well as reckless. The warning sounded almost amusing. "What?"

She let her hand drop, though she wanted to go on touching him. To have him hold her again. To let what seemed to be hovering just on the fringe take over and progress naturally. A small kernel of impatience struggled to peek out from behind her calm demeanor. "You look as if you're afraid of me."

He shook his head slowly, his eyes remaining on hers. "It's not you I'm afraid of, Funny Face. It's me."

Slipping his hands into her hair, he just lightly touched his lips to hers and then turned away.

Rachel could feel her very blood humming in her veins. She stared after him as he walked away, wondering what he had meant.

When she awoke the next morning, Rachel remembered feeling emotionally drained and exhausted after Kirk left. She'd had just enough energy, when Cameron went home, to check on Ethan and then peel off her clothes. She didn't even remember climbing into bed.

Questions buzzed through her head as she clung to the warming blanket of sleep. Questions about Kirk. Was she reading things into his actions, or was there something there? Something on the cusp, that he was afraid to release? Something that would take them beyond the plateau where they were?

She thought she was ready.

Anticipation stirred deliciously throughout her semiconscious body.

Morning spilled into her bedroom unannounced, like a bucket of sunbeam that had been accidentally kicked over. One moment she was buried in a soothing dreariness, the next moment there was sunlight all over, prodding away misty half dreams.

With a surrendering sigh, Rachel rolled over in her bed and focused on the bright red oversize digital numbers on her clock.

Eight o'clock.

She couldn't remember when she had slept so late. It was definitely time to stop hibernating.

Throwing off the covers, Rachel sat up and dragged her hand through her hair. It struck her as odd that she hadn't been woken up earlier by the sounds of Ethan puttering around. He was always dropping something or banging it. By nature, Ethan was like her, an early riser, even on weekends.

As she got out of bed, Rachel heard a crash. But it came from outside, and sounded as if it were some distance away. It sounded vaguely like metal hitting pavement. Absently she wondered what it was.

Stretching, she reached into the closet for a pair of cutoffs and a baggy sweatshirt. After tugging them on, she went downstairs to see what Ethan wanted for breakfast. Maybe she could get him to talk about the videos, she mused hopefully. Any conversation was better than none.

He wasn't there.

"Ethan? Ethan, where are you?" She went from one room to the other, looking for him. He wasn't in the kitchen, or planted before the television in the family room, the way she expected him to be.

A tight feeling began to wrap invisible fingers around her throat. Something was wrong. Six months ago, she thought as she hurried upstairs again, she wouldn't have felt panicky like this if Ethan wasn't around. She'd just have assumed that he was out playing. But life wasn't that simple anymore.

She knocked once on his door and then opened it. The room was empty. A quick search of the rest of the house yielded the same information. No Ethan.

Had he decided to run away? He'd been upset last night, after seeing that last video. But when she had gone into his room to check on him, to talk if he wanted to, he'd been asleep.

Or he'd been pretending to be, she thought now.

Rachel was just about to retrace her steps to his room, to see if he had taken anything with him that might indicate that he had run away, when she heard another clatter out front. It made a continuous noise, like a hubcap spinning around before it settled down on the sidewalk.

Impulse had her turning on her bare heel and hurrying to the front door. Ethan wasn't supposed to take his bike out for a ride without telling her first. Maybe he was just tinkering with it.

Her heart sank when she saw that her driveway was empty.

Rachel pressed her lips together and let out a ragged breath. *Ethan, where are you?* Rachel dragged a hand through her hair and turned to go back into the house. She'd call Cameron and see if he would help her look for Ethan. Two steps toward the house, and she stopped as impatience rose up within her. She didn't have time to wait for Cameron. Kirk could help.

Rachel was halfway down the driveway when she heard his voice.

"No, hand me the smaller wrench."

He was with someone. Ethan? It didn't seem likely, but she was ready to clutch at any straw. She picked her way around the patch of dirt that separated their two properties, circumventing the border of cypresses that blocked her view of his house.

And then she stopped just at the perimeter of the last tree.

Kirk's minivan was in the driveway, jacked up on one side. A pair of worn cowboy boots—Kirk's, she recognized—were sticking out from underneath. It looked as if the car had partially ingested him.

And crouched down beside the worn boots, a profusion of tools scattered next to him, was Ethan. There was a semi-empty toolbox just beyond his reach.

Rachel didn't know whether to laugh or cry with relief. She did neither. Instead, she just stood where she was for a moment, watching.

Without anyone around to observe him, Ethan's face was devoid of its perpetual frown. He looked almost animated, she thought. And involved.

"Okay." Kirk's voice sounded a little strained as it drifted from beneath the vehicle, as if he were struggling with something. "Now get in and turn the wheel all the way to the left, then all the way to the right."

Ethan gaped at the driver's seat. "You want *me* to turn the steering wheel?"

"You don't see anyone else around, do you?"

Ethan shook his head in response, though Kirk couldn't see. "No."

"Then do it."

Ethan was quick to scramble up to his feet and follow orders. Like a kid on a joyride, he twisted the wheel first one way, then another. "How's this?" he called out happily.

He seemed so carefree. Rachel could hardly believe that this was her son.

Kirk sighed. "That about does it."

Another turn on the bolt, and he was satisfied. Kirk snaked his way back out, hoping he wouldn't tear his worn jeans. That was his last clean pair. Emerging, he threw down the wrench next to the others.

"Thanks." He wiped the back of his wrist across his forehead, leaving a small, dark streak across it. "You were a great help."

Ethan shrugged self-consciously. "I just handed you some stuff."

Kirk rose to his feet, brushing off the dust and dirt he'd acquired. "When someone tells you that you've been a great help, don't contradict them. It makes them look foolish. Just say thanks."

"Oh. Okay." Ethan seemed to fight with a smile, then let it take over. "What are you going to do now?"

Kirk looked down at his hands. They were black. He hated getting dirty, but he hated not having a vehicle in running order even more. Necessity had taught him how to make basic repairs. Triple A didn't make pit stops in Somalia.

He was getting rather good at it, too, he thought.

"Wash up." He looked down at Ethan. The boy had wandered out earlier to watch him work. He'd made a point of getting him involved. He had no intention of letting go of his edge now. "Want to come in?"

Ethan attempted to appear nonchalant. "I guess." But he couldn't manage to hide his curiosity. It rose up to shine in his eyes.

She'd hung back long enough, Rachel thought, stepping forward. "Can you see your way clear to stretching that invitation to include two?"

Startled, Ethan spun around to face his mother. Before her eyes, he seemed to withdraw into himself. He began to edge away from both of them.

"I got other stuff..." he began.

She'd be damned if she was going to let him drive this wedge farther between them. What she'd seen just now gave her hope that the bright, happy boy she'd known was still in there somewhere.

Rachel placed a firm hand on his shoulder, stopping him in his tracks. "No, you don't. You don't have to run away every time I come near you."

The pugnacious chin that echoed hers shot up. "I can do what I want to."

Kirk dropped a tool into the box, and it clanked loudly, drawing two sets of eyes in his direction. "As long as it doesn't mean talking back to your mother." He hadn't raised his voice an iota, but there was no mistaking the fact that it was a direct order.

Ethan looked down at the ground, embarrassed, confused. He thought he liked the man who was his mother's friend. At least he liked the way Kirk treated him as if he was a grown up.

But he didn't like being told what to do.

Kirk's eyes skimmed over Rachel slowly, lingering on her legs. Her long, firm, tanned legs. She was barefoot, wearing a pair of faded white cutoffs that had lost a little more of themselves with each washing. They were now dangerously close to shredding completely. As it was, they adhered to her body like a soft second skin and brought an itch to his hands that shouldn't be there. Kirk looked away, aware that his mouth was dry.

That shouldn't be, either, he thought.

Rachel felt as if she had suddenly been divested of her clothing. Licking her lower lip, she nodded toward the house behind them.

"Do you realize that in all the years we've lived next door to each other, I've never been inside your house?" She said it only to have something to say, to smooth over the nervous ripple she had felt. She knew damn well that Kirk was aware that she had never stepped inside his house. Nothing that really mattered ever slipped past Kirk.

He shrugged. "There wasn't much to see." Except a drunken father, he thought. Kirk dropped the rest of the tools into the battered box he normally kept in the back of his van. He looked at Rachel, careful to keep his eyes on her face. "There's even less now."

She rocked back on her heels, hooking her thumbs in the loops of her shorts. "As long as you don't charge admission, I won't feel cheated."

Rachel hid her surprise when Ethan picked up a tool from the far end of the driveway and deposited it in the box. She thought it best not to comment, but her eyes met Kirk's in a silent thank-you. Somehow, he seemed to have gained more influence over her son in a short two days than either she or Cameron had managed to exercise in the past six months. But then, Kirk had always had a presence about him.

When Ethan began to head toward Kirk's front door, Rachel laid a hand on his shoulder. "You gave me a scare this morning, Ethan."

Small, dark brows drew together. "How?"

He really didn't know, did he? "When I couldn't find you."

He shrugged and managed to slip away from beneath her hand. "No big deal."

"Yes, it is," she insisted quietly, her eyes intent on his. "Not finding you is a very big deal."

He flushed, embarrassed. Ethan slanted a look toward Kirk to see his reaction.

Kirk wondered what was going on in the boy's head. When he was Ethan's age, he would have willingly cleaved to his mother if she had displayed the slightest inclination to take his side. Instead, she had left him to fend off his father himself.

"In case you don't recognize the signs," Kirk told the boy as he closed the toolbox and snapped down the two locks, "it means she loves you."

Ethan shoved his hands in his back pockets awkwardly, caught between being a little boy and being a man who had burdens to shoulder that he didn't quite understand.

"I really gotta go do stuff," he mumbled to both of them without looking at either. Ethan toed a pebble with his sneaker, pretending to be riveted by the task. His stomach rumbled loudly.

"How about breakfast?" Rachel suggested. "I'll make you both breakfast." She looked up at Kirk. "Provided that you have something to work with."

He had bought a carton of eggs, a loaf of bread and some orange juice when he went to the store to pick up the wine yesterday. "I've got a few things," Kirk volunteered. "But I haven't gotten around to finding where the pots and pans are."

He'd been back—how long? Two days? "How have you been eating?"

"I took most of my meals with you," he reminded her. "That fast-food place right outside the development took care of breakfast yesterday."

She winced. "They use lard to make everything." Then she grinned as she flicked a finger down a bicep that was accented by his sleeveless sweatshirt. "Of course, on you it hardly shows."

"Hardly?" he echoed, raising a brow.

She laughed, enjoying the playful mood. "I think I came along just in time to rescue you from a fate worse than death. How about French toast?" The question was directed more to Ethan than to Kirk, since she knew that was his favorite.

The indifferent shrug wasn't quite convincing. "Sure."

Kirk held up a hand before she could work up a full head of steam, the way he knew she was wont to do. "One small problem, I haven't got powdered sugar or syrup. And I'm not sure if I bought any margarine."

She nodded. It sounded as if he kept the same sort of refrigerator Cameron did. Cameron took most of his meals with her, bringing armloads of groceries along and looking like a helpless puppy. She fell for it every time.

"Lucky for you two, I do. Just give me ten minutes to get everything together, and I'll be right over."

Kirk glanced over his shoulder at the house. He wasn't really prepared for company. Ethan was one thing. Rachel was another. For Rachel, things had to be . . . different. "Won't it be easier just to make breakfast in your kitchen?"

"Uh-uh." Mischief played at the corners of her mouth. It looked incredibly appealing and tantalizing to him. "I already know what my kitchen looks like. It's too late to back out now."

With that, she hurried away.

Kirk wondered if her words were somehow prophetic.

Chapter 9

Rachel quickly gathered together all the things she needed in order to make breakfast for Kirk and her son. Depositing everything in one of the grocery bags that she kept stashed in the kitchen drawer, she hurried back to Kirk's house.

It felt odd, standing on the Callaghans' doorstep, ringing the bell. To her recollection, she had never done it before. Mr. and Mrs. Callaghan had not received visitors, had not welcomed uninvited callers. Cameron had told her that years ago. She couldn't remember if it was something he had heard, or had been told firsthand by Kirk. She just knew that neither of them had ever been invited over to Kirk's house.

Rachel smiled to herself as she hugged the bag closer. She would be lying if she denied that curiosity was coloring her eagerness to make breakfast for Kirk and Ethan in the Callaghans' kitchen.

She rang twice before the door was opened by Kirk.

"Hi." She peered around Kirk's shoulder and saw that what furniture there was was covered with sheets. Still? It seemed unusual to her, and just a little creepy.

She shifted the grocery bag as it began to fall. "I was beginning to think that you'd changed your mind about breakfast."

"We were just in the back room and didn't hear you." He took the grocery bag from her as he stepped back, allowing her to walk in.

Kirk studied Rachel to see her reaction to the house. There was no reason why there should be this tiny chord of anxiety strumming through him. Yet it was there, vibrating insistently. He hated this house, but there was no denying that he was part of it, that his life was tangled up with it and had been formed by the events that had transpired here. He didn't want it to repel her.

Whatever she thought would be there for him to see. Rachel had a very expressive face. It reminded him of a flower opening up to the sun, or a child's face, absorbing the various sensations around her.

He'd always enjoyed watching her face. In a movie theater, the few times he, Cameron and Rachel had all gone to see a show together, he could gauge the action taking place on the screen just by looking at Rachel's face. She could keep nothing locked inside.

Honesty. There was no other word for it. Hers was the face that honesty wore.

Rachel glanced about. In a way, what she saw was exactly what she had expected without fully knowing why. It was a house people left, a house people came *from*, not a house people came *to*. The building felt cold to her, and it had nothing to do with lack of heat. It was almost as if the sun were hesitant to enter, reluctant to embrace the room.

Sorrow had lived here, she thought. Perhaps, in a way, it still did.

Kirk rested the bag on his hip, waiting for Rachel to make a comment. When she didn't, he prodded her. "Well, what do you think?"

There was no pride in his voice, no attachment of any sort. It was the kind of tone a homicide detective might use when asking the coroner to speculate as to a victim's cause of death.

She wanted to say something genial, something nice. But they had been much too close for her to assume the role of the polite, distant visitor now.

Rachel turned toward him and saw the look in his eyes. She had the distinct feeling that even the worst comment would have no effect on him. Not about this house. "I think I saw this room in *Great Expectations*. Just before the fire."

He knew exactly what she meant. It was a cold, bloodless place. "That's kind of the way I see it." He turned and led the way to the kitchen.

Rachel followed, still looking around. The kitchen was neat and clean and completely devoid of personality. She tried to envision the way it might have been when he had lived here with his parents. She couldn't.

"Why don't you take off the sheets?"

He set the grocery bag down on the counter before answering. "I'm not sure I'm staying that long."

His words saddened her. Even after just two days, she had gotten used to the idea of having him back. She sighed, forcing away the pang.

"You could still take off the sheets, you know." She gestured toward the room they'd just walked through. "At least out there." From where she stood, Rachel could see the back of what looked to be an armchair, covered by a faded white sheet. "It looks like a scene from a grade B horror movie. All you need is a ghost to pop up."

Her assessment seemed in keeping with the way he felt. "Maybe it will." He began to unpack the bag.

Rachel stared at him. "What?"

"Hmmm?" He looked up, as if she had interrupted some train of thought. "Did I say something?"

Rachel shook her head. "Don't play innocent with me. You know you did." She crossed to the refrigerator. "I think you like being mysterious." With a tug, she opened the door, and was pleased to see that the light came on. "Well, at least the power's on." She surveyed the interior. Except for a carton of eggs, a container of orange juice and a loaf of bread, there was nothing there. Rachel took out the carton of eggs and then released the door. "Looks like you're going to have to go shopping for food, or your next meal is going to be the light bulb."

He was opening cabinets, looking for a pan for her to use. Kirk glanced at her over his shoulder. "I can always go next door and beg a meal."

"You would never have to beg." Folding the bag, she tossed it to one side. Like a surgeon preparing for an operation, she carefully laid everything out on the counter. Behind her, Rachel heard the sound of a pan being placed on the burner.

They were in business, she thought.

Rachel glanced up at Kirk as he moved past her. "By the way, what have you done with my son, aside from making him human."

The boy had had a difficult time masking his interest as Kirk began unloading his van. It was filled to capacity with camera equipment and everything necessary to transform his van into a studio on wheels, right down to the chemicals used in the darkroom.

"Ethan's human on his own, Funny Face."

Rachel moved the bowl closer and broke an egg over it. "Yes, I know, but I haven't seen or heard him do anything but scowl and grumble for so long, it was getting rather hard for me to remember."

Since there didn't seem to be a place for garbage, she opened the folded grocery bag. Dropping it to the floor, she tossed the empty eggshells in it. "You didn't answer my question, where is he?"

He nodded toward the other side of the house. "I left him in the back room. I'm thinking of using it for a studio. Temporarily." He'd felt bound to toss in the qualifying word. "Ethan's helping me set up my equipment."

Rachel stopped beating the egg and stared at him in disbelief. "You trusted him with your equipment?"

Was the boy clumsy? He hadn't appeared to be. Amused, Kirk leaned a hip against the counter and watched Rachel work. It occurred to him that watching her soothed him. And stirred him at the same time. "They're not exactly the crown jewels, Funny Face."

She began listening for the sound of things falling. Breaking.

"They might as well be." Well, if he wasn't worried, why should she be? It wasn't as if Ethan were going to have a fit and start throwing things. Fortunately, they were past that stage by a couple of months. "They're your claim to fame." She poured oil into the pan and turned up the heat. "That and your unerring eye."

Kirk frowned as he thought of his failing. Of how he had watched when he should have acted. Of the life that had been lost because of him.

"It's erred plenty."

He said it so solemnly, Rachel instantly knew she'd treaded somewhere that was too tender to bear any traffic, at least for now. She retreated.

Satisfied with the consistency of the batter, she dipped in the first slice of bread. "Shouldn't you be supervising him?"

He'd rather be out here with her. "I gave him a few basic instructions. Don't worry, he's just unpacking some boxes of supplies." Kirk smiled at her concern. "There's nothing in his hands that can be damaged seriously, and it makes him feel good."

Testing the oil, she watched a bead of water dance on it. The reaction reminded her a great deal of the way her pulse felt whenever Kirk touched her. Gingerly she deposited the coated slice of bread and picked up another. "I don't know how to thank you."

Compliments and gratitude of any sort made him feel uneasy, as if he didn't know what to do with himself. "For what?"

Rachel laughed. Was it so hard for him to just say "You're welcome"?

"Endangering your equipment, for one thing." A second slice joined the first. "I think you're giving his self-esteem a tremendous boost."

He attempted to shrug off her words. "I could use the help."

A skeptical look entered her eyes. "Yeah, right." Rachel shook her head. "I never knew you to need help in anything." In all the years they'd known one another, she couldn't remember Kirk ever asking for help. Not even when she'd felt he needed it.

I need help now, Funny Face. I need it and I don't even know how to ask, or what to ask for. Everything's so damned messed up.

"Now there you're wrong, Funny Face."

The smile faded from her lips. Rachel stopped dunking the bread and let it slip back into the bowl. Her eyes were on his. He wasn't teasing her. He was serious. "You've never admitted something like that before."

It had just slipped out. He hadn't meant to let it. Instant regret urged him to shore up his defenses. "Must be hunger." He dipped a pinkie into the box of powdered sugar and sampled it. "They say they get their best confessions from people who are being starved."

She was going to have to proceed very lightly if she didn't want to frighten him off, she thought. Like a naturalist attempting to get a close look at a deer, she moved cautiously forward.

Rachel raised a brow in his direction as she resumed working. "What else will you tell me if I threaten to withhold your French toast?"

He'd already said far too much. As willing an ear as she was, his problems were his own to work out. She had enough to contend with without his burdening her. Just being around her was enough.

Perhaps, he thought, suddenly catching a whiff of her perfume, more than enough.

He nodded toward the frying pan. "Start cooking." He began to edge out of the room. "As you pointed out, maybe I'd better get back to supervising."

"Coward." But her eyes were laughing at him. Whatever was bothering him, she had a feeling they'd get to it soon enough. She sensed that, beneath it all, he wanted to talk. She'd just have to be patient.

He only grinned. "I'm not rising to the bait, Funny Face."

"Damn," she muttered good-naturedly.

With a toss of her head, she attempted to send her long hair over her shoulder. Both her hands were covered with batter and unsuited to the task. Hair rebelliously fell back into her face. With a huff, Rachel tried again. And failed.

"Want help?" he offered.

"Please."

He crossed to her and slowly threaded his fingers along her temple, then pushed her hair back. Rachel thought that she had never felt anything so sensual, so unsettling, in her life. She had to struggle to keep her eyes from drifting closed. Fingertips coated in batter, oil snapping in the pan at her back, Rachel had transcended the kitchen and was in a place that had nothing to do with food or cooking.

And everything to do with desire.

She let out a long, languid breath that hitched in her throat at the end. "Much better," she murmured.

He sincerely doubted that, he thought. Not for either of them. But he was beginning to have difficulty keeping his distance from her. Keeping from touching her.

Once again he shoved his hands into his pockets to keep himself from giving in to his feelings. It was getting to be a tiresome habit, Kirk thought, but a necessary one. He didn't want to abuse what was offered in friendship. He already knew he couldn't ever be Rachel's future. She deserved better than a burned-out shell of a man.

"Don't mention it," he told her, turning to leave the kitchen.

Rachel began humming, and Kirk stopped just beyond the threshold to listen to her. The tune she was humming seemed to waft into his system through cracks he'd had no idea were there, as if he were a watertight vessel that had somehow developed fissures.

There was something hypnotic about Rachel, he felt it every time he was near her. He was going to have to watch his step at all times. Even though he enjoyed being with her, there was a price to be paid for that enjoyment. And he knew that, if he allowed himself to let go, she would be the one paying. She, and possibly her son.

He could never allow that to happen, not to Rachel. She didn't need another liability in her life. She'd already had one.

Straightening, Kirk forced himself to turn around and return to the back room. Ethan should be finished unpacking all the boxes by now. He wanted to show the boy his camera. From all indications, Kirk had a feeling Ethan would enjoy that.

* * *

Rachel leaned back in her chair and surveyed the kitchen table. She was careful not to lean back too far. The table leg next to her seemed ready to collapse at any moment. It had shuddered once when she accidentally hit it with her foot.

"All right, we've eaten and cleaned up..." she began, and got no further.

"Under protest," Kirk interjected. He made eye contact with Ethan, and the boy nodded in reply. "At least as far as the latter goes."

She'd commanded both of them to stack and wash. Ethan had looked ready to refuse until Kirk acquiesced.

"Cleaning up is good for you," Rachel insisted.

Kirk blew out a breath as he glanced at the empty dish rack on the counter. She'd insisted not only on washing everything, but on drying it all and putting it away, as well. "I don't mind dirty dishes in the sink."

Her eyes narrowed. "*Learn* to mind." Rachel rose. "As I was saying, now that that's out of the way, let's get to the sheets."

Kirk looked dubiously at Ethan. A contented, full feeling was curling through him. He couldn't recall having felt that way in years. "Does she always order people around like this?"

Ethan was willingly pulled into the scenario as a confidant. He took to sharing feelings with another male surprisingly easily, Rachel thought—although, unfortunately, it was at her expense. Perhaps especially since it appeared to be at her expense. She didn't care. She'd endure anything as long as it meant that Ethan would come around again.

Ethan nodded, his blond hair swaying like the fringe of a grass hut in the strong spring breeze. "Yeah."

Kirk sighed and then rose to his feet. "Then I guess we don't stand much of a chance if we try to resist. Might as well give in."

Ethan wasn't as easily convinced. A stubborn expression took over his face. "But it's your house." His stance showed that he clearly sided with Kirk. "You can if you wanna."

He was enjoying the boy, Kirk thought. Almost as much as he enjoyed Ethan's mother. And for a whole host of different reasons.

"Sometimes," Kirk confided in a conspiratorial tone, "it's a whole lot easier just going along with things than fighting the inevitable." Kirk noted Rachel's pleased expression.

Ethan frowned and cocked his head. "What's that? In-inevitable..."

Kirk placed a hand on the boy's shoulder. He didn't flinch this time. That was a good sign. "Your mother, for one." Kirk raised his eyes to Rachel's. She looked sure of herself, he thought. He hadn't had any intention of ever lifting those sheets. But if it meant that much to her, what harm could it do? Maybe it would even make him feel a little better, though he doubted it. "It means something that you can't avoid or escape. Like your mother getting her way."

"Smart thinking." Rachel pushed her chair in, then led the way into the living room. "I take no prisoners, remember?"

Ethan made sure he kept up with Kirk. He looked from one to the other now. "What are you guys talking about?" he demanded.

Rachel wrapped her fingers around the edge of a sheet. "Old childhood games." She had been a fierce competitor, always desperate to win. Desperate to show her brother and Kirk that she was their equal, even if she was younger and smaller. "And it certainly wouldn't hurt to try to make this place more inviting."

"It'll take more than removing sheets to do that."

She heard the dark note in his voice. What had gone on here? she wondered. If it was so terrible, why had he returned? Why hadn't he just sold it?

Maybe she was just reading things into nothing, she thought. "It's a start."

His eyes shifted to hers. "Why start what can't be finished?" He hadn't meant it as a challenge, but that was the way it came out.

She chose her words carefully, for Ethan's sake, as well as his. "Because you just might be able to finish it after all. You'll never know if you don't try." Rachel pulled the sheet completely off the armchair. It didn't look particularly comfortable or inviting, she thought as she folded the sheet mechanically.

Kirk took the sheet from her and let it drop onto the coffee table. "Anyone ever tell you that you're terminally cheerful?"

She smiled at him. The look in his eyes made her want to soothe him, to chase away whatever it was that was troubling him. She had very few weapons at her disposal, but she would use what she could.

"Must be the company I keep." Her smile faded a little around the edges as she remembered another time. "I wasn't always."

She couldn't deny what he knew to be true. "You have been for as long as I can remember."

She was already tugging off another sheet, this one from a sofa. "You were gone for a while, remember?" She sensed her son's retreat. Turning, she saw Ethan at the front door. "Speaking of going—" she raised her voice just a little to catch Ethan's attention "—where are you headed, Ethan?"

The defiant look was back in his eyes. He kept his hand on the doorknob. "Out."

Two steps forward, one step back. Rachel controlled her impatience. "Can you be a little bit more specific than that?"

Ethan shifted from foot to foot. "I'm bored."

It had been good while it lasted, she thought. Avoiding Kirk's eyes, she looked in Ethan's direction. "All right, go back into the house and play video games for a while. I'll be home soon."

His expression indicated that she could stay away indefinitely, for all he cared. "Yes, ma'am."

The door slammed in his wake, and she winced, both at the sound and at the unspoken display of rebellion it symbolized.

She sighed as she turned toward Kirk. "I'm not a mother, I'm a drill sergeant." She finished pulling the sheet away with a vengeance.

He laughed at the comparison. "Video games are hardly K.P. duty."

"No, that's not what I meant. He won't listen to me if I ask him to do something nicely. I have to order him around before he obeys."

The sheet she was folding was long, and she was having trouble with it. Kirk picked up the other end and folded one edge over the other, then brought his end to meet hers. Their hands brushed against each other, and a pleasant, electric feeling reinforced the contact. A feeling of inevitability coursed through him. He remembered the definition he'd given to Ethan.

"At least he obeys."

She dropped the first sheet on top of the other. "For now."

Words of hope were not something he was accustomed to doling out. For her sake, he tried. "He doesn't seem that bad."

Bad wasn't a word she wanted to attach to Ethan. He wasn't bad. He was troubled. Like Kirk.

A lot like Kirk, she thought suddenly. "No, not with you," she agreed. "Not when he thinks I'm not around," she amended. When she was there, Ethan was inflexible, stubborn, as if her very existence repelled him. "He seems a great deal more relaxed around you."

There was a reason for that, Kirk thought. He followed her to the last covered piece of furniture in the living room. "Maybe because we understand each other."

The comment lingered in the air between them for a moment. Rachel debated asking Kirk about something that had been preying on her mind.

It wasn't curiosity that won out in the end, it was concern. And the knowledge that sharing pain helped to diminish it far more than the passage of time could.

Each word seemed to stick in her throat. Rachel had to coerce the question out. "Did your father beat you, Kirk?"

A dark, distancing look entered his eyes. "What makes you ask?"

He was being evasive, and he knew it. It didn't make any sense. The fact that his father had beat him, had abused him, shouldn't bother him anymore. After all, he'd shed that skin. All of that was in the past.

But it did. It bothered him a great deal.

Rachel shrugged. She didn't want to tell him about that time she had witnessed it without his knowledge. Instead, she shrugged. "I don't know...some of the things you say, the way you seem to relate to Ethan so well."

Kirk avoided her eyes. "Most fathers hit their kids once in a while."

She placed a hand on his shoulder, drawing his eyes to her. "Mine didn't," she told him softly. Unspoken sympathy filled her.

"You were lucky." He laced his hand over hers, but then, very gently, removed it. He didn't want pity, even from her. "Luckier than you realize. People can be cruel to one another inside and outside of the family. I saw a lot of it in the last nine years." And he'd relived it in his nightmares, nightmares that came all too frequently.

He hadn't really answered her question, but at least he was opening up about his work. It was definitely a step in the right direction.

"Tell me about it."

He sighed and dragged his hand through his hair. If he closed his eyes, he could still see it, the despair, the poverty. The fear.

"I saw men and women so eaten up by frustration, by their own inability to control their lives, that they took it out on anything that was smaller and more defenseless than they were. Children, each other..." He looked down into her face and fought the temptation to frame it with his hands. Fought the temptation to kiss her. "It's a very cruel world out there, Funny Face. You don't know how insulated you are here."

She pressed her lips together as she thought of Don. She hadn't had to go halfway around the world to find the human frailties Kirk cited. "Not so insulated."

How could he have been so insensitive? he thought, cursing himself. "Yeah, right, I forgot." The last thing in the world he wanted was to cause her pain. "I'm sorry, Funny Face."

She knew he hadn't meant to hurt her. "Don't be." She wanted to divert the conversation. Don was old territory. She wanted to explore uncharted frontiers—Kirk's uncharted frontiers. "If you felt the way you did about what you were doing, why did you keep doing it? Why didn't you just stop?"

She was asking a question he'd asked himself a hundred times. And he gave Rachel the same answer he'd given himself. "What else would I do?"

He paced around the room slowly, unconsciously reacting to the echoes of the past he still felt. "I can't explain it exactly, but the first time I touched a camera, I knew. I knew that this was what I wanted to do. It was as if I'd found a piece of myself that had been left out all this time." His mouth curved at the memory. "Everyone ridiculed Mr. Miller, but to me, he was like a magical gnome in that photography workshop, unlocking a world for me I'd never seen." He looked at Rachel, trying to make her understand. "I could trap time, highlight injustice, capture a laugh, all through the eyes of a camera."

He made it sound wonderful, but he had still shifted the focus. "All through your eyes," she pointed out.

His smile deepened. Did she have any idea how incredibly sweet she was? "Yeah, that's what made it special. I could observe and show, all without intruding."

Rachel heard more. She heard what he wasn't saying. "Or being part of it? Didn't you get lonely, standing on the outside?"

The amusement faded from his smile. She had hit it right on the head. That was the part that had been so appealing. Being on the outside. Untouched.

"I didn't stand very much. Most of the places that I've been to the last few years required a great deal of running." Kirk thought of his last harrowing escape. "Usually without any warning."

She knew that a collection of his best work had won an award several years ago. It had evoked words such as *poignant, poetic, powerful,* and *incredibly moving* from the critics. She also knew that Kirk had taken none of it to heart. He was the least self-absorbed person she had ever known.

"I saw a great deal of that work. They've used your photographs in magazines, newspapers, anthologies. You couldn't have put that much passion into it without feeling some of it yourself."

He knew what she was trying to do, and he appreciated it, but there was no point. "The passion was already there, Funny Face, I just captured it."

Rachel wasn't going to let him elude his due. "Even so—"

"Even so," he echoed, "you're doing a great deal of prodding this morning."

She looked at him with an expression of complete innocence. "Is that what I'm doing?" Rachel drifted from the living room into the hall. "I thought we were just having a conversation."

He arched a skeptical brow as he followed her. "A conversation starts out with 'Say, how about those Dodgers?' "

Rachel refused to be evaded. "Only if you have nothing else to talk about."

He shrugged. A curtain had gone down, as surely as if she had watched the material fall, separating him from her. "Maybe I don't."

She tried not to be hurt. He had his reasons, she told herself. "Meaning the subject is closed?"

It sounded too harsh when she said it that way. "How about tabled?"

Rachel accepted the terminology. "Speaking of tables, you need to buy a new one for the kitchen. The one you have really wobbles. I thought the leg next to me was going to give way while we were eating."

"If I stay."

Maybe he just needed to be coaxed, she thought. To be made to feel that someone cared whether he came or went.

"Why don't you? Stay for a while, Kirk." She turned so that her body was just a breath away from him. A small, tantalizing breath. "I think it would be good for everyone." She could feel her pulse accelerating again when she looked deep into his eyes. This had all the earmarks of an adolescent crush. Except she was light-years away from being an adolescent. "Certainly Ethan. And Cameron, because you bring out the boy in him." Her eyes held his. "And you, because I think you need to remember that it isn't all pain out there."

He felt his body reacting to her, felt the urge to hold her growing. "How about you? Would it be good for you if I stayed?" It was stupid to ask, but somehow he couldn't help himself.

There was no point in being either coy or evasive. "Me especially."

"Why?" The word glided along her face, making her breath stop in her lungs.

She smiled, and it seemed to seep into his bones. "Because I always liked having you around. Because you're good for everyone."

It was the last thing he would ever have expected to be said of him. His father's mocking words rang in his ears: "You're nothing. You were born a nothing, and you're going to die a nothing."

She saw the denial rising to Kirk's lips. "You are," she insisted. They were standing too close to each other. And to something he didn't seem ready to explore yet. Drawing herself away, she turned and placed her hand on the knob of the door to the closed room. It would be best if she remained busy. "I wouldn't mind having you live next door to me forever."

He stiffened when he saw what she was about to do. "Leave that alone."

He made her jump. "What?"

His voice was far rougher than he had meant it to be. Emotion had rung it out of him. "I want you to leave the door closed."

She raised her hand in surrender. "Okay, but why?"

"It's my father's den."

She didn't see the reason for his sudden shift. "And—?"

He blew out a breath. "I'd just rather not go in there." He looked at her, an apology in his eyes. "I'm sorry, Funny Face. I didn't mean to yell."

Was that what he called yelling? His voice hadn't gone up at all. It was the low warning tone that had had her backing away. "It's okay. After all, as Ethan pointed out, it's your house."

"It was never mine." Before she could ask him what he meant by that, he retraced his steps into the living room. "I think we've cleared off enough sheets for the day."

She knew better than to argue.

Chapter 10

Rachel was seriously thinking of having Kirk canonized. What was happening—what had been happening for the past three weeks—couldn't be described as anything short of a miracle.

Granted that it might be viewed by some as a *small* miracle. There was no flash or fire accompanying it, and it couldn't be termed earth-shaking. But it was a miracle, pure and simple nonetheless.

Rachel saw a piece of it taking shape every day. Ethan was beginning to slowly change. Or rather to slowly revert. Her son was becoming more like the boy he'd been before the whole horrible business of the divorce and his father's death had taken place.

And Kirk was the reason.

No matter how much he shrugged it off, Rachel thought as she sat in her den, grading the mountain of test papers on her desk, Kirk was the cause, the source.

It had been only four short weeks since Kirk had returned to Bedford and reentered her life. In that time, their former relationship had taken on yet another dimension. He was now her baby-sitter, though she would never have put it that way to him *or* to Ethan. Neither of them would appreciate it.

It had all begun with Mrs. Gillion.

Mrs. Gillion was the woman who watched Ethan three days a week after school let out. Those were the days when Rachel taught classes that ran too late for her to be able to pick up her son herself. Mrs. Gillion picked Ethan up and brought him to her house, where he stayed until Rachel could come for him. He had never been happy about the arrangement, balking at having a "sitter." But he was far too young for her to leave alone—especially since his behavior had taken such a drastic turn. Rachel wanted to be certain that she knew where he was at all times. Mrs. Gillion had seemed perfect for the position.

And then it had all fallen to pieces.

When she'd picked up Ethan at the woman's house, Mrs. Gillion had informed her that she had to have a gallbladder operation immediately. Rachel had come home feeling particularly defeated. She'd had absolutely no idea who she could get on such short notice to take care of Ethan. He wasn't exactly the sunniest child to cope with. She'd felt as if she were out of options and, for the time being, out of hope.

Kirk was outside on his porch, repairing a broken front step, when she had pulled up in her car. He noticed her mood immediately, even at that distance. Abandoning his chore, he crossed over to her property and was at her car door when she opened it.

"What's the matter, Funny Face? You look like you have the weight of the world on your shoulders."

"Not quite," she murmured, getting out.

Ethan scrambled out of the car. "Hi, Kirk!" he shouted before bolting for the house and the bathroom.

"Hi," Kirk called after him, then looked at Rachel. "Is it Ethan?"

She sighed. "In a way. Mrs. Gillion has to have an operation."

As far as he knew, Rachel wasn't related to anyone named Mrs. Gillion. Was she talking about a friend? And what did it have to do with Ethan? "That sounds like a title for a Movie of the Week."

He managed to make her smile with that. In the past few days, Kirk's mood had softened somewhat. In her heart, Rachel knew that they were getting to him, she and Cameron and Ethan. They were easing him back into civilization and away from the jungles of his mind.

"Close, but not quite." She leaned against the car, not quite ready to go inside. Maybe if she discussed the situation with Kirk, an idea would come to her. "Mrs. Gillion is the woman Ethan stays with until I can pick him up on my way home from the college."

Mrs. Gillion had the disposition of a kindly grandmother. A kindly, unflappable grandmother. The unflappable part was an invaluable attribute. It was absolutely necessary in order to get along with Ethan.

"And now she has to have an operation."

It wasn't hard to fill in the blanks. "And you don't know what to do with Ethan."

It made Ethan sound like a thing instead of a person. She was glad he was inside and couldn't overhear them. "In a nutshell, yes."

Kirk was silent for a moment, debating the wisdom of what he was about to suggest. He really wasn't accustomed to sharing his space, or his time. But this was Rachel, and she was clearly in need. This much he could do for her.

"I can watch him."

She looked at him, surprised by the offer. And by what she knew it meant. "On a regular basis?"

"Until Mrs. Gillion gets back on her feet." The hedge against any hint of permanency came automatically. Then he shrugged. "But sure, why not? He can stay with me until you get home."

She was afraid to let her relief bubble up just yet. This was almost too good to be true. "Won't he get in your way?"

He watched the way the breeze flirted with the edges of her hair, and felt an urge to do the same. He kept his hands at his side.

"There's nothing to get in the way of," Kirk reminded her. "It's not as if I were doing anything at the moment except puttering around, fixing a few things here and there."

"It's about time you had a little time to yourself," she pro-tested, but there wasn't a great deal of conviction in her voice. Hope, despite the safeguards she tried to impose, was taking root quickly. She'd gone from having no options to having one that opened up a host of greater possibilities. "You sure you won't mind?"

"I'm sure."

Overwhelmed, relieved, Rachel threw her arms around his neck and hugged him. "God, but you are a lifesaver, Kirk."

Her choice of words roused a memory, a very painful mem-ory. But the warmth of her quick embrace blotted out the stab of pain.

Very gently, he drew her back so that he could look at her. "I'm going to get used to this hugging, Funny Face," he said teasingly.

Rachel left her arms around his neck a moment longer. A sliver of pleasure was dancing through her that had nothing to do with his having come to her rescue. She wasn't quite ready to give it up just yet.

"Good." Slowly she let her arms drop to her sides, her eyes on his. Her pulse was beating just a little faster than was nor-mal. "A person can never be hugged enough." Impulsively she turned toward the front door. "C'mon, let's go tell Ethan. I think for once he's going to be happy with a decision I made."

Lacing her fingers through Kirk's, Rachel eagerly walked into the house. "Ethan," she called. "Ethan!"

She ran into her son at the entrance to the kitchen, directly off the living room.

The moody look on his face brightened when he saw that his mother had brought Kirk with her. His eyes slid warily toward his mother. "Yeah?"

He'd lose that wariness someday soon, she thought. An edgy impatience surrounded her silent promise.

"Ethan, Kirk's going to be watching you after school until Mrs. Gillion's back on her feet."

"Watch me?" Ethan's voice held a hard edge.

Kirk picked up his cue from Ethan's tone. "Not unless you do tricks." He saw the slight glint of humor in the boy's eyes, and knew he'd guessed correctly. "Otherwise, I expect you to be helping me."

"Helping?"

Kirk nodded. The cracked wood on the front step was only one thing that needed seeing to. "I'm doing a few repairs on the house—"

Rachel grasped at the implied meaning behind his statement. "Then you've made up your mind to stay?"

Funny Face, if you knew, the last thing you'd want me to do is stay.

"No." He watched as the light slowly receded from her eyes, and felt a pang because he had caused it. But he knew that there would be even greater remorse for both of them if he stayed. He wasn't the boy she remembered. "But you can't sell a fixer-upper for a good price, and I might as well get the most I can."

Rachel nodded, trying not to appear as disappointed as she felt. It was silly to feel that way. She'd known he wasn't one to be pinned down to one place for long. Still, there was a part of her that hoped . . .

She pushed all that aside. What would be, would be. Right now, Kirk was helping her out with Ethan, and that was the important thing.

Kirk laid a hand on the boy's thin shoulder. "I'll need help. You up to it?"

Rachel could have sworn Ethan puffed up a bit. He was struggling not to look pleased or excited, but both pleasure and excitement were evident in his body language.

"Can I use a hammer?"

Kirk lifted a shoulder and let it fall, indicating that he was open to the situation. "If you prove that you can handle it the way it's supposed to be handled, I don't see why not."

Ethan's eyes all but shone. "Cool."

Despite how well this was evolving, Rachel knew that she had to put in some ground rules at the beginning. "I'll want homework done during that time, just as you're doing now. Or better, actually." Homework, as light as it was in the third grade, was a bone of contention she and Ethan went round and round about almost every night.

"Yeah, yeah . . ." Ethan's tone was rude and dismissive. But when he raised his eyes to Kirk's, he sighed. "Yes, ma'am," he added.

Rachel had to consciously work at keeping her mouth from dropping open. She looked from her son to the man standing indolently at her side.

Another miracle to be attributed to Saint Kirk, she thought incredulously.

If she had had any doubts that the new situation would work, they were soon erased. Each day, at exactly 2:15, Kirk would walk to the elementary school, which was located at the end of the development. There he would wait on the outskirts of the playground area until Ethan emerged from the school.

Kirk had told Rachel that Ethan was almost always the first one on the grounds. Shooting through the doorway, Ethan would hurry over to Kirk like a homing pigeon, eager to pick up where they had left off the day before.

In time, Ethan had even allowed some of the eagerness to show. Rachel was beginning to pick up latent signs at home. Nothing she could directly point her finger at, just small, telling signs.

It was nothing short of a miracle, Rachel thought, with the flood of gratitude that always accompanied the realization.

Her eyes shifted wearily to the papers on her desk. She'd need another miracle, she mused, to get this stack read and graded tonight.

Tired, Rachel leaned back in her swivel chair and stretched her arms overhead, trying to work out the kinks in her back.

If she closed her eyes and inhaled deeply, she could swear that she could still smell the cherry pipe tobacco her father used to favor. This had been his den once. He had sat here, night after night, grading papers just as she was doing now. He'd taught math at the community college in Costa Mesa.

The apple didn't fall far from the tree, she thought with a smile.

Except in Kirk's case, of course. From the little bit she'd known of his parents, predominantly garnered through hearsay, Kirk was completely different from the people who had given him life.

He never really spoke of them, and that, she thought, could be part of the problem he was harboring now. In fact, she was almost sure of it. He was doing such wonders with Ethan, she wished she could return the favor and help him somehow. But Kirk had never been an easy man to do anything for.

All she could do, she thought with a sigh, was be patient and be there. And hope that someday he'd choose to really confide in her.

The sigh sent the top paper on the stack closest to her wafting from her desk to the floor. With a grunt, she leaned over and picked it up. She'd been at this since dinner. It had been rather a quiet meal. She and Ethan had eaten alone. Kirk had left right after she arrived home tonight, saying he had something to take care of.

He had a perfect right to be busy, but she couldn't help wondering what he was doing.

And couldn't help missing him, she thought. As had Ethan. Her son had easily grown accustomed to having Kirk in the house from the time he arrived home from school until almost bedtime.

Well, not tonight. Tonight they'd had to make do without Kirk's company. She'd done some long-overdue yardwork, and then, after dinner, she'd left Ethan alone in the family room, communing with his video games, while she surrounded herself with test papers in her den. Time had slipped away from her. When she had gone to tell Ethan it was his bedtime, she'd found him asleep on the floor, the control pad clutched in his lax fingers.

A twinge of guilt had pricked at her conscience as she picked him up and carried him upstairs to his room. They needed to spend more time together, she thought. Except that he didn't seem to want it. Even tonight, without Kirk, the conversation had eventually dwindled to nothing.

And there seemed to be so little time to spare these days.

Feeling oddly sad, she had returned to her den and tackled a second stack of test papers.

The papers seemed to have a life of their own, she thought accusingly. It was almost as if they were multiplying capriciously when she wasn't looking. From where she sat, there seemed to be no light at the end of the tunnel.

Just like her life, she thought, looking up at the ceiling as if she could see into Ethan's room which was directly overhead.

The words on the paper were beginning to swim before her eyes. Served her right for giving essay questions, she thought as she rubbed the bridge of her nose. Next time, it would be multiple-choice.

Rachel rose and rotated her shoulders. The kinks refused to leave. Feeling mentally drained, she looked out the window. The den was at the front of the house, and her window faced the end of the driveway. Moonlight was casting a silvery beam along the path. It seemed to flow out to the street, beckoning to her to follow it.

Maybe a little night air would invigorate her. It certainly couldn't hurt. If she kept at this another five minutes, she was going to lay her head on the desk and fall asleep.

It took Rachel only a moment to make up her mind. The debate wasn't even close.

The May night was warm when she stepped outside. The gentle breeze drifted by her like an enticing, seductive kiss. This wasn't a night to spend alone, she thought sadly.

But those were thoughts that belonged to the young woman she'd been, not to the single mother with a demanding career she had become.

This *was* silly. She was indulging a side of herself she seldom even acknowledged. There was nothing to be gained by feeling sorry for herself, or by wishing for things that couldn't be.

Straightening, she decided to go back inside, but just then she saw someone approaching in the distance. As she watched, she realized that it was Kirk.

She waited until he was closer before she spoke. "Restless?"

Kirk looked her way, surprised to find her outside. It was after eleven. He'd been too restless, as she had noted, to remain at home. He'd tried to walk off his agitation, and had succeeded only marginally.

He shrugged away her question, not wanting to get into it. She would ask too many probing questions if he let her. "I like to walk around at night. It's so..." His voice drifted away.

"Peaceful?" she supplied.

The word *peace* and he had only a nodding acquaintance. It was difficult to summon it when he wanted to describe his feelings. A corner of his mouth rose.

"Yes."

He was by nature a loner, she reminded herself. And they had been taking up a good deal of his time, she and Ethan.

"Then I'm intruding." She meant to withdraw politely, but she couldn't quite manage to get herself to do it.

Kirk laughed as he came up the steps to join her. "Like you don't normally."

Since he was smiling, she took it that he thought of her intrusion as a good thing. Did he think of her she wondered, as something other than a friend? She felt a little foolish hoping, but she couldn't help herself.

"Do I? Intrude?"

It wasn't an intrusion, exactly. More like an invasion. And usually, despite himself, he welcomed it. She had a way of scattering his dark thoughts until they were like so many rain clouds breaking up in the face of the sun.

Kirk leaned a hip against the post, studying her face. "You've been intruding in my life, Funny Face, ever since you moved in next door."

She wrapped her arms around herself as she thought back. "I remember that day. I was so mad at my father for moving us here, for taking me away from all my friends." It all returned to her on a wave of nostalgia. The anger she had felt, the fear of the unknown that had haunted her. "I was sure I was going to shrivel up and die here after leaving San Francisco."

Her face was a showcase of emotions. They ebbed and flowed across her face like a never-ending tide. He could have watched her all night. "Pretty deep thoughts for a seven-year-old."

She sniffed as she raised her chin. Only her eyes sparkled with humor. "I was six, and very mature for my age."

He laughed, remembering an entirely different Rachel. "Yeah, that was why you always threatened to hold your breath until you got your way."

She spread her hands wide as she lifted her shoulders. "Hey, it worked, didn't it? You and Cameron always let me tag along."

Cameron had once referred to them as a modern-day version of the three musketeers—with a handicap named Rachel.

"We felt sorry for you."

She ignored his teasing tone, or pretended to. In reality, it warmed her immensely, just as it always had. "Whatever. But you couldn't have felt sorrier for me than I felt for myself that day we moved here." Her eyes shifted to her face. "And then I looked up as I got out of my father's car and saw you staring down from the second-story window."

"I remember." He could picture it in his mind as clearly as if it had happened only a few hours ago, instead of over twenty years in the past.

"You looked solemn."

His father had just ended a drunken all-night binge by passing out on the floor. He had tried to hit him again for daring to talk back, but Kirk had been too fast for him and had gotten out of the way. His father had fallen over, thrown off balance by the force of his swing, and passed out where he lay.

When Kirk had heard the moving van pull up, he had just been thinking of running away from home and taking his mother with him. He had still been young and naive enough at eight to think that she loved him enough to come with him when he fled. At that age, he hadn't realized the full extent of her emotional entanglement with his father's dark moods and demands. Nor had he known the full extent of her apathy toward him.

He hid all this from Rachel now, just as he had always hidden that corner of his life from her. "That's because I was looking down at you as you got out and thinking to myself, here comes trouble."

She didn't believe him. That would have been too light-hearted a response for the boy she'd known. "Know what I thought when I looked up at you?"

"No, what?" He expected to hear something trivial or possibly sexist. At six, Rachel had thought herself superior to every boy she encountered, including her brother.

Her expression grew serious. "That you were the saddest boy in the whole world, and that I was going to find a way to make you happy."

It had been an odd premonition that had floated through her. Or perhaps it had been fostered by her undying belief that everyone should be happy. Whatever the source, she had felt motivated when she saw him, and her thoughts about never speaking to her father for having done this horrible thing to her had vanished instantly.

Kirk arched a very skeptical brow. "At six?"

She nodded, unfazed by the disbelief that was evident in his eyes. "I told you, I was a very mature six." She felt Kirk's eyes on her and tried not to shift in nervous anticipation. "What are you looking at?"

He grinned. She looked slightly messy, reminding him of the way she'd been when they all played together. And rather breathtaking for it. "You have a twig in your hair."

Automatically she reached up to brush it away, even though she hadn't the slightest idea where it was. She missed completely, and the bit of twig stubbornly clung to the strands of her hair.

"I did some yardwork before dinner. When I was a kid, I thought *evergreen* meant that they never lost their leaves, not that they lost them all the time. They should be called everfalling, not evergreen."

She shook her head slightly. The twig remained lodged. "We missed you at dinner tonight."

"I had something to take care of."

Which was a lie. There hadn't been anything to take his attention away. When he had seen her come home today, he'd realized that he welcomed the sight of her a little too much, looked forward to her arriving home too much. It was a dangerous habit, a dangerous frame of mind to allow himself to fall

into. One way or another, their lives were becoming as en-
twined as ivy growing up a trellis. He was becoming too de-
pendent on seeing her, which was bad. For her.

When she took another swipe at the twig and missed again,
he took pity on her.

"Here, let me," he offered.

The twig was stuck in her hair just above her ear. Kirk gently brushed it away. How, then, his fingers came to be tangled
in her hair, he didn't know.

It was as if his hands had a life apart from him. As did his
eyes, which were fastened to the tempting curve of her mouth.

He couldn't seem to take his hands away, so he left them
there, framing her face. The words came on their own. "You
know, most of the time I see life through the eyepiece of a video
camera. Everything is gray. When I'm with you—" his voice
lowered until it was almost a whisper, almost a prayer "—it's
like looking through the eyepiece of my camera. All the colors
come into focus."

Rachel was certain her heart was lodged in her throat.
Speaking was difficult. Not speaking was impossible. "That's
very poetic," she breathed. "Have you ever thought of dou-
bling as a writer?"

He felt his mouth curving in a grin. She could still get in a dig
when she wanted to. "You've seen what I can do with letters."

The rest of the world was swiftly fading away into the darkness around her. All she could see was Kirk. "Maybe poems
will come easier for you."

He shouldn't be feeling these things, he told himself. He
shouldn't be wanting her this way. It wasn't fair to her.
"Nothing comes easy for me, Funny Face."

Her mouth was dry, and she had to force her next words out.
"Should make the getting of it all the sweeter for you, then."
As she spoke, Rachel raised herself ever so slightly on her toes.
She realized that she was holding on to his arms for balance.

"There's nothing sweet about life, Funny Face." God, but
he wanted her, wanted to lose his soul in her sweetness, to lose
himself in her. "Except for you."

Her breath was in very short supply by now. "More po-
etry."

Slowly he shook his head, his eyes remaining on hers. "More truth."

She couldn't take it anymore. If he didn't do something soon, she was going to explode. "Are you going to kiss me, or am I going to have to throw myself at you?"

He couldn't help the grin that rose to his lips. Honest, even now. She was incredible. "Can't have that, can we?"

If her heart pounded any harder, it was going to fall out of her chest. "Nope."

Hesitation overtook him. Whatever his needs, they shouldn't be allowed to hurt her. "But—"

Her patience vanished like a drop of water in the desert. "Damn you, Kirk Callaghan. For a man who doesn't talk much, you can't seem to shut up."

Rachel brought her mouth up to his, but at the last moment, it was he who lowered his mouth to hers.

The explosion, she later judged, could probably have been felt for miles.

By making the initial contact, Kirk had meant to control the action. To provide the brakes that would be necessary to end it. It was as simple as that.

There was nothing simple about it.

Something crackled through him as he tasted her mouth. Electricity, gunfire, something. It had no name, other than *Rachel.*

It was like tumbling off the edge of a cliff. Exhilaration and fear warred within him, and he could do nothing but pray that there was something out there that would break his fall.

Nothing could have prepared him for this, not the women who had come before, not the anticipation that had preceded this.

Nothing.

His mouth worked feverishly over hers. Each pass fed on the last and increased the passion that went through him a thousandfold.

Her lips parted, tempting him, admitting him.

Dreams tangled with tongues as her blood heated to the point where she didn't know why she didn't just boil away, evaporating into the clouds overhead.

She delved her hands into his thick hair, losing herself in the infinitely wonderful sensation of his mouth hot on hers. It was like riding the largest roller coaster ever created. Each plunge had her hurtling to the next crest, hanging on with both hands to keep from falling out.

She felt his body seal against hers, felt the hardness of his desire. She could taste it on his lips, feel its mate singing in her veins.

It was everything she had ever expected, everything she had ever dreamed of, but multiplied by an exponential factor too large to conceive.

By now her heart was hammering so hard against her chest that she was convinced it had slammed out of her body and gone into his. Which was as it should be, she thought. Her heart had always belonged to Kirk, one way or another.

This was temporary. She knew that. Knew he wouldn't stay with her. When the time came, he would leave again. But that knowledge made no difference to her now. Whatever he had to offer, she would take and treasure. Whatever would happen tomorrow, she'd have this moment.

Chapter 11

Kirk drew away, even though everything in his being urged him to continue. To hold her soft body against him and drink in the wild, intoxicating wine of her lips. With considerable effort, he forced himself to take his hands away from her. Regret, for what he had done and for what he could not do, filled him.

Rachel saw it in his eyes.

"I shouldn't have done that," he told her.

Until it had happened, Rachel hadn't fully realized just how long she had been waiting for Kirk to kiss her. And how much she had wanted it.

"On the contrary, you should have done that a long time ago. And as I recall—and you did burn out a few of my brains cells just then, so I might be wrong—we did it together."

Very softly, he stroked the back of his hand along her cheek. Whatever excuse she gave, it took two, and he shouldn't have been one of them. "I'm no good for you, Funny Face."

Sometimes he made her so mad she could scream. But reason, not emotion, was called for here.

"If I was mature enough at six to know you needed someone, I think I'm mature enough now to judge what's good for me and what isn't." She saw the doubt in his expression and did what she could to alleviate it. "Kirk, you just kissed me. You didn't plight your troth. There are no consequences for this."

But they both knew that there were. Singularly or together, they'd opened a door that had never been opened before.

Kirk avoided her eyes as he edged away. "I'd better go."

"I know that you will," she told him quietly. Her tone made him turn around to look at her. "Eventually. I'd never try to stop you."

That made it all the harder, because she was so good. He didn't want to hurt her. "Rachel, there are things you don't know about me."

She laid a hand on his arm, mutely communicating things she couldn't quite put into words yet. He could never tell her anything about himself that would make her back away from him. Anything that would make her feel any differently about him.

"I know all that I need to know about you, Kirk. I always have." As she said it, she knew that she had never stopped being in love with Kirk, not really. It had just been dormant all this time. "The rest, you can tell me. Or not," she added simply. "The choice is yours. I won't pass judgment on you. I never have." She smiled her encouragement. "I'll just be here when you need me. The way I always was."

He knew she was telling the truth. She *had* always been there for him, even when she hadn't realized it. It felt so one-sided. He couldn't take, not when he had nothing to give. He was so empty inside. "And what about you? What about your needs?"

She wanted to hold him, to hug him and make whatever doubts he had go away. She remained where she was, afraid of pushing him even farther away.

"Silly." Affection flooded her voice. "Don't you know that you've always helped me, no matter what was wrong, just by being there? By listening when I talked. By making me feel special? You gave me a great deal."

"Gave." The word hovered in the air like a eulogy. "In the past." Didn't she understand what he was attempting to tell her? "I have nothing to give now, Funny Face."

How could he underestimate himself so much? "Don't be so sure of that." Resigned for the moment, Rachel stepped back. "Good night, Kirk. I'll see you tomorrow morning."

"I—"

She looked up sharply at the hesitant note in his voice. He was going to change his mind, she thought suddenly. Fresh fear surged through her. He couldn't back away, not from her son. Ethan would never get over having Kirk break his word to him.

Rachel struggled to hide the emotion she felt. "Ethan said something about you taking him out for a shoot early tomorrow. It was the only conversation we had, actually. He talked about you. Just you."

Her eyes held his, pleading with him not to turn her down. Not to turn Ethan down because of her.

"I have to tell you, he was more animated with me tonight than he'd been in a long time." Her hand slid from the doorknob, and she stepped forward again until her eyes were almost level with him. "He's trying very hard not to appear excited, but he is. You're slowly giving me back my son, Kirk." Her expression grew serious. "Don't tell me you have nothing to give, Callaghan. I won't have you beating up my best friend that way."

She stopped, realizing that her voice was growing in intensity. Rachel leaned over the step and brushed her lips lightly over his. It wasn't easy restraining herself when she desperately wanted to lean into him and let things progress naturally from there.

She stepped back. "And you are, you know, and always will be—my best friend."

He couldn't remember ever aching for a woman the way he was for her. Kirk couldn't remember ever aching for a woman at all. Sex had always been casual—no strings, no desires beyond the physical. He couldn't remember the face of a single woman he had slept with.

Though he had done nothing more than kiss her, it was different between Rachel and him. There was another dimension shimmering between them. There was tenderness, and a need to protect her at all costs. "Best friends don't hurt each other."

"No," she agreed softly as she moved away, "they don't."
She stood framed in the doorway of her house, a hazy, warm
light shining at her back. "And you never will."

Rachel closed the door behind her.

He wanted to follow her inside. To take up where they had
left off a few minutes ago. For a moment, he was certain that
if he didn't give in to the overwhelming desire that was racking
his body and pounding in his brain, he'd die.

But he had been to hell and back more times that he could
count, and he knew that deprivation wouldn't destroy him. It
never had before. Only then it had been the deprivation of love.
The deprivation of even the slightest bit of human kindness
from either parent.

In a way, it had helped him, he thought. It had hardened him
for the sights he was to endure in his travels.

As Kirk turned and began walking toward his own house, he
didn't know just how much longer he could go on like this,
harnessing what begged to be set free.

He didn't know how much longer he could go on wanting her
and not give in, especially since she was so willing to let him.

With a sigh, he shoved his key into the lock of his door and
turned it. Nothing but dark and cold greeted him. It was no
different from all those years when he had been growing up.

Kirk thought of leaving again. Permanently.

But he knew he wasn't ready yet. There was unfinished
business here for him. There were ghosts to finally confront and
lay to rest. The peace he'd sought, he'd found, in part, in Rachel. But what she gave, she also took away, because his desire
for her broke up his peace like ice melting beneath a hot sun.

But there was a different, greater peace to be won. One he
had to attain if he was to go on. One he wasn't certain he *could*
attain. But he had to try. No, he couldn't leave, not yet.

Kirk closed the door behind him and flipped on a light. The
sheets, thanks to Rachel, had been removed. The barriers had
not. That needed more time. He needed more time.

He had been on the phone to the publisher who handled most
of his work, and had extended his leave for a little while longer.

He had time.

But was time alone enough?

He stared off in the direction of Rachel's house, seeing past the walls between them as if they didn't exist. He really had no answer to his own question.

He could only hope. She had done that for him, allowed a tiny kernel of hope to nestle in his soul. He owed her so much.

Which was why he could never allow himself to make love with her. He couldn't begin to repay what he owed her. He was empty inside, and she deserved a man who could love her. A man who could be good to her and her son. And Kirk knew he wasn't that man.

Ethan had been ready since five o'clock. He had gotten up, made his own breakfast and planted himself on the sofa near the front door, all before Rachel ever got out of bed.

She had come downstairs and found him like that, sitting on the sofa, poised and ready. "Big day?" she asked affectionately as she fought to drive sleep away from her system.

Ethan shrugged, though the gesture was growing less pronounced each time he employed it. "You said it wasn't polite to keep people waiting."

"That I did." Rachel struggled with the urge to press a kiss to his serious brow. Not yet, she told herself. Soon, soon, he'd let her back in. Rushing him wouldn't make it happen any faster.

She heard the doorbell ring. "That would be your mentor."

Ethan had popped to his feet like bread being ejected by a faulty toaster. "My what?"

"Mentor," she repeated, moving to the door just ahead of him. "That means teacher. He is going to be teaching you how to take photographs, isn't he?"

"Yeah. He said I had a good eye." Ethan turned to Kirk as Rachel admitted him in. "Didn't you say that? That I had a good eye?" he prompted impatiently when Kirk said nothing in response.

Kirk's greeting had evaporated on his tongue when he glanced in Rachel's direction. She was wearing a worn baseball jersey, and what seemed like nothing else. His mouth felt dry as dust.

"Yeah," he finally said, his eyes still on Rachel, "and so does the man across the street, as I recall." The mailbox before the door still read The Hendersons.

Rachel looked at him, amused. Their kiss had kept her awake half the night. It was nice to know that it wasn't all one-sided. Kirk was jealous. "Are you politely telling me to get out of the doorway?"

"Unless you want to torture the man." He nodded toward the Hendersons' house.

Rachel didn't attempt to hide her grin. "I do believe you've just given me a compliment." Prudently she stepped to the side.

"I'll give you whatever you want," he muttered. "Just go put something on. For everyone's sake," he added, and saw a wide smile taking over her lips. He looked down at Ethan. "Ready?"

Ethan nodded, his blond hair bobbing to and fro. He darted through the open door.

"How long are you going to be gone?" Rachel called after them.

"As long as it takes," Kirk answered. "Don't expect us back before evening." He looked down at Ethan. "Okay with you?"

Ethan was surprised at being consulted. "Super with me." He had to work at forming a frown. "I mean, yes. It's okay."

"See you," Kirk said over his shoulder. And he certainly was, he thought. Far more than he had reckoned on.

Ethan was already at the minivan, eagerly shifting from foot to foot.

Kirk had nothing definite planned as he got in behind the wheel. He intended to drive around the town, which was slumbering beneath the early-morning sun, until something struck him as worthy of being captured on film. For the past few days, he'd been toying with the idea of compiling a book of photographs of Bedford as a present for Rachel. He knew how much she loved the place.

Having Ethan help him, and perhaps even take some of the photographs, would undoubtedly add to her enjoyment of the gift.

Ethan remained quiet as they drove along the empty thoroughfare. He stared straight ahead, trying to guess where it was they were going. Finally, he couldn't hold his questions bottled up any longer.

He turned toward Kirk as they approached a long, empty stretch of road. "How do you know?"

"Know what?" Kirk replied, turning left onto University Drive. He could remember when there had been deer here instead of a network of houses crawling up the hill. The town *had* grown up while he'd been gone.

Ethan waved his hand about airily to indicate the immediate world outside the van. "How do you know when to take a picture?"

Kirk decided to drive down a little farther, toward a fenced-in field he remembered seeing. Untended, sun-bleached grass waved on the crest like the delicate fringe on a newborn's head.

"It comes to you." Kirk smiled as he thought about it. "Not all at once. At first, you just snap anything that moves. After a while, you start to be a little more discriminating." He glanced at Ethan's face to see if he understood. The boy's brow was puckered, as if he were trying hard to make sense out of what was being said. "You start to be picky," Kirk clarified. He laughed softly, remembering. "Also, having only a certain amount of money to pay for film kind of helps make you pick and choose."

Restrained by his seat belt, Ethan twisted around in his seat as best he could to look at Kirk. "Is that how you started?"

A pleased feeling filtered through Kirk. The open field, separated from the road by a forbidding length of barbed wire, was still here. Perfect.

"Mostly. I made myself indispensable to this news photographer I was working for. I made sure that I was always one step ahead of him whenever he wanted anything." It had been a hell of an apprenticeship. The man had been a hard taskmaster. But it had been worth it. "He taught me a lot."

Ethan stared at Kirk with awestruck eyes. "How come you did this instead of something else? Like being a big-league ball player?"

He'd never had that choice to make, and it amused him that Ethan had thought that much of his abilities.

"Well, for one thing, I wasn't all that good at baseball." He saw the doubt rise in Ethan's eyes. "Not good enough to hope for a career, anyway."

Kirk slowly eased his vehicle over to the shoulder. The road snaked off toward the campus before him, but for now he was interested in the lone cow that stood on the hillside, like the last bastion of the rural world that had once existed here. She was munching peacefully, while behind her, just barely visible, was the outline of a tall office building peering out of an industrial complex located in Newport Beach. A shadow of the world bearing down on them, Kirk thought.

"There's something almost mystical about being able to take a photograph. You freeze a piece of time and put it in your pocket, Ethan. It makes you feel powerful, as if you had a hand in creating something." He looked down at the attentive face. "Or saving it for all time."

Kirk leaned over and pulled open his glove compartment. The door all but yawned into Ethan's lap. What Kirk wanted was right on top.

"Here, this is what I mean." He took out a small hard-bound book. It was a collection of stills taken of settlers in the late 1800s. Kirk flipped it open at random. The book was fairly worn. He'd found it in a secondhand store over ten years ago.

"Look at this." He pointed to a photograph of a group of miners standing before a tent in a mining town long since forgotten. "What do you see?"

Ethan stared for a long moment, wondering what it was that he was expected to answer. It was a photograph of a group of men, all with mustaches and beards. It was kind of fuzzy, too.

He raised his eyes to Kirk's. "A bunch of old people, looking pretty stiff."

Some of those men, Kirk guessed, were probably younger than he was. But the facial hair—not to mention the hard life—tended to make them all look older. "What do they all have in common?"

Ethan frowned as he studied the photograph again. "They all have hats?"

He couldn't help the amusement that rose into his eyes as he looked at Ethan. Kirk closed the book and replaced it in the glove compartment, snapping the door shut. "Yes, and they're all dead."

"Oh." He'd figured that part, Ethan thought.

Kirk slanted a look at Ethan, biting his tongue. "But they're all alive, too."

Ethan's eyes grew wide. He stared at the closed glove compartment as if it were going to pop open at any second. "They're zombies?"

Kirk had to bite down on his lower lip to keep from laughing out loud. He knew such a reaction would only hurt Ethan's feelings. Averting his face, Kirk got out of the car. Like an echoing reaction, Ethan quickly followed, jumping down from the van. Kirk waited until he had rounded the hood and joined him.

"No," he began patiently, hoping he could make this simple enough for Ethan to understand. He wasn't accustomed to talking to children. "They've been captured on film forever. So even when they become really old, even when they die, you can see them the way they had been when they were young and vital. That makes them alive. Forever."

Kirk gave Ethan some time to think about the idea as he opened the side of his van. He'd brought various lenses with him, and two cameras. The one he favored, and a very simple model he retained for sentimental reasons. It had been his very first camera. He had bought it in a thrift shop in Santa Ana, with money he'd earned doing odd jobs in the neighborhood. It was the perfect camera for Ethan to work with.

Taking them both out, he closed the sliding door. "Did you know that there were certain Indian tribes who used to believe that if you took their photograph, you stole their spirit, their soul?"

Ethan wondered if Kirk was just teasing him, then decided that Kirk didn't do things like that. "Really?"

"Really." Kirk looked through the viewfinder as he aimed the camera at the cow. The animal obligingly remained in one spot. He lowered the camera to adjust the aperture. "Maybe they had the right idea. You don't steal anyone's soul, but you do get a bit of their spirit, a bit of their immortality."

Ethan dramatically blew out a breath. "Wow."

"My sentiment exactly."

Kirk took a few shots, adjusting the range on his telephoto lens after each shot. The building behind the cow loomed larger and larger. Finished, he glanced at Ethan and then handed him the other camera.

He slid the strap over his neck. "Here, let's get to work."

Ethan stared down at the camera as if it were a huge magical medallion. "You're giving this to me?"

"I'm *lending* it to you," Kirk told him. "Like with the hammer, you have to prove to me that you can handle it."

"Sure!"

Ethan looked around quickly. There was nothing before them except the field. On the other side of the road was a small shopping center with all the essentials, including a supermarket, gas station and restaurant.

The boy's expression was uncertain. "Here?"

"Why not? Your mother passes here every day on her way to the college. I thought she might like to see a few photographs of it in the album." For variety, he aimed the telephoto lens at the supermarket. A woman with a small child attached to each hand as if they had been born that way was hurrying into the store.

"You making an album for her?"

It was a very innocently voiced question. Kirk took a moment before answering. "Yes."

Ethan fingered the camera in his hands reverently, not quite ready to use it just yet. "You like her, huh?"

Kirk thought of several qualifying words to use in place of Ethan's simple one, but decided that simple was best. And most accurate.

"Yes." He took one last photograph of the cow alone. "Don't you?"

"Sure," Ethan mumbled into his chin. "A guy's gotta like his mother."

Kirk slowly lowered his camera and studied the boy's face. He removed the lens without looking at it. He could switch lenses in his sleep. Setting it aside, he put on the macro lens and aimed it at Ethan.

"There's no 'gotta' about it. But from what I saw, I'd say that your mother treats you pretty well."

Ethan's head jerked up at the sound of the click. He seemed surprised at being the subject of a photograph, and he quickly lowered his eyes.

"Yeah, she does. I guess."

Kirk set his camera in the cab of the minivan and looked down at the troubled boy beside him. "So, why do you always seem to be so angry with her when she's around?"

Ethan sighed. A lone car drove by, and he pretended to be interested in that. "I'm not angry with her," he mumbled. "I'm angry with me."

That sounded almost too familiar to Kirk. "You want to talk about it?"

Ethan toed the dirt with his sneaker. His hands were still wrapped around the camera. "Maybe."

Only the soft moan of the wind through the dried grasses was heard. It created a sense of isolation, even with civilization a stone's throw away. It made him feel lonely and yet secure. The security of familiarity.

Kirk knew what pushing would do. "I'm here, if you do."

He turned and selected another lens from his case.

Ethan stared at Kirk's back, hesitating. "You're not gonna make me tell you?"

"You'll talk when you need to." New lens in place, Kirk shut the door and turned to look at Ethan. "Do you need to?"

"Maybe." It hurt his chest, keeping all this in. Maybe if he let it out, it would stop hurting so much. Ethan said the words to the camera, not to Kirk. He couldn't look at anyone when he spoke. "I'm not mad at Mom, I'm mad at me," he repeated.

"Why?" Kirk asked softly.

"'Cause it's my fault."

Kirk heard the tears in the boy's voice. He proceeded carefully, like a man crossing a chasm on a bridge made of eggshells. "What's your fault?"

Swallowing didn't make the lump in his throat go away. "That they divorced." His lower lip trembled as he looked at the yellow dividing line down the long road. "That Dad got killed."

Kirk set his camera aside and fixed his entire attention on the boy. "How do you figure that?"

The camera now swung free, hanging about his neck from the black strap Kirk had fastened to it years ago. Ethan was twisting the edge of his T-shirt.

"Well, if they didn't divorce, then he wouldn't be driving to his house after seeing me. And if he wasn't driving to his house, he wouldn't have gotten killed." Ethan's voice hitched badly in his throat. "So it's all my fault."

How had he ever gotten tangled up in that idea? Kirk wondered. He knew it hadn't come from Rachel or Cameron. "And how was the divorce your fault?"

Tears shone in Ethan's eyes as he raised them to Kirk's face. "She left him after she saw him beating me."

His own past rose up before him in vivid colors. "Did he do that a lot?"

Ethan looked away.

Kirk gently placed his hands on the small shoulders. "Did he, Ethan?"

Ethan bit his lower lip. Only babies cried. "Just sometimes when he got to thinking how much he wanted to be somebody and he wasn't." Ethan was echoing his father's words as best he could. "He got hurt before he could do that."

For a second, Kirk was at a loss as to how to begin untangling Ethan's statement. Anger welled up inside him, anger against Don, and against his own father, for creating these pockets of guilt and pain because of their own shortcomings.

"He didn't have to hurt you, Ethan. Lots of people don't get to do what they want to, and somehow they manage to work things through. They don't take it out on others. It wasn't your fault that you father hurt his leg." His voice became sterner as he tried to break through the resistance he saw clouding the boy's face. "And it wasn't your fault that he beat you. That was *his* fault, not yours. Your mother was right to leave him."

Ethan shook his head fiercely from side to side. "But—"

His hands still on the slender shoulders, Kirk crouched down beside Ethan. "Ethan, none of this was ever your fault. Your dad was frustrated. He was angry. There are ways to cope with that," Kirk insisted. "None of them involved beating up a little boy, or his mother. Real men—real *people*," he amended, "don't do that. They find a way around obstacles. They don't take out their anger on everyone around them. That's not right."

"I know that. But—"

"But what?"

Ethan drew away and turned from Kirk, as if ashamed to let him see his tears.

Kirk could tell by the set of his shoulders that the boy was crying. For a moment, he allowed him to have his privacy and his dignity.

Finally, in a broken voice, Ethan said, "On the day he was killed..."

"Yes?" Kirk prodded.

Ethan drew in a ragged breath and rubbed the heel of his hand hard against his eyes. "When he left, I wished he was dead. He hit me again. Mom didn't see," he added quickly. "I hated him so much, I just wanted him dead. And then... he died."

He swung around, the horror of what he believed to be his fault evident in his eyes. "I did it. It was me. I killed my father."

Damn, the guilt that must have been tearing him up all this time, Kirk thought, numbed.

Kirk drew Ethan into his arms and held him tight, attempting to form a barrier and shut out all the boy's pain.

"It wasn't you, Ethan," he said fiercely. "God's very busy." Kirk sat back on his heels. He took out his handkerchief and offered it to Ethan. "Blow," he instructed. Ethan did. "God doesn't do away with people on a little boy's say-so."

Ethan wiped his nose, his eyes never leaving Kirk's. "But he died."

Kirk took back his handkerchief, tucking it into his pocket. He remained crouched at Ethan's level. "Your father died because someone lost control of their car and ran into him."

Ethan remained unconvinced as he shook his head again. "But I wished it."

Kirk took another approach. "Have you ever wished for anything else?"

The boy shrugged. "Sure."

Kirk arched a brow. "Did you always get it?"

Ethan thought for a moment, then shook his head. "No."

Kirk rose. "What makes you think it was different this time?" His mouth curved slightly as he looked at the boy. "You're special, Ethan, but you're not magical. You had nothing to do with your father's death, just like you didn't make your parents get a divorce. Your *father* was responsible for that."

Kirk spoke slowly, hoping the boy would finally understand and find some peace. "If he hadn't hit your mother and you, she would have never left him. You mother's a very loyal lady. She sticks by people she loves." He brushed a hand over the boy's hair. "Like you." His expression grew more serious. "Your father was just reaping what he sowed."

Ethan squinted as he looked up. The sun seemed to be directly behind Kirk now. "What does that mean?"

Kirk searched for a metaphor Ethan could relate to. "It means he swung too hard at the pitches and struck out."

Ethan studied his sneakers again. "Then I didn't kill him?"

"No." He hugged the boy to him one more time. "You didn't kill him." Kirk released Ethan, then straightened the camera around his neck. "Okay—are you ready to get down to some real work now?"

Ethan gave a sharp nod of his head. "Anything you say, Kirk."

Kirk laughed, and prayed that the headway they'd made would take. Ethan's all-consuming guilt had been Don's final revenge against his son. "That's what I like to hear from an assistant."

"Am I really?" Ethan's voice was filled with all the enthusiasm an eight-year-old was capable of. "Am I really your assistant?"

Kirk pretended to look at him as if that were an unnecessary question. "You're here, and you're assisting. That makes you my assistant." He looked across the road. The shopping center had an outdoor restaurant. There was one lone man having breakfast there, sharing it with a sparrow. The scene looked rather poetic. "Think you're up to carrying that case of lenses?" He jerked a thumb behind him at the front seat of the minivan.

"Sure."

Kirk eyed him. "You'll have to be careful."

Ethan couldn't have been more solemn if he was taking a pledge. "I'll be real careful."

Kirk couldn't resist tousling the boy's hair. "I know you will."

He took out his camera again and handed the case, with only one lens in it this time, to Ethan. They'd take a few shots here, he decided, then head for the campus. Saturday should be a good time to roam around without running across students.

As an afterthought, Kirk took Ethan's hand, and they hurried across the road, though there were no cars on the road yet. "I could have used someone like you on my last assignment."

"Tell me about it," Ethan begged him as they reached the other side.

Kirk hesitated. Almost all the things he had experienced were things that a young boy couldn't hear. But then, Kirk decided, Ethan was probably a great deal older than his years. Guilt aged a person, no matter how young. He knew that firsthand.

The service station attendant was watching them curiously. Kirk nodded toward the man before turning his attention to Ethan. "All right, but don't blame me if you get bored."

"I'd never get bored listening to you, Kirk." He said it so sincerely, Kirk was moved. "Do you think I could come with you next time?"

The restaurant he was looking for was just off to the side. Kirk remained where he was and raised his camera. The older man sitting nursing his coffee as he read his newspaper was completely oblivious of them. What a contrast this was to the scenes he had captured in his viewfinder two months ago, Kirk thought.

"Sure, if it's after school."

Ethan rocked back and forth on the balls of his feet as he watched Kirk work. "No, I mean next time you leave Bedford."

Kirk took his photograph, then looked at Ethan. "We'll talk about it."

"Great. Now tell me about the last assignment, like you said."

There was a sparrow patiently waiting by the man's table, unaware that there was no food on the man's dish to throw. Kirk snapped another photograph. "You drive a hard bargain."

As he worked, Kirk talked, censoring himself as he went along, making it a story that was suitable for a boy Ethan's age.

The day went by very fast, and before Kirk realized it, he and Ethan had gone to more than half a dozen different locations and Ethan had urged approximately a dozen different recollections from him. They had stopped and eaten at a local fast-food place and topped the day off with a box of a dozen doughnuts. It sat between them in the van, steadily becoming depleted, as they headed home.

Kirk was satisfied that they had made a good dent in the project. He glanced at Ethan. More than that, they had brushed away a good deal of debris that Ethan had been harboring.

"This is the best day ever," Ethan enthused, his mouth rimmed with raspberry jelly.

Kirk smiled, satisfaction, the kind he had never known, permeated him. It felt good, very good. "It was good for me, too."

His response pleased Ethan most of all. His eyes grew large. "Really?"

"Really."

Ethan decided to risk one more confidence. "My dad never took me anywhere."

Kirk turned the minivan down the main thoroughfare. "Neither did mine."

The answer surprised Ethan. He digested the implication slowly. "Guess that gives us something in common, besides Mom."

Kirk was amused by the way Ethan lumped the two together. "I guess it does at that."

Ethan settled back and contentedly polished off his fourth doughnut.

Chapter 12

Rachel had spent the whole day waiting for Ethan and Kirk to return. She had been working around the house, catching up on chores, attempting to keep her hands, if not her mind, occupied. Tension danced through her relentlessly, like electricity traveling along a power line.

It was ridiculous to feel this way. Afraid that they would return too soon, afraid that they would return too late. But no matter how hard she tried to keep an open, positive mind about the day, unease continued to nibble small holes in her resolve.

This day had been so important to Ethan. What if it somehow turned sour for him? She knew that she'd never be able to reach him if that happened.

She didn't want to think about it.

She couldn't help thinking about it.

When she heard the light rap on the door at almost seven o'clock, Rachel quickly abandoned the dust rag she had been pushing around over and over on the same spot for the past fifteen minutes.

Rachel took half a moment to compose herself in a last-ditch attempt to bridle her eagerness and glanced at her reflection in the hall mirror. She still looked unsettled, but, with luck, Ethan wouldn't notice. Kirk, she knew, would.

She unlocked the front door and was greeted by the sight of a very tired, contented-looking Ethan on the doorstep, a tiny streak of what looked like jam along one cheek. Kirk was behind him, looking somewhat weary. There was a hint of satisfaction in his eyes.

"So, was it a success?" She stepped aside to let them in.

God, as tired as he felt, she still looked good to him. It made him come to life. He needed to get home and take a long, cold shower, he decided. To wash away the dust and the desire.

At her question, Kirk exchanged looks with Ethan. "We cruised, we took photographs, we ate."

She couldn't help noticing the way Ethan puffed up when Kirk said "we."

"It was a success, then." Rachel looked at her son. He appeared different, she thought. Definitely more like the way he used to be. She'd obviously spent the day worrying for nothing. "Hungry?"

At the mention of eating something else, Ethan groaned long and low, clutching his stomach with both hands. "No."

She arched a wary brow as she looked at Kirk. "What did you feed him?"

He felt restless, and had no idea why. Something felt different tonight. As if he were waiting for a storm to break. He hadn't been with her for more than a fleeting moment since he kissed her last night.

He wanted to kiss her again. Now.

Kirk lifted his shoulders and then let them fall, struggling hard to keep his mind from wandering back to last night. "Whatever he wanted."

"Oh-oh," she replied. Ethan, when undistressed and unsupervised, generally had an appetite that was greater than his stomach capacity. While his snacking was a healthy indication that his spirits were up, it didn't bode well for his stomach.

Rachel studied her son's face. "How do you feel?" Sympathy laced her voice.

It was almost as if the past six months hadn't existed. There was no bravado, there were no barriers between them. This was her little boy turning slightly green in front of her. "Not so good."

Without thinking, she brushed his hair from his eyes as she looked down at his sickly complexion. "Maybe you should go to your room and lie down for a while. It's almost your bedtime, anyway."

Mustering his failing strength, Ethan looked up at his mother. "No, please, Mom. I want to stay here."

She could only stare at him.

"Please, Mom," she echoed in disbelief. Ethan hadn't shown her a shred of politeness, or even called her "Mom," since Don's funeral. Joy sprang up and raced through her on winged feet.

Swallowing the lump in her throat, she took Ethan's chin in her hand and raised his head ever so slightly. Her eyes met his. "All right, who are you, and what have you done with my son?"

"Aw, Mom..."

She dropped her hand and ushered him over to the sofa. "Sorry, I just couldn't resist. Sit down and get comfortable." She turned toward Kirk, gratitude shining in her eyes. "How about you? Would you like to have some dinner?"

He shook his head. The day had involved a parade of tacos, fries and doughnuts. He wasn't feeling all that hot himself, although he'd kept it down to a minimum, eating only to keep Ethan company. "I'm not really hungry."

"All right, how about a medal?"

Her eyes were so blue, he thought he could swim in them. He knew he could drown in them without any effort at all. Yet he couldn't make himself pull his own eyes away.

"For what?"

She smiled as she looked toward Ethan. The boy seemed oblivious of everything except finding a comfortable place for himself on the sofa. "I don't think I really have to explain that to you."

He shrugged carelessly. "I'll take a beer, if you have one."

Since Cameron dropped by frequently, Rachel always kept a supply on hand. She'd never managed to develop a taste for the brew herself.

"Beer it is." She looked toward Ethan. "How about some ginger ale?" He definitely looked as if he were in need of some bubbles.

He just gave his mother a woebegone look and nodded. With a sigh, he stretched his feet out on the coffee table, still searching for that comfortable niche that eluded him.

She'd told him not to put his feet up on the table a dozen times or more. This once, she said nothing. Furniture could always be replaced. A precious relationship was something else again, and theirs was just beginning to mend.

Rachel went into the kitchen and returned a moment later, a can in each hand. "Ginger ale." She placed the green-and-white can in front of Ethan. The boy's eyes had slid closed. If she didn't miss her guess, he was nine-tenths asleep, which was just as well. With luck, when he woke up in the morning, his stomachache would be gone.

"And, for the gentleman, a beer."

She handed it to Kirk, then sat down on the love seat beside him, tucking her legs under her. She'd kept on the baseball jersey he had seen her in this morning, and added a pair of shorts that were badly frayed at the cuffs. A fringe splayed along her thigh like so many delicate, caressing fingers.

Kirk took a pull on his beer and told himself she wasn't driving him crazy.

Rachel watched him in silence for a moment. She felt exhilarated, wired and at peace, all in the same instant. A little, she realized, like the way she'd felt when Kirk kissed her last night. That, too, had been on her mind all day.

She waited until he was cradling the can between his hands. "So, how did it go?"

"Pretty well, I think."

If he was going to attempt to maintain his sanity, he was going to have to stop looking at her eyes. Or at her legs. It didn't leave a whole hell of a lot of places for him to look. He settled on the can.

"I've never seen such an enthusiastic kid." Kirk laughed shortly as he hazarded a glance at her. "Except for you, of course."

"Enthusiastic?" She clutched the word to her. It sparkled in her hand, like a precious diamond. "Ethan? Ethan was enthusiastic?"

He nodded, leaning back in the seat. Even then, he couldn't seem to relax. She was sitting too close to him. Every breath he took was filled with her.

"He didn't want to stop." Kirk thought for a moment, reconstructing the day. "I think I must have gone through twelve, fifteen rolls of film today."

She chewed on her lower lip, hardly able to contain her happiness. She felt like hugging the world. And the man responsible for her joy.

"Did you manage to get anything good?"

He watched her teeth bite her lip, and longed to do the same. Longed to kiss her neck, and to taste the bright, womanly flavors he knew he'd discover along her body. Kirk clutched the can so tightly it began to dent beneath the pressure of his fingers.

He forced himself to relax. "I think so."

She shifted, and her leg brushed against his thigh as she resettled herself. "What are you working on?"

He should be going, Kirk thought. He should definitely be getting up and going. Before he couldn't. "This and that."

Rachel shook her head and laughed softly. "God, but you are closedmouthed when you want to be." She looked over toward a sleeping Ethan. "How was he, besides energetic?" She lowered her voice, in case he woke up suddenly. Her eyes shifted to Kirk's face. Hope began to move forward. "Did he talk to you?"

He'd been wondering when to tell her, and how. He might have known she'd be the one to pick the time. And that it would be almost immediate.

"Yes."

There was something in his tone that had her anticipation rising. Her words, instead of tumbling out, emerged slowly, as if coated in fear. "What did he say?"

Kirk took another pull of the beer, then toyed with the can. He knew the capacity of her sympathy, and that what he was about to say would hurt her. "I found out why he acts the way he does with you."

The mere thought brought a fresh stab of pain to her. She pressed her lips together as she looked off at her son. Her voice was scarcely above a whisper. "He blames me for the divorce, doesn't he? For Don's death?"

"Wrong on both counts."

Rachel looked at him sharply, confused, afraid to read anything into his words.

This much he could do for her. He could take away the burden of guilt she was needlessly carrying around. "He blames himself."

Rachel felt as if all the air in her lungs had suddenly been sucked out. Disbelief filled the space as her eyes darted over toward her son. Ethan was now slumped over to one side, his face buried in one of the cushions on the sofa.

"Himself?" She spoke the word, though she hardly heard it. Confusion battered her. "How could he possibly blame himself?"

Kirk knew that she'd grown up with love. She had no idea what it was like to endure anger, to endure resentment and feel it was your fault. Things were born in that environment that children of love had no knowledge of.

"Because he thought you divorced Don because he hit him."

It still made no sense to her. She placed her hand on Kirk's arm, as if that would reinforce her words. "I did, but that was because Don's mistreatment of Ethan was the final straw."

He knew what she meant, but he also knew that Ethan had seen it differently. "And because after he wished his father dead, Don was killed."

Rachel looked at the sleeping boy in horror. "Oh, my poor baby..." She felt her heart twist within her as she realized what her child must have been feeling. She struggled with the urge to wake him, to hold him in her arms and reassure him that he was blameless. "Did you manage to straighten him out?"

He nodded, rising. "I think so. He's going to have to work it through some more, find his own way past the sorrow." No matter what kind of father Don had been, he had still been Ethan's father. Kirk knew the boy loved him, for nothing more than that. He'd loved his own father once, too. "But I really think he knows now that he had nothing to do with it."

Impulsively, since words didn't seem to be adequate, Rachel brushed her lips against his cheek. Then, to forestall the action from becoming something more, she crossed to the sofa. She tucked her arms around Ethan, ready to lift him from the sofa.

Kirk had every intention of leaving, but he couldn't very well let her carry Ethan upstairs by herself, no matter how strong she thought she was.

"Here, let me," Kirk muttered under his breath, edging her out of the way.

"I can carry him upstairs," she insisted, but not too hard.

Even when they were growing up, she had always tried a little too hard. "Anything you can do, I can do better" could very well have been her credo.

"And bend steel in your bare hands when no one's watching," he told her, picking Ethan up. "Don't worry, Superwoman, your secret identity is safe with me."

Ethan's arm was dangling, so she tucked it in against Kirk. Her fingers brushed against Kirk's chest, and she dropped her hand self-consciously. "And what's that supposed to mean?"

"Maybe it's an observation," he suggested charitably, shifting the boy against him.

Rachel led the way to the stairs. She glanced over her shoulder at Kirk. "About what?"

Ethan murmured something in his sleep, but it was too low for either of them to hear. "That you try to do too much."

"I'm a single parent," Rachel walked up the stairs ahead of Kirk. "Nothing I do is too much." She sighed as she stopped at Ethan's door. There were days when she felt so overwhelmed, so unequal to the burden. "It's usually not enough."

Kirk entered the room and placed Ethan on the bed. He watched as she lovingly removed the boy's sneakers. There was love in everything she did. "If I know you, it's enough."

She looked at him, touched. "I take that as a very huge compliment."

Rachel left the rest of Ethan's clothes on the boy, deciding that it was more important that her son get his rest than for him to dress for the occasion. He usually slept like a rock, but she didn't want to take a chance on tonight being an exception. She wanted him to sleep off his stomachache.

Tiptoeing out of the room, she shut off the light and closed the door. She looked up to see Kirk watching her as if what she was doing were completely out of the realm of his experience.

It probably was, she guessed. It didn't take a detective to figure out that Kirk had never known much parental love and attention.

She sighed, contentment flowing through her, as she went down the stairs behind him. "I have absolutely no idea how to begin thanking you."

He didn't want her thanks. What he wanted was to leave before he gave in to the urges that had been multiplying within him at a furious pace since last night. "You gave me a beer."

She threaded her arms through his and gently guided him toward the living room. "A beer is a very small payment for what you've done."

Being thanked for anything made him uncomfortable. He wasn't any good at being on the receiving end of gratitude. "I was just there at the right time. He would have told someone sooner or later."

Rachel sat down on the sofa and tugged on his arm, urging him to sit down beside her. "I don't know about that. You didn't."

Kirk didn't understand what she was driving at. "Didn't what?"

"Tell anyone about your life," she said softly.

She saw the protective barriers go up, and it hurt more than she would have thought it could. After all this time, he didn't trust her. Why? Whatever had happened to him was long in the past. Why couldn't he just tell her and be done with it? They'd always exchanged confidences before.

Or at least she had thought they had. Thinking back, she began to realize that there had been gaps that Kirk purposely left blank.

Kirk picked up the can of beer, but it was empty. He set it down again, refusing to look at her. "You knew all there was to know."

The hand she laid on his arm was gentle, entreating. She felt him stiffen ever so slightly, the way Ethan had when he braced for a blow.

"You never told anyone your father beat you." Rachel saw Kirk's face harden instantly, shutting her out. "Don't try to deny it, Kirk. You're too much like Ethan not to have that in common. Besides," she went on when he didn't say anything, "you never talked about your home, never invited us over. Not even Cameron."

Survival instincts had him evading the truth. "There could have been lots of reasons for that."

"There could have been," she agreed quietly, "but there weren't."

He looked at her, his face inscrutable. "Sure of yourself, are you?"

She hadn't wanted to tell him, but he'd left her no choice. He *had* to set this free, just as Ethan had had to set his guilt free. Secrets left in the dark only festered and she had only to be with Kirk to know that *something* was troubling him. She could only guess that this was the cause.

"My bedroom window faced yours," she began quickly. "I saw your father come into your room one night." She took a breath. It hurt her to say it, almost as much as it must have hurt him to endure it. "I saw him beat you." She had wanted to run, to tell someone, that night, but in those days, parents hadn't been questioned when they administered corporal punishment. She had remained by her window, frozen. Horrified. "You never uttered a sound."

Kirk had no idea which time she was referring to. His father had beaten him in every room of the house more than once. But he did remember his method of coping. He'd clench his teeth together and will himself not to cry out.

"It was the only way I could get back at him."

She remembered the horror she'd experienced, watching. She'd quickly buried her head under a blanket, unable to look on any longer. She'd been ten or eleven at the time. "Why did he hit you?"

There was such love in her eyes, such sympathy, that it drew the words out of him.

"Frustration, I guess." He shrugged, wishing he could shrug away the entire topic. "Same excuse Don used with Ethan." He got up, feeling restless, cornered. "Look, I really don't want to talk about this."

Rachel rose with him, her body brushing against his as she gained her feet. Heat flared through her, demanding an outlet. Demanding him. He didn't trust her, but he couldn't deny what there was between them without exploring it. She wouldn't let him.

Surrendering to her feelings, she threaded her arms around his neck. "Kirk."

Kirk couldn't let this begin. He knew he wouldn't have the strength to stop it once it did. He drew her arms away. "Don't."

She didn't understand his reluctance. He'd kissed her, and she had tasted his desire. He wanted her as much as she wanted him. "Why?"

She was making it so difficult. It was hard to deny them both. "Because it's no good."

"I told you, I'm old enough to decide that for myself." Loosening her hands from his, she lightly skimmed her fingers along his temple. "I'd like to think you need me, just a little."

Her words, her very breath, shimmered along his skin. He felt something in his stomach tightening into a knot that would have defied a sailor's expertise.

"I do." She had to be made to see reason. She was just vulnerable, perhaps even rebounding after what she had gone through with Don. He didn't want her to be hurt again. And he knew he'd hurt her. "But I can't let you in, Funny Face."

If he wanted her, if he could admit that he wanted her, then why was he still retreating? "Why?"

He held her at arm's length, not trusting himself to let her get any closer. "If I let you in, I might never let you go."

Her eyes searched his for a clue. She found none. "Would that be such a bad thing?"

He fought the urge to bury his face in her hair, to breathe in the fragrant perfume and let himself do nothing but feel. "It would. For you."

Ever so slowly, she drew closer, until her body was less than a breath away from his. "There you go again..." she murmured against his neck, pressing her lips to his skin. She felt him tremble, and a feeling of triumph zigzagged through her. "Making decisions for me..."

His mind was fogging over faster than the coastline in spring. "Rachel, if you keep this up..."

She pressed another kiss to his throat and saw the pulse there jump. Her excitement escalated. "Yes?"

He felt heat surge through his loins. Damn, he wanted to spare her, not to draw her any farther into his murky world. "I'm not going to be responsible for what happens."

She wanted him to trust her. To trust her judgment. To trust her heart. It had to begin somewhere. "Fine, because I know I am."

With effort, his breathing ragged, his resolve breaking down into tiny pieces, he drew away. "I think it's a mistake."

She touched his face. He was so kind, so good, how could he possibly believe that this was a mistake? "There is no consensus on that. It's a split decision." Rising on her toes, she nipped lightly along his lower lip. When he groaned, she felt herself melting in response. "You know what that means."

He wanted to undress her, to run his hands along her supple body. To make slow, passionate love to her until heaven and earth faded away into oblivion. She was driving him crazy.

"No. What does that mean?"

"It means we're going to have to have a debate." Her heart pounding, she slowly slid the tip of her tongue along his lips. "Each side is going to have to try to convince the other." She feathered a kiss lightly across his brow. "I go first."

He caught hold of her hands, not certain how much more he could endure without breaking down completely. "Are you trying to seduce me?"

Her body pressed against his, Rachel could feel his reaction to her. Just how much longer was he going to attempt to resist?

"Trying my damnedest." She smiled up into his eyes. "How am I doing?"

He didn't answer her. Instead, as his willpower cracked into a million pieces, Kirk swept her into his arms. The movement was as swift, as strong, as a flash flood unexpectedly surging through the desert.

Rachel's breath was gone instantly. She felt herself drowning in the whirlpool created by his mouth. When he stopped, an eternity later, her head fell back. Her breath emerged in gasps as he rimmed her throat with a necklace of small, ardent kisses.

She had to concentrate to form words. "I guess that means I'm doing pretty well." She dug her hands into his shoulders to keep from sinking to the floor. Her knees had completely ceased to function. "I don't mind telling you that I'm completely seduced on my end."

Kirk drew back for a second, waiting for his heart to catch up to the rest of him. He looked at her and saw before him the girl she'd been, and the woman she was. The person he'd always cared about so deeply.

"This can only end in one place." He meant it as a final warning.

She didn't trust herself to withdraw her arms. She knew she'd fall if she did. "That's what I'm counting on."

I'm sorry, Funny Face. This shouldn't be happening. You deserve someone who can love you the way you should be loved.

"Do you still sleep in your old room?"

Rachel shook her head. "I've got my parents' room now." Turning from him, she took his hand. She meant to lead him up the stairs. He needed to be coaxed out of his wariness.

When he didn't move, she felt disheartened. "What?"

She deserved better, but since it was now inevitable, he would do what he could to ease her regret when the time came. "If we're going to do this—"

Her breath caught in her throat when she saw the desire smoldering in his eyes. "Yes?"

He smiled at her. "Let's do it right."

Suddenly, her feet left the ground. Kirk lifted her into his arms and carried her up the stairs.

Her heart pounding with anticipation, she nestled against him. "Do you know how many times I had this fantasy when I was sixteen?"

He brushed his cheek against her hair. "How many?"

She smiled against his neck. He could feel her lips curving. "I lost count."

He stopped at her door. As long as they remained outside, he could still withdraw. Or at least he told himself he could. "You could lose more than your count this time."

"Shh..." Rachel laid her finger against his lips. "Don't be negative, Kirk," she pleaded. "One step at a time." The words feathered seductively along his mouth. "Just one step at a time."

He glanced toward the room where they had just placed her son. If the boy should wake up and come into her room— "Ethan..."

"Is sound asleep," she assured him. "He sleeps just like Cameron. Once out, that's it for the night. Dynamite couldn't rouse him." Her eyes caressed his face. "He sleeps through thunderstorms."

"Is that what this is?" he asked. "A thunderstorm?" It felt more as if an earthquake were going on inside of him. He edged the door closed with his shoulder.

It was happening, she thought, elated. It was really happening. "It's anything you want it to be, as long as you make love with me."

He set her down on the floor beside her bed. "With?" he echoed.

She placed her hand in his, as if she meant to lead him somewhere he had never gone. "With. Equal." A smile curved her lips and rose into her eyes. "I take off your clothing, you take off mine. Equal," she repeated.

He tried not to let her see just how much the image of that affected him. "Funny Face, you can still back out—"

She was long past that now. She'd passed that when he first kissed her, last night. "I don't want to. And for tonight, I'm Rachel. Say it, Kirk," she breathed. "Say my name. Rachel."

He felt as if he were being hypnotized. As if she had cast a spell on him. "Rachel."

Waves of desire, of passion, swept over her one after the other at the sound of her name on his lips.

His voice, low and throaty, evoked sensations from her. It felt as if everything within her rushed to the surface. When he stroked the palm of his hand over the swell of her breasts, she could feel her very blood rise to the boiling point.

Kirk put his hands under her shirt. Slowly he moved them along her back to her waist, then reached up to cup her breasts. His eyes on hers, he lifted the T-shirt up slowly. It moved over her skin like a whisper, until she was free of it. He tossed it aside and pulled her to him. Rachel groaned.

The groan turned into a gasp when he nuzzled her breasts, his mouth hot on her skin, savoring the dusky flavor he found there.

With fingers that trembled, Rachel somehow managed to undo his shirt without ripping off any of the buttons, though she wasn't sure just how. Urgent needs pounded through her as she finally worked it free and off his shoulders. She splayed her hands over his bare chest. The slight sprinkling of hair there tickled her palms.

His mouth found hers again, and again, until she felt as if she were drunk. Words emerged in short, tiny gasps.

"You know, I never liked the taste of beer before." She pressed her lips together and tasted him. "I guess you were the missing ingredient."

Kirk still felt that this was a mistake, but mistake or not, he could no longer bridle the desires that screamed to be released. Not when she welcomed him with both arms this way.

His only hope was to make her turn him away. He framed her face in his hands. "Rachel, I'll hurt you."

"No, you won't. Not ever. You're not capable of it." He could never make her believe that.

The trust she was handing him overwhelmed him. "You don't know."

"Then you'll tell me." She wanted him so much that she could hardly bear it. "Later. Much, much later."

She had always thought that he had hands like an artist. As they passed over her now, discovering her secrets, taking what she so urgently offered, she felt herself melting. All coherent thought was just beyond her reach. All that existed was this wild, insatiable craving.

She hadn't been with a man since Don. It made no difference. She could have been with a hundred men, or she could have lived the life of a celibate nun. The effect would still have been the same.

Rockets. He was making skyrockets go off in her head every time his lips touched hers. Every time he touched her.

As if they had a life of their own, her hands groped for his belt buckle. Fumbling, she undid it, then eased the jeans down his hips. One thrill after another leaped through her.

He swore to himself that he would go slow, that he would love her the way she deserved to be loved. He knew there would be regrets once the passion subsided, but he wanted her to remember this with a measure of tenderness.

Desire built on desire as Kirk guided first her shorts, then her underwear, down her body. Her skin felt like cream, like satin, to his touch. Reverently he passed his hands over her. When she trembled against him, he found it hard to keep his pace under control.

Her body was molded to his as he tossed aside the last of her clothing. Heat passed between them, mingling, scorching them both. Sealing them to one another.

His body throbbed from wanting her. Tenderly he brushed her hair from her face. "I don't suppose this is the right time to tell you that you'll be sorry."

He felt so strong, so powerful, as he lowered her onto the bed. Rachel arched against him. Tempting him. "You'll be sorry if you talk any more."

"I never meant for this to happen when I came back." If he'd known, he would never have returned. He'd die before he'd ever hurt her.

"Didn't you?"

"No."

She laced her hands together around his neck and pulled him to her. "Then consider it a bonus."

Unable to resist another moment, Kirk trailed his mouth along the column of her throat as he explored what was already his. What had always been his.

He wanted to race to the end, he wanted this to go on forever. He didn't want to think, only to feel. To feel her tenderness, her love. She was his salvation, for she held his soul in her hands.

Rachel raised her hips to his, and control was wrenched away from him. He sheathed himself in her, and with a mutual muted cry they rode the crest of the wave together, fast and hard, until it spiraled and threw them onto the beach, spent, dazed and sated.

"I love you, Kirk," she murmured against his shoulder.

"What?" He thought he'd heard something, but there was a buzzing in his head, and he wasn't sure. "Am I hurting you?"

"I told you, you could never hurt me, silly." For now, she would keep her feelings to herself.

But he would know, someday.

Chapter 13

Kirk shifted and lay down beside Rachel. Her body felt warm, inviting, like a safe haven on a stormy night. *His* haven. In a way, he supposed she always had been. Gathering her to him, he attempted to seal in the sensation. But even as he tried, he knew it was only temporary.

"I should go."

"I know." Everything in her wanted him to stay. She raised her head slightly and pressed a kiss to his shoulder.

Kirk drew her even closer, grazing her temple with his lips. He heard the moan she swallowed.

Rachel tightened her fingers on his arms. "In a minute," she breathed.

In a very long minute, she amended silently, as she felt herself being aroused again. She buried her hands in his hair, coaxing his face down to hers.

Common sense told him to leave. Desire whispered, "Stay." Desire was tenfold stronger than any message his brain transmitted.

With effort, Kirk tried again. "I really should be going."

Her body seemed to curve into his on its own, seeking his warmth. Seeking him. She looked into his eyes and saw herself mirrored there. "Do you want to?"

"No."

What he wanted to do was to remain here and make slow, languid love to her until there wasn't an ounce of energy left in his body.

Her mouth curved as she sensed what he was thinking. Desire curled in her veins like smoke.

"Then don't." Rachel twined her fingers together around his neck, moving beneath him. "Stay here with me. Stay the night." Her words shimmered seductively along his skin.

He wanted to remain with her more than he could possibly have put into words. He knew that it was an illusion, but he had never felt as if he belonged somewhere as much as he did at this moment.

"Ethan..." he began to protest.

Rachel loved him for his concern, for his sensitivity. She loved him for a host of reasons. "You'll be gone before Ethan wakes up."

Temptation warred with sense. "I wouldn't want him to find us like this."

"No," she agreed. "Not like this." And then she grinned when she thought of her son. She had a feeling that Ethan would more than welcome the idea of Kirk being in her life. "But he's a pretty mature kid, all things considered. I think he might like the idea of my seeing you. I know he likes you." Gently she outlined his lips with her fingertip. "And he knows you were my friend before you were his."

Kirk pressed her fingers to his lips, kissing them. He felt her shiver in response. Amusement entered his eyes. "Is that what we are? Friends?"

Rachel poked her tongue into her cheek to keep from laughing. "I think we've gone a little beyond just friends." But then she grew serious. He had to know this, above all else. "But no matter what does happen, we will always be friends."

Would a friend do something like this to another friend? Take advantage of the situation, of them? He knew the an-

swer to that, and yet he couldn't make himself leave. Not yet.
Not when she smelled like heaven and tasted like sin.

He hadn't a clue as to how to handle what he was feeling. He
knew what was right and what he wanted. The two had nothing to do with each other. "Rachel, I'm very confused right
now."

She smiled, love brimming in her eyes. "There's a lot of that
going around."

This wasn't something that could be swept away with a flippant remark. This was serious. With serious repercussions. He
wanted her to try to understand what he was struggling with.

"I feel things for you, Rachel. Things I never felt before. I
came back to Bedford because, trite as it sounds, I had to try
to find myself." And he knew the answers were somehow here,
in his roots. The smile on his lips was sad around the edges. "I
think I'm more lost than ever, now." Lost, but for the first time
in years he didn't feel alone, not the way he had been before.

He wondered if he could somehow manage to freeze time,
just this once.

Rachel refused to accept his negative view. "No, I think that
perhaps you're discovering a great deal about yourself that you
never knew before."

He saw the knowing smirk hovering on her lips. "And you
did."

"Maybe." Her eyes narrowed as they held his. As they
searched for his soul. "Maybe I just hoped I did."

He couldn't resist touching her, couldn't resist skimming his
hand lightly over the swell of her breast, toying with the curve
of her hip. It was as if he were attempting to absorb her, to re-
create her in his mind's eye, through his fingertips. The way she
moved in response thrilled him.

Needs struggled against gallantry. "This isn't going to work,
you know."

*Yes. Yes, it will, if you just give it a chance. Trust me, Kirk.
Love me.*

She bit back her impatience. "Don't make long-range plans,
Kirk." He was making her eyes flutter shut as she steeped herself in the sensations his hands were creating within her.

Her heart was slamming against her chest as she felt her body being primed for him once again.

"One minute at a time," she begged. "Just take it one minute at a time. That's all any of us can do." She grasped his arm when she felt his fingers delve into her, stirring her. Bringing her up to another plateau. "Tomorrow there might be a giant earthquake that'll swallow us all up and change everything."

He watched, fascinated, as her indigo eyes grew smoky. Smoky with desire. And the desire belonged to him. "I think there already was one."

She was barely aware of the grin that rose to her lips. But she was aware of opening her arms. "Want to make the earth move again?"

Kirk didn't answer. He showed her instead.

Before morning's first light could creep into the room, Kirk left her bed. Though she was sound asleep, she still knew the moment he withdrew. The emptiness engulfed her, leaving her cold and alone. It seeped into her dream until she awoke to discover that her dream was a reality.

He was gone.

The place beside her was still warm, and she laid her cheek against it, savoring the feel of it, imagining him still there.

"Oh, Kirk," she whispered softly to the darkness, "where do we go from here?" She knew where she wanted them to go, to the next logical level. But it was never simple with Kirk. There were still layers to remove and secrets to uncover.

If he let her. If he trusted her.

Rachel refused to let the bereft feeling that hovered about her eat away at her. She knew he'd had to leave before Ethan woke up. This wasn't the time for sadness. Instead, she dwelled on the night they had spent together. On the passion that they had shared. She vowed silently that it would happen again. All she had to do, she thought as sleep began to revisit her, was keep a positive attitude. She'd never given up hope on Ethan, and look where that had led.

She didn't doubt, not even for a moment, though she knew his emotional baggage was far greater, that the same would happen with Kirk.

* * *

Kirk spent Sunday in the dark. Literally. He had set up his studio, complete with a makeshift darkroom, in the back bedroom. After leaving Rachel, he had gone directly there.

It soothed him to work with what he knew. Calmed him. He developed roll after roll of the film that he and Ethan had taken, scrutinizing each shot carefully. He selected only the very best for enlarging. Still, as the hours passed, the pile of photographs on his worktable increased steadily. Kirk was careful to keep the ones Ethan had taken separate from the others. They would be subtly mixed in later, to reflect the child's perspective on the town they had all grown up in.

Rachel would like that, he thought. It was the kind of thing she enjoyed.

It would make a good farewell gift. When he left Bedford the last time, he had given Rachel a leather-bound collection of Agatha Christie's novels. This time, he would give her Bedford, bound up with a ribbon, with her son's imprint on it.

He would give her the album, and a piece of his soul he knew he wouldn't be taking with him when he left.

Kirk shut out the thought as he continued to work. Behind him, the shadows slowly lengthened on the walls.

She hadn't seen him in two days. Two long, miserable, endless days.

Rachel knew that Kirk hadn't left town. In her heart, she told herself that he couldn't possibly leave so abruptly, without saying goodbye. Her belief was reinforced by the light she saw in his room at night.

She wanted to go over and demand to know what was going on. Demand to know why he was hiding from her.

She didn't.

Somehow, though she was given to barging into the lives of people she cared about, she just didn't think it was right for her to intrude on his privacy. Yet.

Maybe, she thought, he just needed to work all this through. There were times when he was far too intellectual for his own good. Or hers.

Waiting around was killing her.

He didn't return all day Sunday, the way she had hoped he would after he slipped out of her room like a wisp of a dream. Monday was one of her two early days, so she didn't need Kirk to pick Ethan up.

She just needed *him*.

Kirk had obviously used that as an excuse not to come over at all. By then it had been all she could do to restrain Ethan from bounding over to Kirk's house and presenting himself at his front door. Just the way she wanted to.

Today was Tuesday. Per their agreement, Kirk had to pick Ethan up. That meant he would be there when she arrived home. But would he be there because he had to be, because they had a bargain, or because he wanted to be?

Their night of passion had put an entirely different spin on their relationship. Had it destroyed it altogether?

She chewed her lower lip thoughtfully as she sat at her desk, facing her nine-o'clock class. Had she and Kirk crossed a line by making love the other night? A line he wouldn't cross back? Had making love frightened him away permanently? God, she hoped not. She had no idea how he was reacting to what had happened between them, but she knew that, for her, once wasn't enough. Once only served to make her want him that much more.

It wasn't the sex, though that had been breathtaking. It was the tenderness that called to her, the reverence in his touch that had her aching for more.

Damn it, Kirk, don't turn your back on this.

"Ms. Reed?"

Horrified, Rachel suddenly realized that she was staring at a student, and that he had been asking her a question. Repeatedly, from the expression on his face. A question she hadn't heard.

Rachel blinked, suppressing the embarrassment she felt. "I'm sorry, yes?"

The young man exchanged a look with the girl on his left. Both looked somewhat confused by her behavior. "Will that be on the test?"

She had absolutely no idea what the student was referring to. Rachel debated making a confession, then decided to bluff her way through. Her smile was nothing short of mysterious.

"Why don't I just leave that as a surprise?" she suggested. Her words were met with a communal groan that she was certain echoed out into the hall through the open classroom door. She refused to be drawn in by the plaintive looks. "Always study as much as you can. Remember, it's better to be over-prepared than underprepared."

The bell rang just then, mercifully saving her from having to continue with her charade. The past forty-seven minutes were a blank to her. She sincerely hoped she hadn't sounded like a complete idiot.

The last student shuffled from the room, and she let out a sigh. Automatically she began piling her books and notes into her briefcase. She was going to have to get back on the ball, Rachel thought, upbraiding herself. She couldn't let her students suffer, just because their instructor was suddenly behaving like a love-sick puppy.

"Is that your general rule of thumb? Be overprepared?"

Her heart became swiftly and firmly lodged in her throat as she swung around. Kirk had come to see her.

"What are you doing here?" But joy instantly evaporated as Rachel fell upon the only plausible reason for his appearance. "You're not going away, are you?"

Kirk couldn't recall when he'd seen such pronounced disappointment on her face. He suspected it was vanity that caused him to feel pleased.

"No." He shoved his hands into the front pockets of his faded jeans and pretended that her smile of relief didn't warm his heart. "I should be, but no, not yet." He felt awkward, being here. Awkward because he wanted to be here so much—because she was here. "I thought I'd haunt your stomping grounds for a while."

"Fair enough."

Kirk watched as she snapped the locks on her briefcase. That was what he was straining against, he thought. Locks. Locks on his soul. Locks on his freedom. Locks like the ones on the closet his father had habitually pushed him into as a child, even when he begged to be let out.

Kirk looked around the room, noticing everything. And seeing nothing.

"The truth is—" he lowered his voice so that she had to strain to hear "—I told myself to stay away." She said nothing as she picked up her case. He struggled on. Words were not his medium. "But I wanted to see you." He shrugged his shortcomings away. "I thought it was safer in a public place." His eyes skimmed over her mouth. His own felt like dried-out cotton. "That way, I wouldn't be tempted."

She knew him well enough, or thought she did, to read between the lines. Locking the classroom door behind her, she turned to him. "Is it working?"

"No." He shook his head as he fell into step beside her. "I'm still tempted, but at least here I can't do anything about it."

Her laughter slipped effortlessly under his skin, branding him. Unsettling him further.

"I have a tiny office," she offered. "It just about fits two."

He took her arm, and they moved toward the exit, a little more quickly. He figured she was kidding, but he wasn't taking any chances. "You're not making it any easier, Funny Face."

She'd always taken the name to be a term of endearment. But it was different now. It signaled his retreat. "No more Rachel?"

"Not for now." Not ever, if he could help it. It was her sake he was thinking of. Not his own. He would have wanted nothing more than to take her now in the first out-of-the-way place he could find.

There was a small coffee shop just off campus. Rachel opted to go there with him, rather than to the cafeteria. It was quieter.

She shrugged as they took the footbridge that connected the campus to the shopping area. It hovered over the street traffic like an arched brow. "Well, I don't intend to make it easy for you Kirk. Running away shouldn't be."

A green sports car zoomed by just as they reached the other end of the stone bridge. The coffee shop stood just a few feet beyond it.

Kirk scowled. "Who's running away?"

"You, if you'd left immediately." She placed her hand just beneath the word Jeffrey's on the shop's glass door and pushed it open.

Kirk followed her inside. "Two mocha coffees," he told the man behind the counter. They sat down at a tiny round table for two.

Rachel smiled. He remembered the fact that she liked mocha coffee, she thought, warmth permeating her.

She waiting until he was seated. "Let someone love you, Kirk," she urged softly. "You deserve it."

"Someone," he echoed. "You?"

She wasn't quite ready to admit that. She feared that if she did, it would frighten him away. The man behind the counter brought over their coffees and set a steaming mug down in front of each of them. She waited until he retreated before saying anything.

"Me. Ethan. Cameron." There was safety in numbers. Being loved by them wasn't as intimidating, she judged, as being loved by her. "We all care about you, Kirk."

He wrapped his hands around the hot mug in front of him and stared at the steam. "I don't know how to deal with that. I never had to before."

"Yes, you did."

Though it had never been verbally expressed, it was no secret that the three of them had all cared about one another when they were growing up. That they could all always count on one another.

"Nothing's changed." Saturday night whispered softly in the corners of her mind, and she smiled. "Well, maybe some things, but not the essence. I always loved you. So did Cameron," she added quickly. "You *matter* to us. There might not be any blood between us, but that doesn't mean anything. Just because you're related doesn't automatically mean someone cares about you."

How well he knew that, he thought.

"Being family doesn't always mean you're related," she continued. "Let Cameron and Ethan and me be your family, Kirk. We are anyway, whether you want us to be or not," she added. "You might as well enjoy it."

In her innocence, she didn't quite know what she was tacitly getting into, he thought. "I'd ask a few questions before I drew up the adoption papers, if I were you."

She studied his face for a moment. "If I asked, would you answer?"

He had walked right into that one, Kirk thought. He paused as he took a long sip of his coffee, regarding her over the rim of the white mug.

"Maybe," he finally said.

It was a start. "I'll hold you to that."

She was incredible. "To a maybe?"

Rachel grinned. "You'd be surprised what I can do with it."

A smile rose to his face of its own volition. "No, after Saturday I don't think anything would manage to surprise me."

She laughed as she set down her mug. "Don't be too sure." The tension she'd been living with for two days had completely left her. She felt back on her old footing with him. With a delicious bonus. "Tell me, where were you Sunday? You left while I was still asleep."

He toyed with the dangling earring at her ear. "If I had waited until you were awake, I wouldn't have left."

The bell above the door tinkled as a lone student walked in. Rachel took no notice. She was completely intrigued by Kirk's admission. "Sounds promising. So where did you go?"

"Back to the house. I wanted to work on the photographs that I took with Ethan." Mostly he'd wanted to work her out of his system. He'd discovered that it was impossible.

"That was what Ethan thought." She remembered how eager he'd been to join Kirk. And how disappointed he'd been when she refused to let him. "He couldn't stop talking about you the next day. I think you've been elevated just above Jose Canseco. He wanted to go over and help you develop the films. I practically had to tie him up to keep him from coming over."

"Why did you?"

She shrugged, watching the whipped cream dissolve in her coffee. She knew that he was really asking her why she hadn't come over. "I thought perhaps you might like some time to yourself."

She knew him so well, he thought. Up to a point. "Thanks."

"Don't mention it. I owe you." Kirk raised his brow, and she knew what he was thinking. "Not that," Rachel added quickly, her eyes sparkling with amusement. "For the conversation you had with Ethan. The difference in him is absolutely incredible. It's like night and day."

He didn't want her being grateful to him. It only complicated matters. "I told you, you don't have to keep thanking me."

She wasn't going to let him push her away, no matter how hard he tried. She was accustomed to digging in. "I will, until you learn how to accept it. You've got a lot of good things to offer, Kirk. To everyone you come in contact with."

Her words struck a nerve. "You wouldn't say that if—" He bit off the rest of it.

Almost, she thought. He'd almost told her. Rachel covered his hand with her own. "If what?"

He slipped his hand from hers, pulling into himself. "If you knew."

She frowned. So near, and yet so far. She was at a loss as to how to persuade him to trust her. She only knew he had to. It was the one thing she needed. Besides his love. "Did something happen that made you come home?"

He toyed with his mug. "In a way, yes." He drained the last of his coffee and set the mug aside. "In another way, it was just a steady compilation of things."

No more excuses, she thought. "I have an hour until my next class. We can order more coffee."

He shouldn't have said anything. It was funny how she always managed to draw things out of him. "It would take more than an hour."

Her eyes wouldn't allow him to retreat. "An hour would give you a start."

He shook his head, avoiding her eyes. "It isn't as easy as that."

She wasn't going to let him shut her out any longer. This was more important than their making love together. It went beyond the physical. This involved a melding of their souls.

"It's as hard as you make it," she insisted, quietly, firmly. "Ax murderers can confess in under an hour, Kirk. They start out by saying, 'I did it.'"

In his case, he thought, he hadn't done it. And that was where the whole problem lay.

Kirk was quiet for so long, she was certain that he wasn't going to answer her at all.

"I saw a man die," he finally told her, in a voice so soft and distant, it hardly seemed to be coming from him at all.

She saw the anguish in his eyes and struggled with her conscience. Her inclination was to pull away from the painful subject, to spare him this. But her heart urged her on.

"You covered a lot of different conflicts, or whatever they choose to call them officially. I would have thought that you saw a lot of men die." Her hand offered mute comfort as she laid it on his. "What was different about this one?"

For a moment, he thought of dismissing it, but it was too late to back away. Perhaps if she knew what he'd become, she'd understand why he was all wrong for her. Why he wasn't capable of loving her.

"I saw him die through the viewfinder of my camera." He could tell by her expression that she didn't understand what he was telling her. "Don't you see? He wasn't a person to me, he was a photograph. I was so intent on getting the shot, I didn't stop to save him."

Her voice was low, calming. "Could you have?"

He blew out a breath as he dragged a hand through his hair. "Maybe."

Maybe wasn't good enough. "But not for certain."

He understood what she was trying to do, and was grateful to her. But it didn't negate what had happened. "It was in Bosnia. Nothing's certain there." Or in any of the half-dozen other places he'd been that had been just like Bosnia. Or worse.

Rachel refused to let go. She worked the tapestry of what he had said like a skilled craftsman. "And you could, in all probability, have been wounded, killed or captured, if you'd tried."

His conscious denied it, but his common sense agreed with her. "Maybe."

Rachel folded her hands before her, struggling to keep her emotions out of her voice. Only reason would have any effect on him. "As I see it, you taking his photograph, you preserving that moment of horror for the world to see what was going on in this man's country, might have done the greater good."

His anger rose, not against her, but against himself. Against his fatal inertia. "Tell it to the man's widow. Or his kids. Or his mother."

As determined as he was to blame himself, she was more determined to absolve him. "How many more widows and orphans would there be if no one knew about these wars, these conflicts?"

The wings and halo didn't fit. He knew that without trying them on for size. "I'm not the only one taking photographs of the world's trouble spots."

He was minimizing his work. "No, but you *are* contributing to the world's awareness of them. Photographs are used to make people aware of things they might rather not see. You've won awards for your work." She saw the disparaging expression on his face, and pressed on. "And if everyone suddenly abandoned their cameras, their videotapes, we'd be plunged into mental darkness," she insisted. Her voice throbbed with emotion she wanted to deny. "With that kind of reasoning, inhumanities would go undetected, except by the perpetrators and by the victims. That's not the kind of world either one of us wants."

She sounded so fierce, so sincere, she almost succeeded in making him believe in himself. The way he had once. "So you're saying I shouldn't feel guilty."

Rachel knew it was too easy, but she grasped at it anyway. "That's exactly what I'm saying."

He laughed softly. And felt, oddly enough, somewhat at peace, as if a little of the guilt had been siphoned away. "You always had a way of twisting things around to fit in with your view."

"No, I always had a way of being able to look at something from all angles," she told him smugly. "You told me that. You were annoyed at the time, too."

No, he'd never been annoyed with her, only with the situation. "Funny Face, I appreciate what you're trying to do—"

"No, you don't." She knew that he didn't want her taking his side at all. But that didn't stop her. "And I'm only trying to make you see reason. You didn't do anything to condemn yourself for. Who knows if you could have even saved that man—"

His mouth hardened. Every night for a month afterward, he had relived that man's death, had seen the pistol being raised by his executioner and then being fired at point-blank range. It had haunted him, waking and sleeping, melding into his nightmares, until he had finally come home.

"If I wasn't looking through the viewfinder, I might have seen what was going to happen before it actually did. I could have tried—"

"Yes," she agreed, barely suppressing her annoyance at his stubbornness. "And you could have died. Two men dead, instead of one. I don't see that as a plus." She leaned over the small table, her eyes intense. "You were just doing what you were supposed to do. Bringing the news home. The only way we can fight something, change something, improve something, is by being made aware that it exists. You do that very well."

Though he didn't fully agree, for the moment he let her win the round. He had a feeling they'd be here all day otherwise. Rachel was like a junkyard dog when she believed in something. She wouldn't let go. It both humbled him and awed him that she believed in him to such a degree.

He smiled at her fondly. "And you could argue the ears off a stone statue."

She leaned back in her chair. It wobbled a little. "We all do what we're good at."

Saturday night flashed through his mind. Her skin, soft and silky by moonlight. Her mouth, hot and feverish against his. He felt himself becoming aroused again. "That's not the only thing you're good at." He saw the slight blush rise to her cheeks and found it endearing. Kirk felt his blood warming. "Just how large is that cubicle of yours?"

"Not very. And it's also not as private as I'd like." Rachel thought of the evening to come. "You're picking Ethan up at school, aren't you?"

Kirk nodded. He was actually looking forward to seeing Ethan again. "Yes."

"Stay for dinner?"

He pretended to think it over. "What are you having?"

Rachel arched a brow in disbelief. "Are you getting fussy?"

Kirk spread his hands wide. "A man has the right to know what he's going to be eating." As she laughed Kirk glanced over toward the table in the corner. There was a student sitting alone, a book propped up before him. But he was staring, rather intently, over the top of the book and in their direction.

Kirk inclined his head subtly toward the student. "You know him?"

Rachel looked, then nodded a greeting. "That's Stuart Bowman. He's in two of my classes." She thought of the recent session she'd spent with him in her cubicle. "I've been giving him some extra help. He's very bright, but his mind doesn't seem to be on his work. It's as if he's preoccupied with something."

It didn't take a genius to figure this one out. "Maybe it's his teacher."

That had never occurred to her. She looked at Kirk. "Why, Kirk, if I didn't know any better, I'd say you were jealous."

Jealous. It had an odd ring to it. He began to deny it, then realized that he'd be lying if he did. "Maybe that's because I am."

Rachel's mouth dropped open at his admission. But she was no more surprised by it than he was. And far less uncomfortable.

He was quick to attempt to mend the breach in the fence. "I always thought of you as my mascot."

"Very romantic." But the smile on her face told him that she knew she had him.

"I didn't entertain a single romantic thought about you." He had never lied to her. He wasn't about to start now. "Until I returned to Bedford."

Rachel propped her head up on her hand, fascinated. "And after that?"

He had already said more than he should have, on a lot of counts. "I think that this is the part that should be censored."

"Rats."

He looked at the clock on the wall behind her. "Isn't it time for your next class?"

She glanced at her watch. She had just enough time to make it to her class, but not much more than that.

"Double rats. Saved by the bell, Callaghan. Literally. But this discussion will be continued tonight, in one form or another. For now, I've got to dash."

Impulsively, she leaned over and brushed his lips with her own. She felt the quickening in her pulse as his lips moved over hers.

"Later..." she breathed.

He watched her leave, and knew he had no business feeling the way he did about Cameron's little sister. It didn't help.

Chapter 14

Kirk stared at the door, lost in thought, long after Rachel had left the coffee shop. As a stringently obeyed rule, he had never allowed himself to need anyone before, not since he was a child. Not since his parents emotionally abandoned him.

But he needed Rachel.

It was a dependency he wasn't certain he could live with. He wrapped his hands around the empty mug, slowly rotating it back and forth, an outward sign of his internal debate. And if he couldn't live with it, with the idea of depending on her, of needing her, it wasn't fair to her for him to hang around.

Yet he didn't want to go. Not yet. He *couldn't* go.

"You and Ms. Reed got a thing going?"

Kirk raised his eyes from the mug to see a pair of neatly pressed trousers that appeared to be hanging on the thin frame they were adorning by sheer will and little more. The young man standing before him looked to be barely out of his teens. He was painfully slender.

"Excuse me?"

The same student who had observed Rachel and him so blatantly earlier now stood before him. Oversize hands shifted three textbooks from one bony hip to the other and then back again, as if he were attempting to find a home for them.

Bowman. Stuart Bowman, Kirk recalled Rachel saying his name was. If Bowman's Adam's apple hadn't been hidden by the collar of his navy-blue turtleneck sweater, Kirk was certain he would have seen it riding spasmodically up and down the long, thin column of his throat, like a yo-yo in perpetual motion.

A younger version of Don Quixote, Kirk thought, amused despite the man's invasion.

Pipe cleaner shoulders squared themselves, as if Bowman thought he was about to face an opponent in combat. Perhaps in his mind, Kirk thought, he was.

"Ms. Reed," Bowman repeated, the pitch of his voice increasing, threatening to crack like an adolescent boy's. "Are you and she, um, seeing each other?"

He'd been right in his guess, Kirk thought. Bowman did have a crush on her. It should have amused him, but it didn't. The strange, possessive feeling filtering through him *was* jealousy. Kirk examined the sensation like a scientist discovering an entirely new life form. Awestruck and curious, he felt decidedly uncomfortable in its presence.

"And if we were?" The reply was guarded as Kirk studied the elongated, mournful-looking face. Under no circumstances could Bowman be thought of as competition, so why was there this feeling of protecting what was his?

Besides, there was nothing to protect, he insisted silently. Rachel was her own person, just as he was his.

Bowman seemed to know the glint of danger when he encountered it. Comically, he took a half step back. "Then I guess I'd back off. If you were."

Kirk regarded the man before him. Was he one of those obsessive stalkers who periodically surfaced to tantalize the scandal-hungry public? Instinctively he came to attention.

"Back off? As in how?"

Bowman's nostrils flared as he fumbled for words. "Well, seeing her." He swallowed as he shifted his books again. One slipped from his grasp and fell to the floor. He stooped to pick it up, taking another step back. "Or trying to."

This student was no more a threat to Rachel than he was to world security, Kirk decided. He'd just overreacted. Just why he had, he'd examine later, when he was feeling a little more saner.

Now that he wasn't worried about Rachel, Kirk found he was a great deal more tolerant of the awkward young man. "Is she aware of this?" he asked gently.

Bowman looked like a sweater that was about to come unraveled because a single thread had been pulled. He scratched his head nervously and pursed his lips until they disappeared entirely. "Well, I go to her for help." He looked up quickly. "Not that I really need it, but just because . . ."

Bowman's voice trailed off. He seemed to be searching for a way to explain his feelings. Then he brightened, as if the answer had fallen into his lap. "It's her perfume."

"Perfume?" Kirk repeated, intrigued. He couldn't remember *ever* being this young, not even as a child. He hadn't had that luxury.

"Yeah." Bowman sighed. "She wears it all the time, and it just kinda pulls me in, you know what I mean?" His small, marblelike eyes focused in on Kirk to see if the other man understood.

Kirk thought of the way her fragrance had gotten under his skin. The way it had drugged him when they made love. His tone remained emotionless. It didn't betray his thoughts. He'd trained himself that way. "I think I do."

Bowman looked at Kirk's eyes and seemed satisfied. "Anyway, do you have a thing going with her or not?"

Bowman suddenly made Kirk feel very, very old. He doubted that there was more than ten years, if that much, separating them. Ten years, and a world of experience. Bowman's most traumatic experience to date had probably been running out of ink during a test.

"Don't you think you should choose someone your own age to focus your attentions on?"

The sophomore frowned at the advice. "There's nobody else quite like her."

Kirk laughed shortly. "There I would have to agree with you."

The look on Bowman's face said that there had never been any doubt about it. Then his face fell several degrees, as the implication of Kirk's words hit him. "So you *are* seeing her?"

Kirk never discussed his private life with anyone. He didn't mean to begin with a complete stranger. But if he answered negatively, or not at all, Kirk had a feeling that Bowman's attentions toward Rachel would become more ardent. For Rachel's sake, he decided that the best course to take was to make Bowman believe that he and Rachel were involved.

"Yes."

If Bowman's face fell any farther, Kirk estimated, it would have to be physically lifted from the floor. "Damn, you're lucky."

Kirk's mouth curved. He wondered what it must feel like to be so simply enamored with someone. He almost envied Bowman. "I guess I am at that."

"Guess?" Bowman echoed the word incredulously as he stared at Kirk. "There's no *guessing* about it. If she were my girl—my woman," he hurriedly corrected, "there's absolutely nothing I wouldn't do for her. When those gorgeous blue eyes look at you..."

His voice trailed off, and he sighed deeply. Then, as if realizing how he sounded, Bowman clutched his textbooks to his chest and scrambled backward, in the direction of the door, giving the impression of a squirrel running to high ground at the first sign of a flash flood. His eyes never left Kirk's face. "If you change your mind, let her down easy. A lady like that doesn't deserve to be hurt."

"No." Kirk rose and tossed the price of the coffees, plus a tip, on the table. He nodded toward the man behind the counter. "She doesn't."

And she would be hurt, Kirk thought. If they remained involved any longer she would be hurt.

"Nice talking to you," Bowman blurted out as he reached the door. In a moment, he had darted through it, as if he were afraid that Kirk would follow him outside.

"You too," Kirk called after him.

Bowman turned and fairly beamed, reminding Kirk of the Cheshire cat.

* * *

How did he go about pulling out of a life he had always been a part of? Kirk wondered as he hurriedly walked to his car. How did he pull out, Kirk mused, especially when part of him really didn't want to?

The minivan was in the visitors' parking area, standing directly in front of the liberal arts building. All around him, students were rushing by, cutting across the parking lot to get to their next classes. Each represented a life in progress—a life, usually, just beginning to unfold. He found himself envying them, even though he wasn't that much older than most of them.

He *felt* older. A great deal older.

Kirk leaned against his van, watching a sea of humanity shuffle and reshuffle itself. Faces and bodies merged and separated. Nothing really registered, except for the conversation he'd had with Rachel's would-be suitor.

He had only given Rachel the condensed version of part of what had been troubling him. It had been the proverbial straw. Even so, she hadn't flinched, hadn't looked at him with condemning eyes, the way he would have expected. Hell, she hadn't even seen why he was torturing himself, why he was going through such agony over what he had done, or failed to do. With a few words, Rachel had absolved him.

Kirk shook his head in wonder as he thought about it now. Like a cleansing rain falling from the sky onto a dusty, dirty plain, she'd absolved him. Washing him clean.

Just like that, without so much as a moment's hesitation. Not because she didn't care, but because she did.

He wondered what it was that she saw in him that he didn't, and whether there was a chance that she could be right.

Kirk sighed as he felt stirrings within him. The same stirrings that seemed to occur every time he thought of her lately. How the hell did he walk away from a woman like that?

Quickly, he told himself. Before the scars that would be formed by their relationship went too deep into her heart.

He had a sinking feeling that they were already there, just waiting to bleed. Rachel was good for him—she always had been. But he was so different from her, and he feared that, in an everyday relationship, he would drag her down. In her extroverted way, she'd always been able to keep him from going down for the third time. She'd been his life jacket. It wouldn't be fair to inflict a lifetime of lifeguard duty. She needed support, too. She needed a partner, not an anchor.

God, this was getting complicated. He'd come home to heal, to renew himself, not to hurt anyone—especially not Rachel.

In the distance, someone yelled out a greeting, slicing through his thoughts. The greeting wasn't directed at him, but it brought his attention to the people around him. The hurrying clusters were beginning to thin out as students reached their destinations.

He'd never gone to college himself, though he had entertained the possibility for a while. He'd decided that he preferred to leap right into life. Besides, there'd been no money for college then. Money was no longer a problem, not that he cared about it. All he required was food and a place to stay.

Someone jostled him as they hurried by. It was a breathless young woman. She threw a hasty "Sorry" in her wake and ran to join another student just walking up the stairs to the building. Both of them had a glow of excitement about them. Maybe he'd missed something by not finding a way to attend college, he mused now.

Maybe...

An idea began to form, snowballing down the slope of his mind. He wasn't certain where it would ultimately land.

Kirk stared at the liberal arts building thoughtfully. What if he remained? Only for a few months, of course, but what if he decided to remain in Bedford?

He began to walk. Away from his car, and toward the three-story liberal arts building. It wouldn't hurt to entertain the possibility....

A wise man, he knew, always tested the integrity of his net before he even thought of leaping from a tall perch. And while Kirk considered himself far from wise, he wasn't exactly stupid, either.

The idea of leaping was beginning to show some merit.

* * *

An hour later, Kirk let himself into his house. There was a good four hours remaining before he had to pick up Ethan at school. He wanted to work on the album a little more. Perhaps even plan where he would take his next photographs for it.

His thoughts turned to Ethan. It was like leafing through a page of his own past. The boy had taken to photography with the same enthusiasm and gusto that he had. For Kirk it had been a way to find himself, to prove his self-worth, if only to himself. It was the only avenue of expressing himself that he had. And it afforded him a living that let him remain on the outside, without forming attachments. For Ethan, Kirk knew, it was just a wonderful hobby.

Perhaps, in time, it would be more.

Maybe when he picked the boy up at school, they'd drive around and take a few more photographs in the area.

The thought brought a smile to Kirk's lips as he pocketed his key. He was anxious to get into his studio and start working.

As he walked to the back of the house, Kirk passed his father's den. The door was still closed. Still locked. As were his feelings about what had taken place behind that door. He hadn't opened it since he'd arrived in Bedford. The time wasn't right. Maybe it never would be.

Kirk averted his eyes and continued walking.

It was getting to be a habit, Rachel thought, padding up the stairs to her room, not finding Ethan in the house on Saturday morning.

But it wasn't like the first time. Panic didn't set in anymore. Rachel knew exactly where to find her son when she wanted him. With Kirk. It was a wonderful, reassuring feeling, knowing that Ethan was in good hands. Knowing that Ethan was happy and getting along with someone who was very important to her.

This had all the makings, she mused dreamily as she slipped on her shorts, of a regular, bona fide fairy-tale ending.

If they could just work their way through the briars and the brambles to reach the castle. Something in Kirk's past, immediate or distant, had formed those briars, and until she knew, until he trusted her enough to tell her everything, she was just going to have to hack about blindly with her sword.

He had opened up a little to her in the coffee shop that morning, but not completely. She would have bet anything that what he'd said wasn't all that was weighing so heavily on his mind. There had to be something else that he wasn't telling her.

But he would. By and by, he would. She was relentless when she was after something, and this time she was after restoring Kirk's peace of mind.

She owed it to him for returning Ethan to her.

And because she loved him.

Dressed, Rachel pulled her hair through a plastic ponytail fastener and arranged it high atop her head. It nodded there, listing first to one side, then another, like a topknot.

A cursory survey in the mirror told her that she looked more like a eighteen-year-old girl than a twenty-seven-year-old woman, with a teaching position at a prestigious college and an eight-year-old son.

Eighteen.

She'd been eighteen the year that Kirk left Bedford.

Rachel pulled the fastener out of her hair and let it cascade to her shoulders again. Hastily she ran her fingers through it. She didn't want to be reminded of that time. Didn't want to think about the fact that he might be leaving again.

Rachel wanted Kirk to remain in Bedford more than she had wanted anything in a long time. She knew that if he just opened up, if he just talked things through with her the way he had in the old days, she could help alleviate the pain for him. Then he'd stay. She just knew it.

With a sigh, she padded down the carpeted stairs in her bare feet. Forgoing shoes, she went straight out the front door. She'd just check on Ethan and then get breakfast going.

Outside the first thing she saw was Cameron's maroon four-by-four pulling up in her driveway. Grinning, she postponed her trip to Kirk's and waited until Cameron cut off the engine.

"You're just in time," she called out to him as she approached his vehicle.

"In time for what?" He looked at his sister cautiously as he pulled up the hand brake.

"To cook breakfast. I believe you're behind by about a dozen times." Since he dropped by so often, they'd made a habit of taking turns cooking. Ability and willingness, however, usually placed the ball—and the pan—in Rachel's court.

Cameron got out. Rachel noticed that he was wearing his oldest clothes. The ones he favored when he went camping. Had he just stopped on his way to the campgrounds?

"No time for breakfast," he told her, confirming her suspicions. He looked around the driveway and the immediate area. "Where's Ethan?"

"Where he always is lately." She nodded toward the house next door. "With Kirk." When Cameron began to head in that direction, she quickly matched her stride to her brother's. "I was just going over there to see if he was wearing out his welcome." She passed one hand over the other in an imitation of something taking off. "It seems that every weekend at dawn's first light he's over there like a streak."

Her words made him stop on Kirk's doorstep. "Then maybe he won't want to."

She frowned, trying to make sense out of Cameron's verbal shorthand. "Won't want to what?"

Things had been progressing so well with Ethan the last few weeks, Cameron was eager to get back on his old footing with his nephew. "I came over to borrow him."

Rachel rocked on the balls of her feet, still sorting through the words. "You want to borrow my son? Like a cup of sugar?"

He grinned, realizing he had gotten ahead of himself. "Like a camper. I want to take him on a camping trip. Some of the guys at the precinct are getting together this morning. They're taking their sons and going up to the San Gabriel Mountains for the long holiday weekend." He nodded at the closed door. "I thought that maybe Ethan might like to go. It's been a while since we last went camping together."

Before divorce proceedings and their repercussions had gotten under way, Cameron and Ethan had gone camping all the time. Cameron had known that Don, wallowing in self-pity, made little time for his son. Camping had been Cameron's way of attempting to rebuild Ethan's self-esteem. Ethan had al-

ways looked forward to the trips. It hadn't been until everything began falling apart that Ethan began turning down
Cameron's invitations.

Rachel grinned. "Now would be a good time to start going
again."

She knocked on Kirk's front door. When there was no answer, she automatically tried the doorknob. The door wasn't
locked.

Cameron raised a brow as he followed Rachel inside. "I
didn't think it was necessary, but maybe I should give Kirk my
standard Bedford Police Department lecture about locking his
doors."

"Don't. You'd only manage to put me to sleep." Kirk
grinned as he walked into the living room from the kitchen. The
sounds of voices had drawn him. Ethan shadowed his every
step. "What brings you sneaking around? Slow day for
crime?"

"You know we have no crime in Bedford. It's not allowed.
Like in Camelot." Cameron looked at his nephew. "I thought
maybe Ethan would like to go camping."

Ethan grinned. "When?"

Cameron was immensely encouraged by the look that sprang
into Ethan's eyes. "Now. As soon as you can get your stuff together."

The eagerness on Ethan's face was momentarily tempered as
he looked at Kirk. He was obviously torn. Kirk decided to set
the boy at ease.

"Sounds like a good opportunity to take some unique photographs, if you ask me."

Hope sprang up, usurping indecision. Ethan looked from
Cameron to Kirk. "Are you coming, too?"

It had been years since he'd gone camping. He was tempted,
but he knew that if he came along, it would be an intrusion on
the bond that Cameron was trying to reconstruct with Ethan.

"No." He smiled. "But I can let you take my camera with
you."

Ethan's eyes grew wide as he realized what Kirk was telling
him. "The one I used to take the picture of the cow?" Kirk

nodded. "Wow." Reverence and awe shimmered in the single word. "I promise I'll take extraspecial good care of it."

Kirk rested a supportive hand on the boy's shoulder. "I knew you would, or I wouldn't have offered it."

Cameron clapped his wide hands together, signaling an end to the discussion. "Okay, it's settled. Let's get your stuff together, Ethan."

Rachel cleared her throat loudly. Three sets of eyes turned in her direction. "I hate to interrupt all this male bonding, but aren't you all forgetting something?"

Kirk and Cameron exchanged looks. Cameron shrugged his shoulders for Ethan's benefit, showing his bewilderment.

Ethan's face puckered up as he attempted to puzzle his mother's words out. "What?"

She ran her hand over his hair. "Like asking for permission, maybe?"

Ethan blew out a breath. "Oh, yeah, right." He raised his brows hopefully. "Can I, Mom?"

She laughed and shook her head. "How can I turn down such a heartfelt plea?" She looked at Cameron as a little zip of anxiety raised its head. "You promise you'll watch him?"

"Like a hawk." He winked at Ethan, then looked at his sister. "Don't I always?"

"It's been a while," she reminded him. She turned toward Ethan. "C'mon, let's get your gear together."

She slipped her arm around his shoulders. He was growing up, she thought. Faster than she was prepared to accept. But at the same time, along with the bittersweet pang, she felt a wave of pride. She glanced over her shoulder at Cameron.

"We'll meet you out front in fifteen minutes," she promised.

Ethan hurried ahead of her, impatience and eagerness making him do double time. He was down the driveway before she had made it to the front door.

"Nice to see him back to normal again," Cameron commented as he and Kirk slowly walked out behind Rachel. He watched his sister hurry after Ethan. "Rachel gives you all the credit, you know. She says it's like a miracle." Cameron smiled at his best friend. "I guess it is."

Kirk absently caressed the camera he'd picked up from the coffee table and intended to entrust to Ethan. "The word *miracle* is being greatly devalued. He just needed to unload on a stranger."

"Stranger?" Cameron laughed at the idea. Kirk was such an integrated part of his life, Cameron couldn't imagine him in that role. "He's practically adopted you."

Kirk shrugged as he leaned against Cameron's car, waiting for Ethan to reappear. "Things'll settle down after I leave."

Cameron slanted a look at Kirk. He wasn't bandying words about. He was serious. Cameron frowned. "You're leaving?"

In his mind, he'd packed up a dozen times, for everyone's good. His bags still stood by his bed, empty. But it was just a matter of time. "Eventually."

Cameron felt a sadness seeping through him. He always enjoyed Kirk's company. But it wasn't his own reaction he was concerned about. "Does Rachel know?"

There was nothing accusing in Cameron's tone. Why, then, Kirk thought, did guilt seem to well up in his chest? "My going was never in doubt."

Cameron regarded him thoughtfully. "Oh, I don't now. Rachel probably thought the same thing I did. That maybe this time you'd settle down here, or at least make it your home base."

Maybe, just maybe, that had been in the back of his mind, as well. Kirk drew in a breath and said nothing.

"Would it be so bad," Cameron asked quietly, "having a home to come back to?"

Kirk looked over his shoulder at the house he'd been raised in. The house he'd escaped from, only to return, searching for peace.

"This was never my home, Cameron."

Cameron laid a hand on his friend's arm, drawing his attention back. "Home isn't always a place. Sometimes it's a feeling. Or people."

He laughed dryly. "You're beginning to sound like Rachel."

Cameron raised a brow at his friend's use of Rachel's name. "Why not? I taught her everything she knows." He looked away for a moment, weighting his words. "Kirk, maybe it's none of my business..."

Maybe it was time he started facing things that had lurked in shadows for too long. "Ask."

"Are you sleeping with my sister?"

It wasn't what he'd expected Cameron to ask. Kirk looked at him, surprise and a hint of unease mingling within him. "What makes you think that?"

"Body language. And I saw the way you two looked at each other."

He would have answered any question that Cameron asked him—except that one. It wasn't his answer to give. He wasn't the only one involved. "Maybe that's something you should ask her."

Cameron paused for a moment. "I don't have to. You just gave me my answer."

Kirk felt awkwardness rise up between them in a way it never had before, not even when they had first met. So where did that put them? On opposite sides?

He looked at Cameron, wondering why he wasn't saying anything. "So now what? Are you going to tell me to stay out of her life? Because if you are, I've already made up my mind about that."

Cameron wondered how two people could be as close as he and Kirk, and still miss a call like that. "To stay in it, I hope."

Kirk looked at Cameron incredulously. "You're not angry about this?"

"Only if you hurt her," Cameron answered honestly. If he could have handpicked someone to love his sister, it would have been Kirk. "Hey, this isn't some grade B movie where I suddenly turn on you and beat you to a pulp behind the barn."

Kirk felt his mouth curving in a relieved smile. He would have hated losing Cameron as a friend. "As if you could—"

"You'd be surprised what they taught me at the police academy." Cameron grew serious. "I always thought the two of you would have wound up together if you hadn't left Bedford." He voiced out loud what he had thought a hundred times in the last few years. "Maybe if you hadn't left, Rachel would never have fallen for Don."

The same thing had occurred to Kirk since he'd made love with her. "Great, more guilt. Just what I need."

"Nothing to feel guilty about. Things happen. Mistakes get made. The main thing is not to let them take over your life."

Cameron couldn't begin to understand what he was wrestling with, Kirk thought. Neither could Rachel. He didn't want to ruin her life by staying. "I'm a loner, Cameron."

"You only think you are. Everyone needs someone."

Kirk looked at him skeptically. "Great advice from a bachelor."

"Hey, just because I'm not married, that doesn't mean I'm alone."

Kirk thought of their high school days. "Still maintaining an active social life?"

"Active enough, but I'm not talking about that. I have a terrific sister, a nephew who's finally coming around, and a great best friend." His eyes held Kirk's. "That's not being alone in my book."

Kirk knew what Cameron was saying, and resisted being won over. He was doing this for Rachel's sake. "Look, I taught myself a long time ago not to need anyone. People disappoint you."

"Rachel wouldn't."

Kirk looked at him, but said nothing.

"Your parents disappointed you." Rachel hadn't shared Kirk's confidence with him, but it didn't take a great stretch of the imagination to guess that much. "Are you going to let that color the rest of your life?" For the first time in his recollection, Cameron felt himself losing his temper with his friend. "Because if you do, then you've given them a hell of a victory over your spirit. And disappointed a fantastic woman in the process."

Rachel approached them just in time to hear the last sentence. "Who's a fantastic woman?"

"You are," Cameron told her easily, brushing a kiss to her temple. His manner gave no indication of the intensity of the conversation he and Kirk had just had.

Rachel grinned. "It only took him twenty-seven years to realize that," she confided to Kirk. Behind her, Ethan deposited his sleeping bag and a cloth traveling case stuffed with items he'd need for the trip. Rachel turned around to give her son one last round of instructions. "All right, you promise not to wander off or do anything silly?"

Ethan rolled his eyes, embarrassed. "Mom, I'm eight years old."

"My point exactly. Hey." Rachel cupped his chin affectionately in her hand. "Moms worry. It's part of our job description." She dropped her hand and regarded him thoughtfully. "Tell you what, you make sure to keep an eye on your uncle. Don't let him wander off, either. Deal?"

Ethan slanted a look toward his uncle and grinned. "Deal."

Kirk draped the camera's strap around Ethan's neck and pressed three rolls of film into his hands. "Bring me back some great photos. Something unique."

King Arthur sending off Sir Galahad to fetch the Holy Grail couldn't have had a more dedicated minion. "You bet!"

Rachel suppressed a smile and secretly blessed both Kirk and Cameron for her happiness.

Chapter 15

Issuing another barrage of instructions, Rachel deposited her son beside her brother in the four-by-four. Locking the passenger door, she stood back beside Kirk.

"God, just look at him." She gestured at Ethan, feeling so happy that tears were beginning to form. "He's grinning from ear to ear."

Kirk slipped his arm around her, noticing how naturally it came. "Why shouldn't he be? He doesn't have to comb his hair or brush his teeth or take a shower for two whole days. Little boys like being dirty."

Waving, Rachel smiled, catching Kirk in a contradiction. "You didn't, as I recall."

Kirk maintained a mild expression. "That's because I was always afraid of tearing my clothes." He waved back at Ethan as the boy twisted around in his seat, slicing the air madly with his hand.

"Sounds exceedingly conscientious." Rachel moved into the street to watch the four-by-four disappear around the corner.

"Not really. I just didn't like getting hit."

Rachel turned and looked at Kirk. She was tempted to step through the door Kirk had inadvertently opened, but she thought better of it. She wanted to spend the day with him. If she pursued the matter he'd let slip, she might find herself alone. She'd ask him about it later.

Rachel hooked her thumbs in her belt loops and gave Kirk a look of studied innocence. It was still quiet. The neighborhood hadn't fully awakened yet. Only the birds were out, screeching angrily at one another. Somewhere in the distance, Rachel heard the sharp cry of a cat. Probably out looking for breakfast, she thought.

Kirk turned away from the street, and Rachel followed him to his driveway. "I guess this leaves me with a free weekend."

Somewhere far away, an alarm went off, calling for a retreat. Kirk ignored it, giving in to other feelings. "No papers to grade?"

Rachel thought of the mountain of tests she'd finally plowed through and returned. Her sigh of relief was automatic.

"Mercifully, no." She looked at him brightly. "Not even a lesson plan to wrestle with." She waited for him to say something. When he didn't, she prodded him. "How about you?"

He opened the front door and went inside. He knew that no invitation was necessary. Rachel was right behind him. "No wrestling with lesson plans for me, either."

He was deliberately being obtuse. She suddenly had a free weekend, and she wanted to spend it with him. "You know what I mean. Do you have anything planned?" Playing along, she enunciated each word carefully.

Kirk thought of teasing her a little longer, then decided against it. He dropped down on the sofa. It was a hard, uncomfortable piece of furniture that did nothing to accommodate the body. Somehow it seemed an appropriate sofa for his parents to have chosen.

"No, it seems that I don't. My assistant and one of my two best friends just drove off and left me alone for the weekend."

The smile began in her eyes and worked its way over her face. "Funny, I could almost say the same thing."

She moved around the living room slowly, trying to discover something about it that made her feel at home. There was nothing. It was as if she could feel the vibrations of past discord here.

She blocked them out as she turned toward Kirk. "What do you say we join forces and try to figure out what to do with ourselves until they return?"

Kirk knew what he wanted to do. What he shouldn't do. Like a stone rolling down a hill, he felt as if he had no control over his fate.

When she sat down beside him, he felt that control slipping further away. Bowman was right about her perfume. It was heady stuff. "I have a good idea."

Rachel shifted closer, drawn there by a force that was far stronger than she. "You tell me your idea, I'll tell you if it's good."

He'd never been noble before. It wasn't easy now, not when he wanted her so much that everything within him ached. "That's just the point. It isn't. Not for y—"

She covered his lips with her fingers, stilling them. "Nope, I absolutely refuse to get into another discussion on that subject." Deliberately attempting to keep things light, Rachel rose again. Needing an edge, she fell back on the familiar. "Tell you what." She looked toward his kitchen. "Why don't I make breakfast?"

He didn't want her to think that she had to cook for him all the time. He'd only been back a little over a month, and half his meals had been at her table. Fair was fair. "I could try my hand at it, if you like."

She raised a brow and looked at him doubtfully. "Define 'try.'"

She made him laugh. She always could.

His coffee could double for asphalt filler, and his fried eggs could be mistaken for coasters. He cooked only as a last resort. "Admittedly, I don't do it very often."

She was very good at picking up what wasn't being said. "Translation—you also don't do it very well." She turned on her heel and began heading for the kitchen. "You've convinced me. I'd rather slave a little over a stove than have my stomach pumped."

He pretended to take exception to her assumption as he followed her. "It's not that bad. I'm still alive."

She opened his pantry and decided that it was too much to hope that he had bought a box of pancake mix. She glanced at him over her shoulder, a superior lift to her brow. "I noticed that you had dropped a few pounds or so when you first returned to town. Is that a testimonial to your abilities?"

It was a testimonial to the fact that some days the business of survival took priority over everything else and he forgot to eat. Other days there wasn't anything to be had. It wasn't as if there were a grocery store on every other corner on the beat he had maintained.

"I did a lot of running," he reminded her. He banished the serious thought, preferring, instead, to indulge himself and simply tease her. "But if you're volunteering . . ."

"Yeah, right, volunteering." She closed the pantry door and sighed. She could always make eggs, she thought, provided he had any. "It's like the army. You volunteer or suffer the consequences."

Anticipating the worst, she opened the refrigerator, and was pleasantly surprised. Success. He had a carton of eggs. Probably the same ones he'd had four weeks ago, she guessed.

Rachel took the carton out and placed it on the counter. "I'm not much on consequences," she concluded. She saw the serious look enter his eye. Wrong choice of words, she told herself. "Except in some cases."

Being alone with her would only lead to one thing. He knew that. And he knew that to indulge himself like this wasn't right. Conscience struggled with need.

"Rachel . . ."

She heard the beginnings of a dismissal in his voice. It was something she wasn't accustomed to hearing from him. Something she feared.

"Why don't you go back to calling me Funny Face for the time being?" She purposely kept her back to him as she hunted around in the cabinet for a pan. "I think you're more at ease when you think of me that way."

He'd meant to keep the length of the kitchen between them. Or at least the counter. How they both came to be on the same side, he had no idea. Just as he didn't know how he managed to tangle his fingers in her hair, savoring the silky feel of it.

"I don't think I'm at ease around you at all."

"Oh?" It wasn't easy keeping the anticipation from her voice. It was already reaching out and engulfing the rest of her. "Is that a good observation or a bad one?"

A smile formed without thought. "I'm trying to make up my mind about that."

"It shouldn't take that much of an effort." She abandoned the pan she'd just uncovered. The counter was at her back, and Rachel used it to brace herself as she looked up into his eyes. And felt herself getting lost. "If I excite you, that's good. If I make you uncomfortable, that's bad."

"You excite me…" It was a poor word to use to describe the upheavals that she was creating within him.

Rachel licked her bottom lip, her eyes never leaving his. "So far, so good."

He knew that touching her was his downfall, yet there he was, touching. It was as if he had no say in it, as if all the control he'd exercised all these years had snapped like so many brittle twigs. "And you make me feel uncomfortable with myself."

She wanted just to enjoy what he was doing to her, yet she knew she had to understand what was going on in his head, as well as his heart. And she hadn't a clue. Not anymore. "Now you've lost me."

Ever so slowly, he brushed the hair from her face, his palm caressing her cheek. "I shouldn't be having these feelings about you."

Yes, yes, you should. Her mouth was dry as she asked, "Why?"

It was so hard to explain, to put into words. They were just feelings, moving through him like dark rain clouds. "Because I grew up with you."

It became a little clearer to her. Or at least she thought it did. Rachel twined her arms around his neck. "I'm not your sister."

"I treated you that way." And it felt as if he were trading in one set of feelings for another. He wasn't certain he wanted to do that. To lose his friend and gain a lover.

And yet he couldn't stand being without her.

"But I'm *not* your sister," Rachel repeated, her voice a shade firmer. Didn't he see? They were just adding another dimension, another layer, to what already was. "I'm your friend, Callaghan. We began as friends." And now they could be so much more, if only he'd let them be. "I can't think of a better basis for a love affair, can you?"

He released her and, with a sigh, moved away. He couldn't think properly when she was so close. Couldn't be held responsible for his own actions. "That's all it can be, Rachel. An affair. It can't be permanent."

If she was to believe him, it would hurt too much. But she knew that *he* believed what he was saying. Or wanted to. Did permanence frighten him so much? Or was it the fear of risking his heart that made him refuse what she offered?

"I said no strings," she said slowly. "But, speaking purely hypothetically, why not? Why not something permanent?"

She knew that he hungered for the comforting warmth of home and hearth. There could be no other reason why he had blended in so well with her family all those years he was growing up. No other reason, she thought now, why he had returned. He'd come back to her and to Cameron, the only real family he'd ever known. She wanted to give him a different family now. She wanted to give him a wife and a son, in one neat package.

Her eyes narrowed as she looked at him. She could sense what was on his mind. "You're not going to give me that garbage about you not wanting to mess up my life, are you?"

How could he make her see that he was pushing her away for her own good? "It's not garbage."

"No," she agreed, "it's not." Her mouth hardened. "I'd use a stronger word, but I wouldn't want to shock you."

And then she softened. Kirk had been battered about emotionally all through his life. It was obvious that he'd come to expect nothing good to enter his life. Well, he had a surprise coming. She wasn't about to give up, easily or otherwise.

"When will you get it through your head that you are very, very good for me?"

He thought of the other night, and a bittersweet yearning slashed through him like the jagged edge of a thunderbolt. "Anyone can make love to you."

"I wasn't referring to that, and even then, you're wrong." It wasn't his way to ask, but she wanted him to know. "It's been a very small club. You're the second." Regret mingled with love. If she was giving away secrets, so be it. It was past the time for secrets. "And you should have been the first. I always wanted you to be the first. And the only."

The look in her eyes made him understand more than she could ever have hoped to. It had been so long since he had even thought of being loved. Or of loving. He'd convinced himself that he could do just fine without it. And now, here she was, turning everything on its head. "Oh, God, Rachel, you make this so damn hard for me."

She laced her hand through his. "I'm hoping to make it impossible for you." Her eyes shone with amusement. "But that's just my perverse nature." She glanced at the carton on the counter. "What do you say we have breakfast later?"

The only thing he was hungry for was her. "I say it's the best suggestion you've made so far."

Rachel returned the carton back on the first shelf in the refrigerator. It had the entire space to itself. The man had no concept of shopping.

She turned, a mischievous smile outlining her lips. "Wait. The morning is still young. I can come up with more good ideas."

As if to show him what she meant, Rachel nipped the bottom of his ear. The responding quickening of breath had her heart and pulse accelerating.

The familiar became the unique as they took one another down the same path, though by a different route.

Rachel hardly remembered leaving the kitchen. It was almost as if they suddenly appeared in the living room, their hands hot upon each other, their mouths greedy for all the wonderful tangy flavors that waited for them. That were theirs for the asking.

It would always be this way, she thought as she felt his hands searing through her clothing, branding her. The curtain of fire that he created with each pass of his hand, each touch of his mouth, threatened to consume her. With Kirk it would always be familiar, yet always be different. And it would always be wondrous.

She was planning on forever with a man who wanted to flee. Rachel would have thought it ironic, if she'd been able to think at all.

All she knew was what lay immediately ahead.

And knowing what was waiting for her, the splendid surge, the awesome power and the overwhelming thrill, Rachel desperately wanted to race toward it. Toward the end that would take her breath away to wipe away her mind.

Yet she wanted to savor it, to cling to this incredible sensation of something building to an eventual explosion, like steam building in an old-fashioned engine.

The anticipation was driving her crazy.

Rachel trembled, trying to stand perfectly still, as Kirk slipped her blouse from her shoulders.

God, but she was beautiful, Kirk thought, slipping her blouse from her shoulders. Her skin as soft as a rose petal. He wanted to rake his hands over her, to steep himself in the wonder of it, of her. With supreme control, he forced himself to go slowly. He owed it to her, if not to himself.

The bra was fastened between her breasts. One fingertip under the tab, he moved it forward, and it gave way. Slowly, painfully slowly, his eyes on hers, awed by the smoky desire he saw there, he coaxed the material from the swell of her breasts. Freed, they spilled into his cupped hands. He felt her tremble, felt her desire.

Kirk was filled with wonder at his own reaction. For him, sex had always been fast and hard, like firecrackers going off on the Fourth of July. There had never been any tenderness to denote its existence. No lasting aura when it was done. There had never been any desire to hold, to cherish, to love.

There was now.

He didn't know what to do about it, and it frightened the hell out of him. He tried to downplay it, and his feelings. His thumbs hooked on to the waistband of her shorts and slowly

moved them down her hips. "I never knew undressing someone could be such an erotic experience."

Unable to hold back, she all but tore his shirt from him. She
pressed a warm kiss to his shoulder and felt the muscle there
tense beneath her lips. She was getting to him, she thought in
triumph.

But no more than he was getting to her.

"Maybe you've been undressing the wrong women." The low
whisper danced along his tanned skin.

He dragged her mouth to his, tangling his hands in her hair.
One kiss flowed into another as his mouth slanted over and over
again on hers. Her lungs were frantic for air. Her body was
frantic for him.

Needing a moment, he moved his head back to look at her.
"There's never been a right woman, until you."

Rachel wanted to cry, to press his words to her breast and
cling to them, taking them as an assurance that he would stay.
But she knew, even in the wild haze that he created, that if she
did, there might only be disappointment waiting for her down
the line.

This was not about disappointments, this was about enjoying him. Later would come all too soon, and it would have to
take care of itself.

For now, she had this moment, and Kirk.

Naked, Rachel shivered. Behind Kirk she could see the faded
white curtains moving in the breeze, like dancers moving to an
unheard melody. She could feel goose bumps rising.

"Your house is drafty."

It always had been. Especially in the winter, even with all the
windows closed, he would feel slivers of wind pass through.

He framed her face and smiled into it. "This isn't the time to
adjourn to yours."

"No." She cleaved her body even closer to his. "That's a hint
for you to keep me warm."

She made him want to smile, to laugh, even though he knew
it was wrong. Even though he knew they'd both regret it—he
because it was over, she because it had happened at all. "You
mean I'm not?"

She wanted to say something flippant, something humorous, but urgency filled her voice. And her body. "Faster, Kirk, faster. I need you now."

He could hold back only so long.

"Funny you should mention that." His mouth covered hers, and the playfulness faded, to be replaced by a burning desire that had him scrambling inside to keep up.

She was like liquid fire in his hands, like captured starlight. Like magic. Everything that had always eluded him.

He caressed and possessed, touched and molded. Rachel twisted and turned, reaching up and endeavoring to press every moment into the pages of her mind.

For later.

Kirk slid his hand over her lower abdomen again and again, lower and lower, gently massaging her until she parted her legs for him. His fingers extended into the velvet softness that welcomed him. Surprised, Rachel gasped and bit her lower lip. He found it hopelessly erotic. He caressed her, driving her swiftly up to a fever pitch, even though his movements were slow, measured.

Rachel's eyes, half closed, flew open as she grasped fistfuls of carpet. With a muffled cry, she crested and then floated to earth, only to have him begin again.

She wanted to scream, "More." She wanted to beg him to stop as the agonizing ecstasy racked her body over and over again.

Her breathing ragged, she combined all her feelings into one word.

"Kirk."

He heard her entreaty, and it humbled him. Her body was slick with sweat as he slid his own over it. Her perspiration dampened his skin and aroused him to a plateau from which there could be only one descent.

When he entered her, an impossible sensation filled him. It was like coming home.

Eager for her, Kirk slid his hands under her hips. He drew her even closer to him than she was. As they began to rock, the tempo quickening, they raced to a place they had discovered together.

Paradise.

Kirk felt his heart pounding against hers, sealing them together, as if they were two halves of a whole.

An eternity later, as the haze parted to admit some sort of thought, Kirk began to shift away from her. He felt annoyed that his desire had exploded so quickly. He hadn't even taken her to bed. They'd made love on the living room floor, like two adolescents.

Maybe, he thought, in a way they were. She certainly made him feel like a kid, not like the burned-out shell of a man he'd been when he returned.

"No, not yet," she protested as he began to move aside. She locked her arms around his neck. "I want to feel you against me just a little while longer."

He shook his head, sliding his body until he was to her left. "I'm too heavy for you."

"You'd be surprised how strong I can be." She curled against him, as if the space there had been created with her in mind.

As if God knew that was where she belonged, he thought. The next moment, he upbraided himself for letting his mind drift to such nonsense. But the very fact that it did surprised him. She was responsible for that, for the tiny notions of hope that insisted on springing up in him. She was responsible for that, and for every good moment he'd ever had.

Rachel trailed her hand slowly along his chest, delighting in the light sprinkling of hair there. "I still don't know what your room looks like."

He gave up trying to shore up his defenses and gathered her against him. He'd crossed this floor a hundred times in his lifetime. A thousand times. It had never felt like heaven before.

"It's nothing special, believe me." He kissed her temple, refusing to think of consequences. Of tomorrow. "We can visit it later."

He was going to make love to her again, she thought, joy leaping up within her. It didn't matter where. "Sounds good to me. Is that where you sleep now, or did you take over your parents' room, like me?"

He could never sleep in his parents' room. He'd heard too many arguments emerging from there. "No. I still sleep in my old room."

His voice was filled with emotions he was denying.

And she heard them all. "Kirk..."

He looked at her knowingly. "You want to ask questions."

"Yes."

He didn't want to spoil the moment, the day. Talking about his parents could only do that. "Leave it alone, Funny Face."

This time, she pushed. "I can't. It concerns you. And I think you need to let it out. Like Ethan."

He shook his head. She was comparing apples and oranges. "I'm not a little boy, Rachel."

"But you were when you were hurt," she insisted. He couldn't keep sweeping this way. They had to face it in order to get past it. If the child was father to the man, she was certain that his past was what was immobilizing him emotionally now.

He looked over her head toward the curtains. They were still moving lightly, gracefully, in the wind. "You seem to think you have all the pieces."

She had the pieces, but she didn't know how they fit together.

"I want to hear it from you." She waited, hoping, but Kirk said nothing. Rachel tried again. "I noticed you still didn't open the door to your father's den." She knew that Kirk's mother had discovered her husband there. Edgar Callaghan had been found slumped over at his desk, a victim of a heart attack.

"I don't have any reason to go in." He had no desire to walk in there, where he had stood, a penitent child waiting to be punished for trespasses, real and imagined. His father had always found reasons to punish him, to make him see how unlovable he was. When he was very young, Kirk had waited for his mother to come rescue him. He'd been seven when he realized that she was never going to shield him from his father's wrath.

Rachel sat up. Her tousled hair spilled out onto her shoulder. As she leaned toward him, a few strands covered his chest. She placed her hand on it.

"Is it because he died there?" she asked softly. "Is it because you can't deal with his death?"

Kirk blew out a breath, struck by the absurdity of the idea.

"Hardly. In a way, his death was a relief." His father had hovered over his life like a threatening force. Kirk paused, sorting, struggling. "All right, you want to know? I don't want to go in because it's *his* room, and he made my life a living hell. He was a drunk, Rachel, a common, ordinary, lying-down-in-the-gutter drunk. And for half my life I was afraid that someone would find out and ridicule me because of it."

He'd even been afraid of letting her and Cameron find out. It had been a secret that burned in his breast during all the years they had known each other.

His reasoning mystified her. "Why? It's not your fault your father drank."

She was wrong. He'd grown up thinking that it *was* his fault that his father drank, that somehow he had failed his father. If he had just been good enough, smart enough, his father wouldn't have turned to a bottle to make him feel good.

But it was far too complicated a subject for a Saturday morning. Kirk was having too much difficulty dealing with the feelings he was having about Rachel to attempt to dredge up the past, as well.

He shrugged it off as best he could. "I hated him for it, and hated myself for feeling that way." He stumbled a little. Somehow she always managed to draw more out of him than he wanted to give. "Part of me felt that if I could somehow reach him . . ."

She was angry with him for even contemplating that. "You were a child. What was a child supposed to do?"

He lifted a shoulder and let it drop, frustrated. "Something."

She feathered her hand along his shoulder. "You expect too much of yourself. You're only human." She laughed softly, then lightly skimmed her lips along his chest. She was delighted when he fell back and pulled her on top of him. "Magnificently so, but only human."

Helpless, aroused, he could only laugh. "You're good for me, Rachel."

She shifted slowly along his body and felt his desire hardening. Rachel raised her chin, triumph in her eyes. "I always knew that."

He threaded his hands through her hair. "No, really."

"Why?" She cocked her head, curious. "Because I always believed in you?"

Kirk considered that. "Yes, I guess there's that, too. No one else did."

He was too quick to dismiss himself. "Cameron did. And my parents," she reminded him.

Her words stirred distant memories. "You have some pretty special parents."

She loved her parents dearly. And never more than when they were kind to Kirk. "I know. They're as proud of you as if you were their own."

He looked at her, completely stunned. "Proud?"

She nodded. For the moment, she just laced her hands together on his chest and rested her chin there, content to look up into his eyes.

"Whenever they see one of your photographs in the newspaper or a magazine." Before he could ask, she added, "I make sure they receive a steady supply. They ask about you, you know."

She had a knack for making him feel good, he thought, when he least expected it. "Give them my love."

"You can give it to them yourself." She saw wariness enter his eyes. "They're coming up for a visit in July."

"July." It seemed a hundred years away. "I don't know where I'll be in July."

July was less than two months away. She'd find a way to make him stay. "Funny, I do."

As comfortable as all this was, it was temporary. He'd made up his mind about that. She had to be stopped before she got carried away. Rachel had a great penchant for getting carried away.

"Rachel, I said not to make plans."

She was undaunted, or appeared to be. Inside, she felt as if she were holding on to a rope with soapy hands. "You say a lot of things. I filter out what's important, the rest I discard." She winked. "It's a secret we women have when dealing with men."

He tried again, thinking of the house, of his father, of the way he felt about things. "Rachel, there's a lot for me to sort through...."

"I know." Her smile was extremely encouraging. "And with two it'll go faster."

He couldn't let her in any farther than he already had. Even that was way too much. "I have to do it on my own."

"Maybe," she conceded skeptically, "but you also have to be coaxed and prodded to do it. That's where I come in."

Kirk arched a brow, amused and wary at the same time. Amusement was winning out. "To coax."

"And prod," she added cheerfully, relieved that she could tease him.

"Like now?"

She smiled. "You catch on fast, Callaghan."

If things were different, if he were someone else, he could go on making love with her forever. For just a little while, he could pretend that he was. "I don't need to be coaxed and prodded about that."

Contentment and anticipation curled through her like smoke lazily emerging from a chimney on a cold winter's morning. "Even better."

Chapter 16

Kirk watched Rachel clear away the remnants of their lunch from the table. Even this simple act filled him with a sense of well-being. It had, he knew, been a weekend that he would always remember. It had been an island of time filled with Rachel and nothing else. No deadlines to meet, no bullets to dodge, no enemy soldiers to elude or attempt to fool.

And no haunting dreams.

That, he felt, was what was unique about this weekend. His nightmares weren't a part of it. They hadn't intruded into his space, into his mind, at all. They'd been part of his life for so long that their absence seemed strange. He could keep things bottled up within him while he was awake. But when he was asleep, all the horror that he carried around with him would emerge. Scenes from his childhood would merge with pieces of the various conflicts he'd witnessed abroad, filling him with dread.

Since he'd returned, the number of nightmares had diminished, but not disappeared. They hung on like a wound that refused to completely heal. It seemed that almost every time he closed his eyes they would come.

But for two nights, while Rachel slept curled up beside him, he'd dreamed of nothing.

Or of her.

He observed her now as he nursed a beer, an empty pizza box lying next to his elbow. Just watching her rinse off a couple of plates and put them away seemed like watching a finely crafted piece of theater.

He was trying to absorb it all, to record it so that he could play it back at will.

And be comforted.

She filled him like sweet mountain air, like the taste of freedom the time he'd made it across the border of one of those newly created countries to his own crew. Unexpected fighting had erupted in the tiny village he'd been photographing. It was a village that had, until that moment, been populated with people content to live out their lives without caring who sat in the seat of power, who governed them.

Peace and tranquillity had been blown up by men whose nationalistic pride clashed. The country had splintered in two, and he had been forced to flee for his life. The momentary exhilaration that had filled him when he reached the safe house had been incredible.

She was like that. She was freedom. Freedom from his past, freedom from all the hellish demons that pursued him. In her arms, he forgot them, forgot everything except her. She was all that had ever been good or clean or precious in his life.

And all that ever would be good.

Which was why he knew that this weekend couldn't have a mate. It would remain a single jewel in his mind, to be treasured on lonely nights. And lonely days. He was going to have to leave Bedford.

He was going to have to leave Rachel.

To stay would be to repay a kindness with treachery, with thievery. She had given herself to him willingly. Her sweetness, her passion, had provided a beacon for him in a dark, rough sea.

He had nothing to give her in return.

He certainly didn't have the kind of love to give her that she deserved. His ability to love had been stolen from him a long time ago. The untapped supply of love that had flowed in his young veins had been taken from him. It had become drier than dust and been blown away, never having been used.

Rachel threw away the empty box. It amazed her how they'd managed to consume such a large pizza with no trouble at all.

Love made you hungry, she thought with a smile. They'd made love over and over again these past two days. She'd made him laugh like the old days. She was filled to the brim with hope, with happiness.

It was almost sinful to feel this wonderful. She felt giddy, capable of hugging the whole world. Rachel sat down in the chair opposite Kirk, her knee brushing his. "You know, I feel guilty."

Now there was an emotion he'd never associated with her. "Guilty?"

She nodded as she placed her hand over his. Such a small gesture, such an infinite feeling of comfort. "Being so happy without Ethan." She bit her lip and then laughed. "Oh, I miss him, but I'm so glad we had this time together."

Rachel sighed as she tilted back her chair, feeling very, very young, and yet womanly at the same time. He'd done that for her. He'd made her feel indescribably marvelous, able to leap tall buildings in a single bound. Able to leap the small wall around his heart.

"Personally, I think three-day weekends are terrific. We should pass national legislation and have them every week." Rachel rose and rounded the table until she stood beside him. She could feel him mentally peeling away her clothing until there was nothing there.

Her heart full, Rachel smiled down into his face. "I feel decadent."

Ever so slowly, Kirk ran his hands along the inviting curves of her body. Curves he had already memorized. "No, not decadent. I'd say you feel like heaven."

His heaven. And his salvation. Because of her, he was momentarily sane.

Because of her, once he left her, he'd have to face the greatest loss he'd ever known.

Rachel leaned over Kirk, her hair raining down and forming a curtain on either side of his face as she brushed her lips over his. She felt him tighten his hands on her waist. And she felt something else.

She blinked and drew back to look at him.

"Something's wrong." She had thought, hoped, that they'd crossed all the hurdles. But there was something else, something still in the air.

He slid his hands lower, on her hips, still holding her in place. "Nothing's wrong."

She cocked her head. The look on her face was skeptical. "You don't lie well, Callaghan."

"Oh, I don't know." They still had today. There was no need for things to wind down until tonight. Tomorrow he'd tell her what he planned to do. But he wanted now. Frozen, the way photographs froze time. "I think I've developed a knack for it." A sensuous smile lifted the corners of his mouth. "That's all we've been doing all weekend, lying around."

She dropped her hands to his shoulders. "Cute, but not diverting enough. Why—?"

Kirk didn't feel like answering questions. Didn't feel like surrendering this feeling yet. He'd have to do without it for a long, long time. Forever.

He rose, taking her hand in his. "How about a sneak peek at what Ethan and I have been working on?"

"All right," she agreed reluctantly as she followed him out of the kitchen. "But we're only tabling this discussion, not terminating it."

Like a junkyard dog, he thought, affection weaving a web in the corners of his soul. "Why doesn't that surprise me?"

Still holding her hand, Kirk brought her to his studio. It was the only room in the house, she thought, that had any warmth to it. The others were just rooms, collected together beneath a roof. There was no life in any of them. Even his bedroom was just a place where he slept and changed his clothing.

Here was the heart of the man, she thought, in this tiny studio, amid his chemicals and rolls of film. She could have felt his presence here, even if he hadn't been standing beside her.

Equipment and supplies shared space with finished works and works in progress. There was a tripod leaning drunkenly to one side. Just above it was a gallery of photographs he'd only hung up in the past week. She took that to mean that he was staying, and reviewed them all with a fondness underlined with joy.

The last one took her breath away. It was a mounted sixteen-by-twenty black-and-white photograph of her. Her hair was blowing about her face, and she was obviously hurrying from one building to another on the campus. Her eyes were wide, and she seemed to be the embodiment of sheer energy.

She turned and saw that Kirk was watching her almost apprehensively. She'd seen the same look on a hopeful student's face when he handed in his term paper. Did her opinion matter that much to Kirk? The fact that it might thrilled her.

"When did you take that?"

He crossed his arms before him. "The first week I was here." He remembered having to lug his lens and set up in the grassy field just across the way from the building.

Rachel frowned. She didn't recall seeing him with a camera. She certainly didn't recall him taking the photograph. "I don't remember."

Kirk pointed to a long cylindrical object that was resting against the cot. It needed its own tripod when it was being used. Rachel thought it resembled a giant telescope. "That's my telephoto lens."

Rachel circled it respectfully for a closer look. The lens was huge. "I'm surprised you didn't get Australia with that thing."

He grinned. "The lighting wasn't right that day."

Her eyes were drawn back to the enlargement. It was almost as if the camera had made love to her, she thought. "It's beautiful." Rachel looked over her shoulder. Vanity born of wanting to be beautiful for him had her asking, "Am I really that pretty?"

Unable to help himself, he threaded his arms about her waist as he stood behind her. She fit against him so perfectly. Kirk rested his cheek against her hair for a moment, breathing in the fragrance. He was probably never going to be able to smell herbal shampoo again without becoming excited.

"No, I just do good work." He laughed as she muttered a stinging retort. "Of course you are. That's the way I see you. Busy, yet beautiful."

Rachel turned in the circle of his arms, absorbing every casual brush against his body the way a battery absorbed a charge. "Anything else?"

"Becoming vain, are you?" he teased. "You want other adjectives?"

Rachel wrinkled her nose impatiently. "No, I want to see other photographs, you dummy." She inclined her head toward the still photo behind her. "There had to be more. This can't be what Ethan's been helping you with."

"No." He released her and crossed to his worktable. Amid the organized clutter, there was a white-leather-bound album. "That's right here."

Kirk handed the album to her. Rachel ran her hand over it, as if she knew there was something very precious inside. And there was. Within those pages was the catalyst that had brought Ethan back to her. Taking a breath, she sat down on the edge of the cot. Kirk sometimes spent his nights on it when work rendered him too tired to even climb the stairs to his room.

Kirk watched Rachel quietly, anxiously, the way a novice applying for his first professional job might watch an editor. He'd had no idea how much he wanted her to be pleased by his work until just this moment.

Kirk saw by her awed expression that he'd been successful.

Rachel slowly turned page after page, looking down at the city she loved. The photographs were all in color. Collectively, they managed to capture the soul of the city, both its rural roots and its urban destiny. The only time Kirk spoke was to point out which photographs had been taken by Ethan.

"It's beautiful." She gently closed the album. "I don't know what to say."

"You don't have to say anything." He couldn't resist touching her cheek. It was soft, like the whisper of a prayer, he thought. His. "Your face said it all."

Rachel rose to her feet and offered the book back to Kirk. "You do wonderful work." She thought of Ethan. *In far more ways than one.*

Kirk shook his head, refusing the album. "No, keep it. I made it for you. I know how much you love this place."

She pressed the book to her chest. "Thank you. I'll treasure it always."

It was no use. He couldn't prolong this for his own selfish reasons. He couldn't mislead her by his silence. Restless, Kirk shoved his hands into his pockets and turned away. He couldn't talk to Rachel, couldn't say what he had to say, if he was looking down into that endless well of love in her eyes.

The words became frozen in his throat, and he had to force them out. "Think of it as a farewell gift."

"A farewell gift?" Stunned, she felt as if her legs were dissolving beneath her. Had she missed something? These past few days had been more fantastic than she'd ever dreamed possible. She had been so certain that the barriers that surrounded his world, his heart, had all come down.

Apparently, she thought with a stabbing pang, she'd deluded herself.

He stared at her photograph on the wall. That was the way he was always going to remember her. Rushing, with the wind in her hair, a smile of anticipation on her lips. "Yes. I've made up my mind to leave."

"Obviously some time ago." Her own voice rang in her head, sounding hollow and distant. "You've been working on these photographs for several weeks."

Kirk heard the numbing pain in her voice, and it hurt to know that he was the cause of it. But it was better this way, far better for her than to be tied to someone like him. Someone who couldn't give, who couldn't love.

He shrugged, attempting to keep his feelings at a distance, as he turned around again. "I told you when I came back that I wasn't staying."

He wasn't going to hide behind that excuse. Rachel felt tears rising in her eyes. "You said that when you thought you couldn't find a place for yourself."

He forced himself to sound cold. He was doing this for her sake, and someday she'd realize that. "Nothing's changed."

Rachel had never realized how much words could hurt. It felt as if each syllable had jagged points around the edges. Somehow, she worked past the pain. "Your place is here, with us. With me."

He wanted to pull her to him. Instead, he bracketed her arms to keep her at a distance. "Rachel, there's no future for us."

"Why?" she demanded, raising her chin pugnaciously, like a bantamweight sparring for the crown. "Why do you keep saying that? There *can* be one, if you let it."

She was so innocent. There was an entire black world that she knew nothing about. And he was going to have to be the one to show her. To make her see why he didn't fit into her good, clean world. "You want to marry me?"

Rachel had never been embarrassed about being bold. She wasn't about to start now. "Yes."

He was leading her to a point, a painful point he'd wanted to avoid. Something that had haunted him for a long, long time. It had made him vow not to ever have children of his own.

"And you want me to be Ethan's father."

"Yes." The answer was given without qualification, without hesitation.

The single word echoed in his soul. It was killing him to refuse. What shreds of integrity he still had left gave him no choice.

"Rachel, have you thought this through?"

Her eyes, filled with desperation, never left his. "Every night since you've come back."

He shook his head, sorrier than she would ever know that he had to refuse the wondrous gift she'd offered. Her faith in him. "Then you haven't thought this through far enough. Ethan's just beginning to heal . . ."

That was exactly her point. How could he twist it inside out?

"Yes! And you did that for him."

He wanted to shake her for forcing him to take this so far. He was saying things to her that he'd never said out loud to anyone, even himself. Things that sat, hidden, in the recesses of his heart. The monster he could yet become.

"And I could undo it all, too." His fingers dug into her shoulders as he struggled to make her understand. "There's a rage inside of me, an anger . . ."

Did he think she believed he could lash out at her? At Ethan? "An anger at what's been done to you," she insisted. That had nothing to do with her or her son.

"Yes, but it might just erupt in the wrong direction. *His* direction." Kirk saw Rachel wince, and he released her. The imprint of his fingers remained on her flesh, and he cursed himself for it. But it proved his point. "I'm a product of abusive parents. People like me have a greater tendency to be abusive themselves."

Her faith was unshakable, though her voice quavered from the emotion smoldering in it. "You won't be."

"How do you know that?" How could she be so sure, when he wasn't? "Do you want to chance that? Do you want to chance Ethan?"

Her hands fisted at her sides, and she fought the urge to beat on him, to somehow break down the wall he was constructing between them before her very eyes.

"This isn't a game of chance we're talking about. It's you. I *know* you. You couldn't hurt me or Ethan." Tears were building within her, and two spilled out, running unheeded down her cheek. "You're too busy hurting yourself."

Now he was making her cry. Damn it, it wasn't supposed to go this way. "Funny Face—"

Frustrated, she hit his cheek with the flat of her hand. "Stop it. I'm not a child anymore. You didn't make love to a child. I'm a woman, Callaghan. A woman who loves you. Who's always loved you." She blinked as tears made her lashes heavy. "Damn it, I'm not an idiot. I wouldn't love the monster you're painting."

He had one weapon left to make her see the flaw in her words. In her faith. "You loved Don."

She paled. "That was low."

He'd told her the truth. Now he steeled himself to keep from taking her into his arms the way he wanted to. "No, desperate."

"All right. All right," she repeated as she began to pace about the small room, struggling not to hit something, not to vent her anger. "Since we're being desperate, I might as well tell *you* something. Don was my substitute for you." She saw sur-

prise enter his eyes but felt no triumph. "I realize that now."
She wiped her tearstained cheek with the heel of her hand. It
hurt to remember any of this. She'd placed it all behind her, in
a neat little box. "I married him right after you left town.
Maybe to coat the ache I felt because you wouldn't stay." She
couldn't help the accusing look that came into her eyes. She'd
kept all this bottled up, but he had forced it out. "That I wasn't
enough to make you stay."

She blew out a ragged breath. "Well, I can't get you to stay
now, any more than I could then. Last time, I waved goodbye." She shook her head, trying to numb herself so that she
wouldn't cry. "I won't wave this time. I won't usher you out
with good wishes, when I know that you're leaving the best part
of your life behind."

Her voice broke, and she thrust the album at him. "Here, I
don't want it. You keep it. Maybe someday you'll want to remember what it was you abandoned."

"Rachel—" But there was nothing to say. There were no
words to fill the void that lay between them.

With a frustrated sigh, she turned on her heel and ran from
the room.

Kirk remained standing where he was, even after the front
door had slammed and the echo had faded away. He was doing the right thing. The only thing.

He'd never felt so rotten in his life.

With an oath, he threw aside the album he had created for
her. It bounced on the cot and then fell to the floor. Landing on
its spine, it opened to a large photograph of Ethan, mugging for
the camera. It was the day Kirk had gotten him to open up.

Kirk blocked the emotions that rose up. He was leaving, and
there was no time like the present.

He left the book on the floor and walked quickly from the
room. He had to go now, while he still could. Someone else
could come and pack his equipment for him. The main thing
was to go. he could sell the house through the agency that had
handled the rental. There was no need to remain and make
things any worse.

No need.

Needs scrambled through his body, and he cursed himself for them, for being weak. Without realizing it, he kicked something, and it went skittering across the wooden floor. When he looked, he realized it was Rachel's earring. She must have dropped it in her hurry to leave.

He wanted something to remember her by, something to hold on the nights when loneliness became so huge it threatened to swallow him whole.

Kirk bent down to pick up the earring. When he raised his head, he was staring straight at the knob of the door to his father's den. Very slowly, he straightened. It was as if his past were daring him to open the door.

To finally confront the rest of it.

Something cold and clammy wrapped its tentacles around him as he placed his hand on the knob and turned it, opening the door. For a long moment, he just stood on the threshold, looking in.

The room smelled stale.

He walked in, expecting to feel something, some wave of fear, of revulsion. Each time he was summoned to this room, it had been to wait for punishment to be meted out.

The room had always smelled of whiskey and anger.

The whiskey smell was gone. And the anger was now his.

Kirk moved about the claustrophobic room as if he'd never seen it before. And perhaps, in a way, he hadn't seen it. Not this way, denuded of the things that had held terror for him. The trophies that had once hung on the walls, a tribute to his father's hunting prowess, were gone. No more dead animals staring at him with unseeing, accusing eyes.

Nothing but the scarred oak desk remained to remind Kirk of his past.

Approaching it, Kirk rubbed his thumb over the corner closest to the door. He'd fallen against that exact same corner that time his father swung out blindly before he could duck. Edgar Callaghan had sent his son sprawling into the desk. Kirk had just barely avoided putting out his eye. There was a tiny scar above his right eye that commemorated the event. He remembered telling Rachel and Cameron that he had gotten the scar fighting a bully. They'd believed him.

Or said they did, he thought now with a tightening of his mouth.

One way or another, they'd always gone out of their way to support him.

If it hadn't been for them, Kirk knew, he would have run away years before he reached his eighteenth birthday. And he would have run away, he realized, before he discovered his talent with a camera.

It was a room, he thought. Just a room. Not a prison cell. Not a chamber of horrors. Just a room.

He stood, looking around, waiting for that old feeling to permeate him. That feeling of dread, of fear, mingled with overwhelming guilt. Guilt that somehow, in some way, his father's failings were his fault. That his father's alcoholism was his fault. That everything bad that had ever befallen his family was his fault.

It didn't come.

Kirk took a deep breath as a cool wind seemed to sweep through him. None of it had ever been his fault. And he realized that the seeds of that knowledge had been nudged into fruition by another small boy who had felt just as he did. That evil had been his own doing.

"It wasn't my fault that you drank, was it, old man?" he said aloud, looking at the chair where his father had always sat. "Just like it wasn't Ethan's fault that his father was a failure. Or that he was killed."

With a shake of his head, Kirk laughed at his own folly. At his own stupidity. He'd wasted all those years feeling guilty for no reason, when the explanation had been so simple, so clear. Edgar Callaghan had transferred his own guilt onto his son, and made him a whipping boy, in theory, as well as in practice. He'd done it so well and for so long, Kirk had grown up believing it was gospel.

It fell into place in his head, like dominoes falling against one another until the whole row has fallen. Or, better yet, like the sun coming into a darkened room and chasing away the shadows with its intrusion.

If he wasn't to blame for his father's drinking, if he wasn't as worthless as his father had always maintained, then he didn't have to taint what he came into contact with. He'd always lived in fear that he would become his father someday. Cruel. Abusive. Heartless.

All his beliefs, the dark foundations of his world, were wrong.

"I guess I just had to see it in another context to realize it for myself. You made yourself a drunk, old man. I had nothing to do with it. And nothing I could have done would have changed it." Just as nothing he could have done would have had a world-shaking impact on the tragedies he'd preserved for history.

Kirk shook his head again at the shame of it all. "You wasted all those years, taking out your anger on me, missing out on what was important. A home. A family. A wife who loved you."

Love. That had been the missing ingredient in this house. Missing only because his father had thrown it away. He had been willing, eager, to love his father, and he knew his mother's love had been all but obsessive. All that love, wasted, misdirected. Abandoned.

Abandoned.

The word echoed in his head. Kirk thought of Rachel, and what she had just said to him.

Wasn't he guilty of the same thing? She was giving him her love, and he was throwing it away under the sanctimonious guise of doing it "for her own good." Whatever the reason, it was still being tossed back in her face.

The way his father had tossed his love back in his face.

Kirk wasn't rich enough to toss a gift like that away. Maybe crazy enough, he reflected, but definitely not rich enough, to toss away the love of a woman like Rachel. And a child like Ethan.

Maybe, just maybe, her love would make him worthy of her. He could only hope so. What he knew was that he planned to love and cherish her and Ethan until his dying day. If he was lucky, that wouldn't be for a long, long time. It would take that long, he thought, to make up to her for today.

Anticipation hummed through him as he left the room. He felt like someone emerging into the sunlight after years in a dark cave. If this were a play, he thought, there'd be music accompanying his entrance.

Or exit, as it were.

Whatever it was, he knew that his life was ahead of him. And it would be with Rachel. If she'd have him, after the fool he'd just been. His mind moving rapidly, he decided on his next move. He was going to get the photo album he'd made for her, and get down on his knees, if he had to, to make her accept it. And him.

A humbling prospect, he thought, begging. But not nearly as humbling as the idea of going through the rest of his life without her.

As he turned toward the studio, someone began pounding on his front door. Pounding as if intending to break the door down.

He frowned as he crossed to the door. If it was someone selling subscriptions or cookies, he wasn't going to find a very agreeable prospective customer.

Kirk pulled open the door. "Hey, what's the idea? Are you trying to break the door down?" His annoyance evaporated immediately. Rachel stood on his doorstep, shaking like a leaf. She looked almost wild with fear. "Rachel!" He caught her as she stumbled into the house. "What's the matter?"

"It's Ethan. Cameron just called me from the campgrounds."

Had the boy been hurt? "What?" he prodded. He'd never seen her like this, and it frightened him. "What about Ethan?"

"He's missing."

Chapter 17

"It's going to be all right." Kirk's tone was firm, assured. It belied the tension working through every part of him, wringing him dry.

Rachel sat beside him in the minivan, staring straight ahead at the road, willing them to already be there.

Kirk glanced at her when she didn't respond. Her hands were clenched in her lap, her knuckles so white he thought they'd break through her skin. They were driving to San Gabriel Mountains Park as fast as was reasonably safe. He kept one eye out for the highway patrol, the other on the road in front of him. Because of the holiday, traffic was mercifully light.

Agitation was beating a sharp drum roll within Rachel, growing in intensity. Would it be? she wondered. Would it be all right? She found her endless supply of optimism completely gone.

"Cameron said Ethan's been out overnight." She swallowed, fighting back the terrifying image that the words evoked. "He said he didn't want to call me, but when they didn't find Ethan by morning, he knew he had no choice." She covered her mouth with her hands to hold back a sob. She had been making love with Kirk while her son was lost somewhere.

Guilt and fear almost overwhelmed her. "Oh, God, Kirk, he's just a little boy."

"A *bright* little boy. This isn't his first time camping." His hands tightened on the wheel, as tight as his control over his thoughts was. He refused to let his mind wander.

How could he sound so calm? This was Ethan they were talking about, not a story she was reading in the newspaper. Ethan. Her only child.

"Experienced campers get lost in the woods all the time." *And some of them die.* She couldn't force herself to form the last words.

He read her thoughts. It wasn't difficult. "That's not going to happen here," he said fiercely. He set his mouth hard as he slanted a look at her. "You've got to believe that."

Her breath was hitching in her throat as sobs clawed to be set free. "Do you?"

There wasn't even a split second's hesitation. "Yes." He forced himself to become detached. A degree of detachment was what had seen him through some very tight situations. Believing you were doomed only set you up for that eventuality.

Rachel hung on to Kirk's strength as if it were a tangible thing, as if it were her life raft, carrying her through shark-infested waters.

She stared at the road, impatient to be there, to be doing something other than just impotently sitting in a vehicle. "Can't you drive faster?"

He was already traveling well over the speed limit. "Not without a pilot's license. We're lucky this isn't a regular Monday, with rush-hour traffic."

"Yes, lucky." She repeated the word hollowly.

Kirk placed a hand over hers and squeezed lightly, never taking his eyes off the road. "We will be."

She nodded mechanically. Numbness was mercifully spilling all through her.

But despite the numbness, she'd never experienced such sheer terror in her life.

Cameron was waiting for them just inside the grounds, by the guard's hut. When he saw the minivan pulling in on the serpentine road, he ran to meet them.

"Any word?" Rachel cried. She jumped out of the vehicle before Kirk even pulled up the hand brake.

Cameron caught hold of her shoulders to steady her. "No, but leaping from a moving car isn't going to help find him, Rach."

She shrugged out of his grasp, waving away his words. She was in no mood for any kind of lecture. Her nerves were completely frayed. Cameron had given her no details on the telephone. She hadn't given him the opportunity, cutting off his words by saying that she was leaving immediately.

"How did it happen?"

Cameron spread his hands helplessly. "I don't know. We were all together at breakfast yesterday morning. Ethan said he wanted to see something. He promised he'd be right back. I didn't think anything of it, until he didn't return."

"How long was that?" Kirk asked quietly. He slipped a protective arm around Rachel's waist. She was trembling.

"Half an hour, maybe forty minutes." Cameron remembered the uneasy feeling that had spread through him when he realized that his nephew hadn't come back.

Rachel's eyes widened. "You let him wander away for forty minutes?"

"Rachel, we're camping. The point of the trip was to unwind, to let him have his space."

"And now he has it. Out there somewhere." She gestured around at the grounds as she struggled to keep from becoming hysterical. Half a dozen news stories raced and collided in her mind, stories about children being mauled by bears while camping, about people getting lost and not being recovered until it was too late.

Kirk saw emotions washing over her face. He gripped her hand hard. "Don't worry, we'll find him."

"Where?" She knew she was lashing out, but she couldn't help herself. She should never have let Ethan go. "Where are we going to find him?" She rubbed her hands over her arms, the chill within her surfacing. "It was cold last night."

"Ethan knows enough to find shelter and try to keep himself warm," Cameron interjected.

Her brother's words held no comfort for her. "He knows enough not to wander off, too, and he did. Why didn't you call me sooner?"

He sighed, dragging his hand through his hair. He'd already explained that on the phone. "I kept hoping we'd find him. I didn't want to alarm you."

Kirk exchanged a look with Cameron. He turned toward Rachel. "Maybe you'd better stay in the car..." he began gently. In her present state of mind, she would be more of a liability than an asset during the search. He didn't want to have to worry about her, as well.

She shook her head, refusing to entertain the suggestion for even a moment.

"No, I'm going with you." There was no arguing with her. "I can't just sit here and do nothing, not when he's out there somewhere, cold and alone. Frightened." Her eyes were pleading with him to help her, to support her. "He needs me."

"Shhh..." Kirk kissed the top of her head. "We'll find him." He turned to Cameron. "Did you notify the ranger station?"

It was the first thing he'd done after it became evident that Ethan hadn't just stepped away, he told them. He began to lead them back to the campsite where they'd originally been. Ironically, it wasn't far from where Kirk had parked the minivan.

"Yesterday. Vikerson, Trask and Delgado are all combing the woods right now," he told Rachel, referring to the men who'd come camping with him. Their sons remained at the campsite, just in case, with a fourth man. "Along with some volunteers, and the rangers."

Cameron stopped for a moment, bracketing Rachel's shoulders. She'd never felt as fragile to him as she did at this moment. "We'll find him, Rach. I promise you, we'll find him."

"We have to." She uttered the words stoically.

"C'mon, let's go. We're wasting time," Cameron said, leading the way back to the campsite.

Rachel looked around, taking in her surroundings, praying the mild weather would continue. Praying they'd find Ethan before long.

* * *

The search party was broken up into twos. Communication would be maintained by walkie-talkies. Cameron paired himself off with one of his detectives, while Kirk took Rachel with him. There had never been any question as to the way they would separate.

Struggling, Rachel did what she could to bury her feelings and maintain a positive attitude.

They had come here, to San Gabriel Mountains Park, a great deal when they were young, she, Cameron and Kirk. Her father had a love for the outdoors that he had passed on to his children. The same love had completely eluded her mother. Mrs. Reed had come along on a few trips, hating every bug-infested minute of it. Her reason for doing it had been simple. She'd done it for the children. Rachel remembered teasing her mother about that, about hating the whole idea of camping.

Now she hated it.

It was supposed to have been good for Ethan to come out here with Cameron, she thought miserably as she made her way up the incline behind Kirk.

She gritted her teeth, scrambling for a hold. Lost in thought, she had missed her footing and almost fallen.

Kirk swung around at the sound of the loosened rocks falling. "Are you all right?"

"I'm fine. Keep going," she ordered. Getting herself hurt wasn't going to do Ethan any good. And neither was upbraiding herself. She could do that all she wanted after it was over.

After they *found* him, she amended, realizing the implications of her thoughts.

A chill akin to a premonition passed over her soul. Rachel angrily dismissed it. There were no such things as premonitions. There were only fears.

They'd been going up the steep path for a while now. The terrain had flattened considerably.

Kirk turned and looked at Rachel over his shoulder. She looked frayed and exhausted. They'd been searching for over three hours with no luck, no indication that they were even going in the right direction.

"Why don't we turn back? Maybe someone's already found him and they just haven't contacted us yet." He glanced down at the silent walkie-talkie strapped to his belt.

She knew he was just saying that. He didn't believe it. Rachel heard the distant sound of a helicopter. They were still searching. "No."

Kirk didn't move any farther. "Rachel, you look exhausted."

No one was going to stop her, not even Kirk. "I said no." Her expression softened, pleading with him. "He's out here. I can feel it. Please, Kirk."

He tried again, though he knew it was futile. If he was in her place, he wouldn't give up either. "I can go on ahead if you want—"

"*We* can go on." Anger flashed in her eyes. "I'm his mother, not you."

This wasn't the time to argue with her. But it was the time to make something clear. "I care about him, too, Rachel."

She felt ashamed for carrying on this way. Kirk was out here with her, looking for Ethan. She shouldn't be biting his head off, just because she was afraid.

"I know you do. I'm sorry." She pushed her hair from her face. "Let's just keep going, all right?"

He nodded and turned back toward the path.

Between men provided by the ranger station, Cameron's men and the volunteers who had joined them, they'd made a complete wide circle around the area where Ethan had last been seen. The men were fanning out farther and farther from the center in their attempt to track down where a small boy might have gone. The helicopter had been recruited earlier that day by one of Cameron's men, whose brother ran a flight service.

No one had seen the boy.

Rachel felt hope ebbing out of her.

Kirk offered Rachel his hand. The incline was growing steep again. On the far side was a narrow path that broke off into a cave. The other path went straight up to high ground.

Every bone in her body ached. She was miles past tired. But she kept pushing herself, hoping that they'd find him in another few minutes. She'd give anything if she could just hear—

Rachel's head snapped up, exhaustion falling away as if it had only been a hallucination. "Wait! Kirk, do you hear something?"

He paused, listening, then shook his head. There was nothing out of the ordinary.

"Just the wind. It tends to be louder up here, remember? Your dad used to say it was angels singing." He'd forgotten all about the silly story until just this moment.

But Rachel was adamant. She strained and heard it again. Euphoria rushed through her.

"Not angels singing—crying!" She looked up at Kirk, her eyes bright with hope. "That's crying! Listen!"

Kirk tilted his head slightly, holding his breath and listening very intently. And then he heard the sound as well. He saw the way Rachel was watching him, hope and fear washing over her face. He wasted no words confirming what she believed she heard.

"That way..." Kirk pointed toward the mouth of the cave. Some distance away, it was partially obscured by brush, debris and leaves.

"Ethan!" Rachel called. Her throat was hoarse from crying out his name. *Please, God, let him answer! Please!* "Ethan, it's Mom! Where are you?"

Nothing but a whimper answered her. But the noise was growing louder.

Kirk made sure he kept Rachel close behind him as he quickly made his way up the incline. His movements were fast and sure, as if he'd been born part cougar.

As they drew closer, the debris turned out to be a mound of leaves. They appeared to have been gathered together just inside the mouth of the cave.

"Ethan!" Kirk cried out. The leaves moved, and Rachel clutched Kirk's hand so hard she broke the skin with her nails.

Leaving Kirk behind, she raced ahead to the cave. Kirk caught up to her and stopped her from frantically digging through the mound.

"Careful," he cautioned. "It might only be an animal. Ethan?" he said softly.

The mound shifted and rose until suddenly a dirty golden head broke through. Leaves rained down from Ethan's hair.

"Kirk?" Ethan blinked, his face puffy and red from tears, both old and new. He'd cried himself to sleep last night, and huddled here, half out of his head, waiting and praying for morning. When it came, he was too afraid to move, too afraid to go anywhere else for fear of missing someone if they were looking for him.

"Mom?" Staring at her as if she were a mirage, Ethan rubbed his eyes. Overcome with joy, he reached out to her just as she embraced him. He squealed as she crushed him to her, for once happy for the contact. The ragged sigh he emitted was heart-wrenching. "I kept dreaming that you came to rescue me, but every time I woke up, you weren't here."

She held him to her, running her hands through his hair, down his back. Rachel didn't even know where to begin to sort out her emotions.

"We're here now." Gratitude brimmed in her eyes as she looked over her son's head at Kirk. "Oh, baby, are you all right?" She held him back, looking him over. "Did you get hurt?"

He shook his head, trying very hard not to cry again. "I'm okay," he mumbled.

Kirk felt emotions he had never realized he possessed threatening to choke off his windpipe. He stroked the boy's hair. "What made you go off like that?"

Ethan's ruddy cheeks became even more flushed. "I thought I saw a deer." He turned toward his mother. "I wanted to take a picture for you." It was only then that she realized that Ethan still had Kirk's camera strapped around his neck. He fingered the strap as he spoke. "But the deer kept moving away. I was trying to be real quiet. I followed, sneaking up on him, and then I didn't know where I was."

He shrugged helplessly and sniffed, then screwed up his face as he attempted to push fresh tears back. His mother was here. His mother and Kirk had come for him. He shouldn't be crying again.

Pressing his lips together, he held up the camera for Kirk's benefit. "I kept your camera safe."

Kirk hugged the boy to him, then tousled his hair. "The main thing is that you kept yourself safe. Cameras can always be replaced."

"Even this one?" Kirk had told him it was the first camera he had ever owned, and that it was special.

"Even this one." Kirk crouched down to the boy's level. "Pretty smart, covering yourself with leaves like that."

"I had to," Ethan said honestly, not bothering with pride. "I was scared that something would come and eat me." He didn't notice that his mother shivered when he said that. "And then it got so cold . . ."

"We'll get you warm again," Kirk promised. He picked the boy up in his arms. "C'mon, let's get you back to the campsite. There're going to be an awful lot of people who'll be happy to see you." He nodded at the walkie-talkie. "Rachel, call in and tell them Ethan's safe."

Rachel unhooked it from his belt. It took her only a moment to reach the other search parties. Then she discontinued communication and wiped away the tears of joy that were falling with the heel of her hand.

Ethan stared at her. "Why are you crying, Mom?"

She touched his arm, as if to reassure herself that he was really there, then glanced at Kirk before answering. "Because I'm so happy."

Happy tears rose to Ethan's eyes, as well. He hid them by burying his head in Kirk's shoulder as he carried him down the incline.

The hospital corridor had pastel walls and was dotted with cheerful lithographs that depicted scenes of children romping with small animals. Kirk barely noticed the decor, so focused was he on what was happening behind the door of room 122.

Cameron stood beside him, as restless as he as they waited for the doctor to emerge from Ethan's room. Ethan had wanted to go home, but his request had been temporarily vetoed. Kirk had convinced him that being checked over would put his mother's mind at ease.

Cameron offered Kirk one of the two candy bars he'd gotten from the vending machine. "I can't tell you what having you here did for Rachel." He unwrapped the chocolate bar, remembering that he'd eaten only sporadically since Ethan disappeared. "And me."

Kirk held his candy bar in his hand. He had no appetite. "Yeah, like you needed your hand held."

"Figuratively." Cameron took a bite of the bar. "Hey, even big detective types need someone to rely on once in a while."

Kirk turned toward him and raised a dubious brow. "You?"

Cameron took another bite, then grinned. "You know any other big detective types? Seriously, thanks for being there for us."

There was no trash can nearby, so Cameron pocketed the wrapper, then looked at Kirk. "Maybe I haven't said it very much, but I couldn't have picked out a better friend than you." Kirk stared at him, a glimmer of surprise in his eyes. "What, all these years you thought maybe it was a one-way street?"

Kirk had always thought of himself as the one attempting to warm himself by the fire. The Reeds' fire. "I was the one invading your family."

"It's only invading if you're not welcome. And you always were. You going to eat that?" He nodded at the candy bar in Kirk's hand.

"No, here."

Cameron unwrapped the second bar. "I always knew I could depend on you," he continued seriously. "No strings attached, no motives. That's a hell of a mind-easer."

Pleased, surprised, Kirk said nothing for a moment. He didn't have to. The look in his eyes told Cameron everything.

"Yeah, me too, buddy," Cameron murmured.

They turned as the door behind them opened. Rachel came out. The lines of tension were gone from her face. Both men gathered around her. They already knew what she was going to say, but they still wanted to hear her say it.

"He's going to be fine. The doctor doesn't need to keep him for observation overnight." She looked up at Cameron. "It seems that his uncle taught him survival well." She placed a hand on Cameron's shoulder. "He's getting dressed now. Why don't you go in and help him?"

"Always bossy," he commented to Kirk with a laugh. Relief making his step lighter, Cameron went in to join his nephew.

Rachel turned to look at Kirk.

"Thank you," she said quietly. He began to shrug, but she placed her hand on his shoulder, preventing him from completing the motion. "It's nothing to brush off." Her eyes held his. "You kept me from going to pieces. You pulled me out of emotional quicksand and helped me look for my son. There aren't enough words in the world to thank you."

She blew out a breath as she dropped her hand and took a step back.

"I know you have to leave, and I won't stand in your way. That would be selfish." She swallowed as she felt her throat threatening to close. "But I just wanted to tell you. If you ever want to come back, I'll be here." She touched his face briefly, then drew away. "I love you, Kirk, and I always will."

God, what a mistake he had almost made. "Stand in my way."

"What?"

"I said, 'Stand in my way.'" He fought a grin as she stared at him in confusion. "I don't want to leave, Rachel."

He drew her to the side of the corridor, creating a small haven for them. He attempted to make it as clear as possible. For both of them.

"I came back to see you because when I remembered you, I remembered feeling good. About myself, about life." He took her hands in his. "And I'm the one being selfish, because I need that. I need you, to go on." He watched, fascinated, as hope began to take root in her face. "What I said before, about being afraid that I would be bad for Ethan—when he was lost, all I could think of was that I had lost him, too. I love your son, Rachel. I love him as if he were my own."

This was far more than she had dared hope for. "He's more yours than he ever was Don's."

He'd sensed that almost from the beginning, from the rapport that had emerged. "I don't want to give either of you up." He framed her face with his hands and struggled with the urge to kiss her. He knew that if he did, he'd lose his train of thought. And there were things he still wanted to tell her.

Reluctantly he took his hands away from her face. "That last time I was on the campus, when I took you to the coffee shop, I stopped by the liberal arts building."

Rachel waited wondering what he was getting at, biting her tongue to keep from asking.

"Joe Frazier's the assistant dean there." They'd both gone to high school with him.

"Yes, I know." Her voice was hardly more than a whisper.

He dropped the bombshell. "I bumped into him by accident, and we began to talk. He's followed my work, and he offered me an adjunct teaching position if I ever wanted it. Said he'd have would-be photojournalists lining up six deep if my name was in the class bulletin." He wasn't one for vanity or flattery, but this one time, he'd chosen to believe it. It worked to his advantage. Taking the position would keep him close to Rachel.

"He tends to be conservative in his estimations." Rachel swallowed, then dared to ask, "Does this mean that you're going to stay?"

"Yes." He watched her eyes, wondering if he'd sabotaged his life earlier.

Rachel kept very, very still. "For how long?"

He looked for signs to tell him what she was thinking and saw none. He pressed on. "As long as it takes."

After wanting something for so long, she refused to believe that it was actually happening. Two miracles in one day was too much to hope for.

"I don't understand. As long as it takes for what?"

"For as long as it takes for you to give me the right answer to my proposal." Kirk watched her mouth soften, and knew he'd been worried needlessly. He took her into his arms. "The right answer, by the way, is yes."

Rachel threaded her arms around Kirk's neck. "I don't need a crib sheet, Callaghan. I've known what the right answer is all along. I was just waiting for you to find out."

It had taken him a long time, but he finally had. "Cameron can be best man."

She shook her head slowly, then watched, amused, as he arched a questioning brow. "No, you are. You were always the best man, Callaghan. It just took you a hell of a long time to accept that."

"I'm a slow learner." He brushed a kiss against her hair and listened to her sigh softly. He found it hopelessly arousing. "But something tells me that I'm going to enjoy learning."

She was so happy, she was afraid she would burst. Rachel nodded toward her son's room. "Let's go tell Ethan that he's going to have a new father."

"In a minute." Kirk wasn't anxious to go anywhere just yet. It was private here, and he wanted to enjoy the moment. He pulled her closer to him and saw a spark of desire flicker in her eyes. As he knew one did in his. "I told you, I'm a slow learner. I have to take this one step at a time."

He had her very curious. "And that first step is?"

"To kiss you."

She grinned, fitting herself against him. "You know what they say."

"What?" he teased, glorying in the feel of her. "What do they say?"

"Watch out for that first step." She rose on her toes, bringing her mouth to his. "It's a doozy."

And it was.

* * * * *

SILHOUETTE

Sensation®

COMING NEXT MONTH

NIGHT SMOKE   Nora Roberts

Heartbreakers

Rugged arson inspector Ryan Piasecki wasn't prepared for the blaze of desire that coolly beautiful Natalie Fletcher had swiftly ignited in him. Could he stop Natalie's dreams from going up in smoke...and could he melt her icy reserve?

WHOSE BABY?   Suzanne Carey

Sweet little Kassie had been abandoned before, and adoptive dad Jack Kelleher was determined that she wouldn't lose her family again. So when the death of his wife caused the authorities to take away the child he'd come to love, Jack knew he'd try anything to keep her, *including* marrying Liz Heflin—his wife's sister.

MAN OF STEEL   Kathleen Creighton

The bottom dropped out of Rhett Brown's comfortable world when he found himself facing parenthood alone. Eventually he asked Dixie Parish to be a temporary nanny to his motherless children. Suddenly his children were smiling again—and *his* heart was stirring with long-forgotten sensations...

SOMEWHERE IN TIME   Merline Lovelace

Spellbound

Air force pilot Aurora Durant's emergency landing had somehow transported her back to the flourishing Roman Empire—and straight into the arms of soldier Lucius Antonius. Though countless centuries stood between them, they soon discovered a love that defied time. But how long could it survive when destiny had different plans?

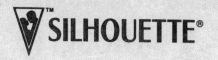

▼ SILHOUETTE®

Who needs mistletoe when Santa's Little Helpers are around...

SANTA'S LITTLE HELPERS

We know you'll love this year's seasonal collection featuring three brand-new festive romances from some of Silhouette's best loved authors - including Janet Dailey

And look out for the adorable baby on the front cover!

THE HEALING TOUCH	by Janet Dailey
TWELFTH NIGHT	by Jennifer Greene
COMFORT AND JOY	by Patrica Gardner Evans

Available: December 1996   Price £4.99

COMING NEXT MONTH FROM

™SILHOUETTE®

Intrigue
Danger, deception and desire

KEEPER OF THE BRIDE Tess Gerritsen
UNDERCOVER VOWS Judi Lind
THE OTHER LAURA Sheryl Lynn
THE RENEGADE Margaret St George

Special Edition
Satisfying romances packed with emotion

MEGGIE'S BABY Cheryl Reavis
NO LESS THAN A LIFETIME Christine Rimmer
THE BACHELOR AND THE BABY WISH
Kate Freiman
FOUND: ONE RUNAWAY BRIDE Stella Bagwell
NATURAL BORN DADDY Sherryl Woods
NEW YEAR'S DADDY Lisa Jackson

Desire
*Provocative, sensual love stories for the
woman of today*

THE COWBOY AND THE KID Anne McAllister
FATHER ON THE BRINK Elizabeth Bevarly
GAVIN'S CHILD Caroline Cross
TWO WEDDINGS AND A BRIDE Anne Eames
THE BRIDE WORE BLUE Cindy Gerard
DONAVAN Diana Palmer

SINGLE LETTER SWITCH

A year's supply of Silhouette Desire®
novels— absolutely FREE!

Would you like to win a year's supply of seductive and breathtaking romances? Well, you can and they're free! Simply complete the grid below and send it to us by 30th June 1997.

The first five correct entries picked after the closing date will win a year's supply of Silhouette Desire® novels (six books every month—worth over £160). What could be easier?

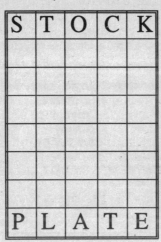

Clues:

A   To pile up
B   To ease off or a reduction
C   A dark colour
D   Empty or missing
E   A piece of wood
F   Common abbreviation for an aircraft

Please turn over for details of how to enter ☞

How to enter...

There are two five letter words provided in the grid overleaf. The first one being STOCK the other PLATE. All you have to do is write down the words that are missing by changing just one letter at a time to form a new word and eventually change the word STOCK into PLATE. You only have eight chances but we have supplied you with clues as to what each one is. Good Luck!

When you have completed the grid don't forget to fill in your name and address in the space provided below and pop this page into an envelope (you don't even need a stamp) and post it today. Hurry—competition ends 30th June 1997.

Sihouette® Single Letter Switch
FREEPOST
Croydon
Surrey
CR9 3WZ

Are you a Reader Service Subscriber? Yes ☐ No ☐

(I am over 18 years of age)

Ms/Mrs/Miss/Mr _____

Address _____

_____

_____ Postcode _____

One application per household.

You may be mailed with other offers from other reputable companies as a result of this application. If you would prefer not to receive such offers, please tick box. ☐

C6L